Prais

You'll Be Fine is a painful and hilarious excavation of queer ordinariness, the tomization and reconstitution of family, and the messiness of survival. I'll be thinking about Michalski's vivid characters for a long time.

— Rahne Alexander, author of *Heretic to Housewife*

Jen Michalski is a stunning writer.

—Laura van den Berg, author of *I Hold a Wolf by the Ears*

Jen Michalski's characters seem to breathe through the pages

—Dawn Raffel, author of The Secret Life of Objects

Michalski never fails to tell compelling stories capable of challenging and surprising readers.

—Baltimore Magazine

You'll Be Fine

Jen Michalski

A NineStar Press Publication

www.ninestarpress.com

You'll Be Fine

Printed in the USA

ISBN: 978-1-64890-310-6

First Edition, August, 2021

Also available in eBook, ISBN: 978-1-64890-309-0

CONTENT WARNING:
This book contains sexual content, which may only be suitable for mature readers. Depictions of Death, homophobia, drug/alcohol use/addiction, child abuse, grief, and sexual assault of a minor (flashback).

"We'll come back some other weekend," their mother said. They sat in the parking lot of Kings Dominion, all four windows of their yellow 1981 Chevy Chevette rolled down. Their mother didn't use air conditioning because she was a true believer, before it was even hip and environmentally friendly, in getting the best gas mileage. The park was scheduled to open in ten minutes, and Alex's denim cut-offs were already soggy from riding for three and a half hours in her own sweat.

"We're turning around?" Alex looked at her in disbelief.

"I'm not paying full price for tickets when we have perfectly good ones at home." Her mother tapped out a Winston and lit it. The whole trip—her mother's chain smoking, the crushed gold and red cigarette packs sliding back and forth across the dashboard, having to listen to the entire Frank Zappa discography on crackly cassette tapes, Alex's legs sliding on the hot vinyl seat as she sat up in front, map spread across her lap in case they got lost while Owen played a hand-held Asteroids game in the back, oblivious to everything but the blip-blip-blip of the machine—had stretched Alex to the breaking point.

"You can use my money." Alex thought of the crumpled ones and fives and the one nice twenty she'd gotten in an early birthday card from Aunt Johanna in Seattle, whom she'd never met. "I won't get any souvenirs."

"It's the principle of the thing." Her mother exhaled a mushroom cloud of smoke between them. Her short dark hair was hidden under a Panama hat, and she wore a Plimsouls T-shirt Alex would steal when she was a teenager. "It's a waste of money, money we don't have. You have no idea of the value of money, Al-ex-an-dra. You got twenty dollars from Aunt Johanna for doing absolutely nothing."

"But we're going to waste gas money going home and coming back here." She pointed out. "So, won't it be a wash?"

Alex glanced back at Owen, hoping he would pipe up. If they were both whiny enough, maybe their mother would take one of her "headache pills" and give in. But instead he frowned in concentration at his video game.

"Maybe if you asked me if I had the tickets before we left, instead of caring about what freaking toy was in the cereal box or wanting to wear your new sandals." Her mother spiked the cigarette in the overflowing ashtray and glared at her. "Maybe if you were more responsible, we would have the tickets, now wouldn't we? You're almost twelve years old, Alexandra Maas. You need to be more responsible."

"I wish I could live with Dad," she mumbled. She hadn't really meant it; for all she knew, their dad was Satan. It was something to say, the same way she might have called Owen diarrhea breath.

The slaps were fast and furious. Her mother's peridot ring, one size too large and always sliding around her finger, cut Alex's cheek as Alex threw her hands up to her face.

"You want to live with your father?" Her mother leaned across her and opened her door. "You think he's such a saint? Then go right ahead. I'll leave you here, with your thirty dollars, and you can call directory assistance in Seattle and ask for Jeffrey Maas, okay? And when you do find him and find out what he's really like and beg me to come back home, I'm not taking you back. Now go—get out!"

Alex grabbed her pink heart-shaped purse, the size of a pancake, and her floppy hat she'd remembered to pack this time because she'd gotten a blistering sunburn when they went to Frontier Town last summer. She didn't want to get out, but she was afraid of getting hit again. There was no way to make things better—this was how things would be until her mother decided they weren't.

Alex set each new-sandaled foot on the asphalt and closed the door so limply the latch didn't catch. Then, meeting Owen's eyes as he stared at her in terror from the backseat, she watched the Chevette screech away, passenger door flapping like a wounded bird.

Chapter One

Even though Owen never calls her, especially at 7:30 on a weekday evening, when Alex sees her brother's name in the caller ID, she drops her phone back into her purse and waits for her metro stop. She figures he'll just leave her a message about his cat. It's been almost the entirety of their relationship the past five years. The week before, he'd texted her a picture of Tortoise, his Himalayan. She was wearing a suit of herbs with terra cotta-colored felt legs. She looked like a chia pet.

> *I am my own catnip receptacle,* Owen had texted underneath Tortoise's picture.

The chia pet text had come after midnight, a time when Alex (like most people) was asleep and susceptible to tragedy, like a call from the hospital, from the roadside after a car accident, or, for Alex specifically, a call from her mother when her mother was completely wasted, one glass of wine away from falling down the steps or worse, keeping Alex on the phone for hours about years-old, completely fabricated grievances.

She hadn't responded to Owen that night, either, mad he'd woken her up about his stupid cat. That he didn't understand she got up at five in the morning for her job as a features writer at the *Capitol Metropolitan* or that her apartment in Adams Morgan was expensive as hell or that the amount of her grad school loans equaled a house mortgage. That she had a life, didn't still live at home with their mother, and didn't have a cat for a best friend.

As she gets up to make her way to the doors of the metro, her phone vibrates again.

"Owen, I just got off work—can I call you back?" She presses the phone to her cheek as she follows the other commuters up the stairs of the station.

"No, Alex—listen."

"You know—I was just thinking about Tortoise—I was worried maybe it meant she had died or something," Alex jokes, cutting him off, even as her hands begin to sweat. She wonders what their mother has done this time to warrant a call from Owen.

"Alex." Owen is silent for a minute. "It's Mom. Mom's dead."

"Dammit, Owen, you shouldn't joke." But she knows he isn't joking. She stops in the middle of the sidewalk. People brush against her, clipping her leg with their totes, her shoulder with their purses and messenger bags, as she tries to remember what day it is again, when she talked to her mother last. What she wishes she could take back.

"You should come home." Owen's words have awkward pauses between them, as if he's too choked up to speak. "Can you come home tonight?"

"I can't." What the hell is she saying? Still, she hears herself go on. "I really can't. I mean—"

"What do you mean, you can't?" She imagines Owen's face on the other end of the line, scrunched like a balled-up tissue. "Mom's dead. What's wrong with you?"

"You're right—all right, okay," she hears herself agree, her voice far away and warbled, like she's in a dream.

As she wanders from the Woodley Park metro station toward the general direction of her apartment, she feels suddenly like an alien life form. *I am experiencing a tragic event*, she wants to tell the dog walker with five French bulldogs who passes her or the woman jogger who pauses at the intersection, drinking from a clear pink plastic water bottle. She wants to grab on to someone, anyone, like a body snatcher, and switch places, away from the kettle ball in her chest, away her knotted intestines and her numb appendages.

Alex has never really done death before. She's thirty-six and never met her grandparents; their father left when she was four. And although their mother had turned sixty a few years back, it was more like Madonna sixty than Medicare sixty. Were Alex and Owen supposed to call Aunt Johanna, other forgotten, faraway relatives in Wisconsin and Arizona, their father, wherever he was? Was some kind of funeral needed for a mother who had flitted between atheism, Wiccan, new age-y crap, and pharmaceuticals like she was at a metaphysics salad bar?

And beyond the details, which Alex is good at, what about the other, more feely things? Like the way her mother had made her *feel*? (Incidentally, like a neon sign, a composition of gasses and other toxic compounds compressed into a fragile glass tube that she has managed to bend into the words *Alex Maas, Successful Person Who Does Not Give a Fuck*.)

Except now she has to give one.

"Crap," she says under breath as she waits for the elevator in the lobby of her building. She brings up her ex Kate's number in her phone doesn't press call, not only because she can't talk to Kate anymore, but because she realizes she can't talk to anybody. If she opens her mouth and voices the words *my mom is dead*, she knows any adrenaline humming through her from the shock will dissolve, adrenaline she needs to get into her apartment, throw a few days' worth of clothes together, call Rowan at the magazine, and get to the Greyhound terminal at Union Station to catch a bus home early the next morning.

Did Owen even mention how she died? In her apartment vestibule, Alex digs her phone out again. She can't remember how they ended the conversation, anything he had said after the words *dead* and *come home*.

"I'm so sorry." Rowan, her boss, sounds like he's outside. "Are you all right? Is there anything I can do?"

"No—but thanks," Alex says as she walks in a circle in her bedroom, staring at her opened suitcase. "I just don't know...I don't know how much time I'll need. A few days? I don't know what's supposed to happen—she always talked about being cremated. But it's not like she wrote a will—she didn't even believe in grocery lists."

"But if you need anything, you'll call, right?" he prods, as if they're friends. Maybe, in some way, because she spends most of her time with him, most of her time at the office in general, he's her friend. It's not like she has many, anyway. Her fingers shake as she opens her underwear drawer.

"Yes, of course. I'm going to get off the phone, though, before I cry."

"Sure, sure. Although you can cry on the phone—it's okay."

"Oh—I might need more time on the ballet company story. Can you give it to me?"

"Don't worry about the story, Alex—we'll find something else to run."

She hears one of Rowan's kids—his little girl—talking excitedly in the background. Then she thinks about the other person she had wanted to call after she got off the phone with Owen. The only person she's ever been able to tell anything.

"Hey," Alex says casually, as if she's just thought of it. "What about Juliette Sprigg—didn't you want someone to interview her?"

"You mean the profile about her restaurant? I thought someone else would cover that."

"Yeah, but..." Alex moves into the bathroom, just in case she might throw up. "Sprigg Restaurant's, like, five minutes from my mom's house. I went to high school with Juliette."

"Don't worry about that. You're going home to take care of what you need to take care of—not work on another story."

"No, it's okay—I can take it. I want to do it." She knows Rowan will give in—he has before—four magazine awards for her stories will do that. "Can you e-mail me her contact information?"

"No," he sighs. "I'm not. You're taking time off. You work too much as it is."

"Jesus, Rowan—are you really saying no?" Her voice rises, like helium, up an octave. "After all I've done for the magazine?"

"Alex," he sounds defeated, like he's speaking to his now-crying little girl. "Your mother just died."

"Fine—I quit then." She hangs up on him and turns on the faucet in the bathroom. As she splashes her face with water, her phone beeps. She hits the speaker with her wet hand as she reaches for the towel. "What?"

"You're not quitting, and I'm not assigning you the story."

She takes a breath and holds it a second before exhaling. "I'm doing the story, or I quit."

"Hi, honey, what sweetie? Will you stop screaming? Daddy can't understand what you want if you're screaming."

Suddenly there's silence, and Alex wonders if Rowan has hung up on *her* this time.

"Rowan, are you there?" she whispers, her neck so tight her head pop off.

"Sorry, Alex, I'm just having some, uh—you know what? Fine, do the story. Only because I have to get off the phone. I'll e-mail you the info of the editor at the newspaper down there—really nice woman. She paired us up with a local photographer when we did that feature on that horse whisperer guy."

"Great." Alex exhales and dabs tears out of her eyes as she sits on the toilet lid.

"—But I really don't want you to do it at all."

"I'll be fine—it's how I get through things." It's been how she's been getting over Kate all these months. And now she's offered, at the supposedly worst time of her life, to interview Juliette freaking Sprigg too.

As she hangs up, her stomach pushes up into her esophagus like peasants storming the Bastille. She sets her phone on the edge of the tub and wraps her arms under her knees, head on her lap, like people in the airplane safety cards do, and focuses on her breathing. Remain calm. Remain seated. Brace for impact.

Chapter Two

Alex doesn't have many mementos of her family—when she left for college, she took one thin, carefully curated packet of photos in case she developed amnesia or died and needed the authorities to identify and contact her next of kin. As she waits in the Greyhound Terminal at Union Station for her bus, she flips through them, sipping her coffee. In one, she's a baby, and her mother holds her in some undetermined seventies-style living room. Her dark, overgrown pageboy falls choppy over her ears and eyebrows, and she's wearing a paint-splattered, faded denim shirt. She looks wide-eyed at the camera, eyes bleary, her smile a mixture of surprise and exasperation. *What have we done?* She seems to plead to Alex's father, who's taking the picture.

She glances quickly at her senior photo, her slightly gapped front teeth peeking out underneath her lip gloss, her traumatized nineties curly big hair, then Owen's, his ill-advised mullet and delicate, soft lips. The second-to-last photo was taken by a park photographer at Kings Dominion. In it, Alex and Owen stand at the base of the replicated Eiffel Tower just inside the entrance. They had a good time that day, Alex thinks; their childhood wasn't all that bad. As she brings the photo closer, though, she's surprised to discover a cut on her cheek. Then she remembers the argument, her mother's peridot ring, being abandoned in the parking lot for half an hour.

Alex frowns and holds her breath for the last picture. Thankfully, it's only of her father's sister, Johanna Maas, the giver of birthday twenties and assorted letters, cards, and trinkets over the years. Alex had included this photo in the unlikely event she, Owen, and their mother met their demise together and someone needed to get in touch with their father. In it, Aunt Johanna sits on their deck, holding a champagne flute. She's wearing large dark sunglasses and a white silk scarf tied over her head, like a movie star. Alex remembers taking the picture when she was twelve.

Say hello to your Auntie Androgyne, Johanna had said on her only visit from Seattle. She was tall, with long hair the color of caramel, cloaked hazel eyes, and wore chiffon scarves of various shades. Although Alex hadn't known what androgyne meant at the time, she'd understood years later Johanna had transitioned from a man to a woman.

> *Have you told Aunt Johanna yet?* Alex texts Owen, hoping he doesn't respond with a picture of Tortoise.

Her bus pulls up, and Alex jostles into line. But she has to pee, and the last thing she wants to do is pee on the bus. She hurries to the restroom at the terminal, which is marginally better than that which she imagines on board. As she crouches over the seat, holding the stall of the broken door closed with one hand, Owen texts her back:

No, I thought you would tell her.

She balances her phone on her knees, reaching for the toilet paper, thinking about what else Owen hasn't done. Called the funeral home? A probate lawyer? Social Security?

She closes her eyes. Don't go, she thinks. You don't have to go. Just walk out of the station.

She hears the final call for her bus over the restroom intercom and stands up like she's been shot out of a canon. Her phone slips off her knees, and with an extraordinary feat of reflexes she hits it with her hand in mid-air, keeping it from falling to the floor, keeping it from breaking. Redirecting it, somehow, through her spread legs into the toilet. In the toilet water, before the screen pixelates out, a second message from Owen pops up. It's a photo of Tortoise sleeping on Alex's old bed. The caption underneath reads

BTW, this is mine now.

Chapter Three

The Greyhound takes three hours from DC. Alex has managed to retrieve her cell phone and shove it, wrapped in a million sheets of toilet paper, into her purse, and grab the last seat on the bus, right across from, ironically, the toilet. As the district recedes and federal buildings, metro stations, and Lululemon stores on every block fall away and are replaced by soybean and corn fields, Alex feels her mother's presence roll over her like a storm cloud. She bites her lip and crouches in her seat, which looks like someone has taken an alligator-sized bite out of the middle of the cushion, and glances at the screenshots on her laptop of Sprigg Restaurant.

But now she's thinking about Juliette, which isn't much better. *It's not too late*, she thinks as she scrolls through the pictures of Maryland rockfish, Chesapeake oysters, crab cakes, and other Eastern Shore cuisine, to abort this particular mission. Although it's unavoidable seeing her mom (in some incarnation) and Owen, torturing herself by writing about what Juliette Sprigg has done with her life is completely within her control.

Her life is manageable right now. She glances at the farmland outside the window. She has a good job at the

Capitol Metropolitan, a DC lifestyle magazine. It's pap, she knows, a vehicle for tony Washington advertisers, but she also knows it's a perfect fit for her. She has a flair for words, a breezy, conversational but also personal tone. She regularly participates in the comments section of her own articles. She's on Twitter and Instagram and has developed a respectable following. Although she's not a quite a celebrity on sight, at least like Kate, people know her name.

The most important thing is her life isn't like her mother's. More specifically, it's completely detached from her mother's, as if they were Siamese twins the first eighteen years of her life and Alex had hacked and sawed and chewed herself free. Her mother had had a way of taking credit for her successes while diminishing them at the same time. *Of course, you got a scholarship to Swarthmore.* Her mother rolled her eyes at Alex's college acceptance letter half her life ago. *Who do you think you got your brains from?*

Alex had discovered from a very early age, when at nine she wrote the winning essay for Sugarman's Pharmacy on what makes a healthy body (something about apples, sleep, and love), that scholastic achievement was her ticket to success. Although the ribbons and plaques and twenty-dollar gift certificates you could use to buy a My Little Pony weren't the same as hugs and kisses from her mother, they counted for something. The world of prize-winning essays, honor roll, Girl Scout badges, and advanced placement also got her noticed by other adults, adults who fawned over her and wished their girls were a little more like Alex. Alex, for her part, would have gladly switched places.

But now she has no mother, and she doesn't know if that's better or worse.

As the bus pulls up to the gas station parking lot outside city limits, everyone stares out the windows as if they've arrived at perdition. Alex scans the parking lot for their mother's ancient Subaru, hoping Owen isn't picking her up in his car. When she spots the lime green Miata with eyes and a blue headband painted on the hood, she closes her own eyes and wills it to disappear.

When she opens them again, it's still there. Owen won the promotional Teenage Mutant Ninja car years ago from the local comic store. Inside, the bucket seats look like turtle shells and the stick shift a sword handle. Owen had named Tortoise after it. It was the kind of car that, left unlocked overnight in DC, wouldn't be stolen, not only because it was conspicuous, but because it was hideous.

"Where's Mom's car?" she asks as soon as she steps off the bus. Owen's gained weight. Not terribly so, but enough to make his stubbled chin round, his stomach bulbous and resting above his jeans. Like a man who is dating mediocrity. His light, layered hair is long over his ears. He looks a lot like their father, actually, at least what she's seen of him in one or two pictures. She, with her curly dark hair, round face, and slightly gapped front teeth, looks like no one in her family, and secretly it has given her hope over the years she was adopted.

"It died—the head gasket cracked," he answers. Before she can react, he's hovering over her, his arms spread as if to bear-hug her. She shoves her laptop bag into his arms and wanders toward the cargo area of the bus, where the driver unloads passenger bags, and watches for her suitcase.

She's not ready to be touched. All morning, her emotions have been shifting inside her like the futures in a magic eight ball, and she isn't sure which one will reveal itself when she opens her mouth. She drinks the rest of her coffee and watches Owen retrieve her suitcase and gym bag and stuff them into the trunk of the Ninja Turtle car. She hopes she doesn't run into anyone she knows while she's home, at least while she's in this car. Why did she not renew her license? She supposes she can Uber if she really has to.

It probably doesn't matter, anyway—Is there anyone here she even knows now, aside from Juliette?

Lewis, maybe. She hopes to God she doesn't run into Lewis.

"Is Lewis still in town?" she asks as Owen gets in. She looks casually out the window, feeling an artery pulse in her throat.

"Lewis?" Owen repeats. "I don't know. Why? You want to tell him?'

"No." She glares at him, slapping his forearm. "Why would we tell the man who almost got Mom sent to prison that she's dead?"

"I don't know," he blurts out, his eyebrows furrowed as he starts the car. "You're the one who brought him up."

"Just forget it." She waves him off. "So how did she die?"

"She was asleep. I got home late, and she wasn't up. When I went to her room to check in, to tell her she was missing *Antiques Roadshow*, she didn't wake up, so I went to bed. She didn't get up the next day, though either."

"Did she overdose?"

"I dunno," Owen answers. "They found some benzodiazepines in her system, and alcohol. So they called it accidental."

Alex picks at the plastic tab on her coffee cup. She can't imagine her mother would do this on purpose. She'd just spoken to her last week. Her mother wanted to come up and go to the Elsa Schiaparelli retrospective at the Corcoran and stay overnight at Alex's place. Alex had agreed but had not committed to a date, hoping her mother would forget. Often when her mother was sober, she'd forget conservations they'd had while she was drunk, and vice versa.

"Did they find a lot of pills?" she asks finally. "Was she acting funny?"

"No more than usual. I mean, she took her nap after dinner. She usually gets up around eleven and does stuff until about three or four in the morning and goes back to sleep. But she wasn't up when I came home, and she hadn't moved when I woke up the next morning. The paramedics came, took her to the hospital, and they pronounced her there."

"Why didn't you call me at work?" Her nostrils flare, like a pit bull. "Did you ask for an autopsy?"

"No." Owen's silent, the way he used to be when he felt like she was going to explode on him. "Should I?"

"Do you think she committed suicide?"

"I don't think so."

"What do you mean you don't think so?" The coffee cup bends under her grip. "You lived with her, didn't you?"

"What—do you think you could have done better? You never even visit." He pulls into Rhubarb Village, the aptly named aging development of townhomes filled mostly now with retirees, and the sight of the rose bush and azaleas that span the length of her mother's brick townhouse make her feel as if someone has shoved a softball down her throat. She counts to ten, waiting for it to dissolve, for her anger to diffuse.

"Owen, I'm sorry," she says finally. "I just... want to know what happened."

Tortoise, a seal point Himalayan, waits for them in the hallway. Their mother had bought Tortoise after she broke up with Lewis. Which would make one think Alex would like Tortoise more, but she doesn't. Mostly because Owen treats Tortoise like she's human.

"Hi honey." To prove her point, Owen scoops Tortoise up and kisses her forehead as Alex drags her suitcase and laptop bag into the house behind him. "I know—mommy's gone; can you believe it?"

Alex expects their mother, in defiance, to burst from the kitchen in a paint-covered T-shirt, in the middle of painting some abstract monstrosity, or with a kitchen knife in her hand. *I'm making super-spicy burn-out your colon guacamole*, she would bark conspiratorially and laugh, sounding like a Scooby Doo villain. *You won't need a cleanse after you eat it.*

But she won't. She wouldn't, ever. This realization intermittently sent rumbling earthquakes through her chest on the bus trip here, ones she'd suppressed by concentrating on the grown woman across the aisle who sucked her thumb without the slightest hint of shame while she played Candy Crush on her phone.

Now that she's at ground zero, the fissures inside Alex feel like the San Andreas fault. Oddly, the house doesn't seem to realize their mother's gone. Everything's just as Alex remembers—the hulking spider plant in the kitchen with a thousand spider babies, the antique Bakelite clock on the hall table her mother had bought at an estate sale, the slightly dusty smell of the Oriental rug—except her mother isn't here. The house, in fact, still seems way too confident of her return, humming with an almost-radioactive sheen, brimming with the bric-a-brac of her mother's short attention span—art projects and empty yogurt containers and filled ashtrays abandoned on tables and in corners like tricycles in a driveway. Its unholy optimism feels like a rib spreader in her chest.

She takes another deep breath, one of hundreds since the night before. The meditation app on her phone reminds her to breathe so much she probably sounds like a hospital respirator.

"Did you eat?" Owen follows her down the hallway toward the stairs. "I'm starving."

"Well, if you could put down the cat and help me, we could actually make plans." She drops her suitcase back on the floor, sending Tortoise out of Owen's grasp and up the steps.

"Jesus, what did you pack?" Owen frowns as he lifts it.

"I don't know how long I'm staying," she answers. Although, judging by the lump her throat, the heaviness in her chest, her irritation at Owen, she could leave right now and not ever come back. "I have a story I need to do for the magazine while I'm here. On Juliette Sprigg."

"Juliette Sprigg?" He looks at her as if she's out of her freaking mind. "Are you kidding? Does your boss hate you? I thought you said you'd rather eat your own eyeballs than see her again."

"Did I say that?" Probably. She stares into space, wondering what other invectives she has shared with Owen about Juliette. "It doesn't matter. I'm a professional."

"Well, you always put your work first." He frowns. "No reason for Mom dying to get in the way."

"Owen." She sighs and put her hand on his shoulder. "I'm sorry."

"About your job?" He turns slightly. "It's not my..."

"I mean about Mom. I'm sorry I wasn't here when it happened."

He's silent for a minute. His eyebrows, as thick and dark as the smudges football players smear across their cheeks, dip toward his noise, like he is an animal in a zoo deciding whether to trust a banana offered from his captor.

"It's okay," he says finally.

She grasps him awkwardly by the midsection. They'd been close once, kind of, before all that stuff with Lewis, but affection now seems so hard, like crossing hot sand barefoot.

"You want to sleep in mom's room?" he asks at the top of the stairs. She's suddenly light-headed, teary, from the telltale creak of certain steps, the smell of the runner (which Owen did not seem to vacuum ever), the cracks of plaster on the wall, patterns she remembers with the same certainty as the veins that forked and vined up her inner arms.

"Why? Is something wrong with mine?" She stares straight ahead, and not into her mother's open doorway. She notes the deadbolt on her door remains, although it'd been years since she remembered where she'd hidden the key.

"No." He shrugs. "Hers has a king, that's all."

The last time she'd come home, maybe eight months before (and only because she'd been on her way to the beach), her mother had been in bed. Which was not unusual for her—she was a night owl and, if anything, now she'd retired, had completely succumbed to her erratic schedule and artistic impulses. But something had been different last time. Not enough to make Alex think death was imminent, but enough to make her think about her mother's mortality in a general way. A way that poked at her at odds moments after she'd returned home, like when she was getting coffee before work or Kate was stroking her back in bed. That her mother would not be around forever, and that Alex would have to make peace with her, find some connection that was pure and confirmed in some way her mother's maternity.

"Honey, make me some coffee, okay?" Her mother lay half in and half out of the sheets, her body angular and thin, like a praying mantis. She still wore clothes from presumably the night before: a pair of dark Capri pants and oversized white V-neck T-shirt (her mother patterned her style after a late 50s tomboy version of Audrey Hepburn). "I just fell asleep, like literally two minutes ago. I thought you weren't getting here until eleven."

"It's noon." Alex stood in the doorway. Honey was the first clue. It was a term her mother used loosely with other women of various ages, from toddlers to grandmothers, but never Alex. "Are you okay?"

"Yeah," she answered, but did not move. "I think I pulled my back out."

"How did you do that?" There were a million ways her mother could have done it, but they were a million ways that were different than most people's.

"I found this great wardrobe at the Salvation Army—it just needs a little staining and one of the legs repaired. It's over there." At this point her mother lifted her arm, half mast, in the general direction of the southeast corner of the room, where a hulking, late-sixties knockoff of a French country wardrobe cabinet, three-legged, tilted against the corner of the wall. "I had a hell of a time getting it up here. Do you like it? I think it would look great in your apartment."

"Why didn't you get Owen to help you with it?" Alex thought it looked exactly like something her mother would get for her and not what she'd actually want.

"It was the day he gets his new comics at the comic store—a couple weeks ago, I don't know."

"You've been having back pain like this for weeks?"

"Not every day. Just sometimes if I make a certain move or something. It's fine."

"Are you faking it?" Alex crossed her arms. It was an easy way, she had figured, for her mom to get prescriptions she didn't need.

"I pulled my frigging back." She looked wild-eyed at Alex. With her short dark hair and small features, she looked like a demented Christmas elf. "Can you just give me some coffee, Al-ex-an-dra, and not the third degree?"

With the introduction of her four-syllable name, her usual moniker, Alex had gone downstairs and dug out a somewhat-stale bag of Gevalia out of the cabinet and made her mother coffee. But she had been worried her mother hadn't moved a muscle, except those in her eyes. Debilitating pain or not, her mother was a tumbleweed. But she was getting older, Alex had reasoned; she would have to slow down sometime. Her next thought had been giving Owen hell about letting their mother go down to the Salvation Army and lug that monstrosity home that she would never get around to refurbishing while he hung out at the comic book store talking to adultescents about Batman and Robin issue number four thousand fifty and which incarnation of Robin were they on now? Had Robin come back to life? Become a villain? Become an alien?

"What the fuck is Robin now?" Alex blurts out as Owen heaves her suitcase onto her bed.

"The fuck what?" He looks up.

"Nothing." She waves him off, looking around and blinking. Her room is still a shrine to her high school years, although not by choice. She had taken down the Replacements and REM posters, shoved her stuffed animals in the closet, and tossed her books—Judy Blume's *Forever, Go Ask Alice, The Outsiders*, in the trash, but when she'd returned home from college (the first and only time) after first semester for break, everything had been restored, like a time machine, by her mother. *It's too weird, you not being here*, her mother had explained. *Now I can pretend you still are.*

"So, do you need like, a minute?" Owen hovers in the doorway.

"Just let me freshen up," she answers, sitting down on her bed. Although freshen up could be interpreted in any number of ways. Take a shower. Reapply her lipstick. Get her shit together. Fall apart. Why are they talking so casually about lunch when their mother had just died, when she was over at the funeral home in a body bag? How could she look at her mother lying there without completely falling into a depth of grief and anger she was not sure she could ever crawl out of?

"You ready?" Owen pops his head back in the door. How long has she been sitting catatonic like this, holding her nonfunctioning phone, praying it will dry out so she'll have the option to call Kate, even though she she'll probably just stare at Kate's contact information like a zombie?

"Yep." She stands, wiping tears from her eyes. "Let's go."

Chapter Four

The funeral home is clean but outdated. Or maybe it isn't outdated, just something else. Everything is white or ivory: the walls, the chair rails that connect to faux Grecian columns flanking corners, the fireplace in the lobby. The only splash of color rests in the framed prints of vaguely timeless pastoral themes that envisioned Heaven as a Thomas Kinkade painting.

"Gary Coons." The man who meets them at the door holds out his hand. He looks like the kind of man who was born to manage a funeral home. "I'm so sorry to hear about your mother, Adeline."

"Thanks," Alex answers. "I don't know if my brother told you, but my mother wanted to be cremated."

"Of course." He nods, hands clasped in front of his crotch. "We can help you with that."

"Can we see her?" Owen pipes up. He's wearing a Dr. Who T-shirt and cargo shorts. Alex wishes she had noticed before and had asked him to put something nicer on before they left.

Gary Coons nods again and leads them to a viewing parlor. Toward the front of the room, covered only by a white sheet, lies what is left of Adeline Maas.

"When you're ready, I'll be just down the hall—third room on the left." Gary Coons closes the door behind them.

Alex takes one step, then another, as Owen remains by the door. Suddenly she isn't in a rush. Maybe if she doesn't see her mother there, dead, her mother could still be at home, or at the art supply store, or at the junior axillary board cafeteria at the hospital, which she insisted had the best coffee in town and spent mornings sometimes chatting up relatives visiting loved ones and doctors she hoped were single (or at least open to having a mistress).

But she's here, in front of her. Alex can see the cow lick on her mother's crown she'd insisted her entire life was just bedhead. It hovers above the table a little, and Alex is mad for a second Gary Cooks or whatever his name is didn't even give her a pillow, letting her head rest on the hard steel instead. Although, she guesses, in his defense, her mother doesn't need it now.

She closes her eyes and smooths her mother's hair, feeling the cool, solidness of her head. She waits for a moment for her mother to roll her eyes and snort. But she doesn't. She looks almost peaceful. Almost loveable.

"Mom," Alex murmurs under her breath. Her mother died alone, in her sleep, not ravaged by cancer, or mangled in a car accident, blown up by a terrorist, or drowned at sea. But she was still her mother, and she shouldn't have died at all. Not, at least, until she had a chance to say goodbye. *Or before you apologized to me,* she thinks in the next breath. The more years that went by, though, the more times Alex picked up the phone and listened to her mother's chatter, her plans for mother-daughter trips to South Beach, or San Francisco, the more her mother seemed to feel absolved, forgiven. Brazen.

She shouldn't be feeling this way now. But what should she be feeling? Unfortunately, she's learned there's no binary emotional scale for important life events. You can feel devastated and relieved at the same time. Or both sad and angry. Or shocked but not surprised. Or, as Alex does right now, all these things at once.

She picks up her mother's hand and squeezes it, over and over. It feels unnatural, stiff and heavy, like hardened clay. Not like a person at all. Her mother is really dead; Alex is really alone. Her mother had not been her best friend, but she knew Alex best, which is its own comfort, she guesses. Someone who always knows who you are and will tell you, whether you want to hear it or not. If that person was gone, who will be there to show you the ugly truths of yourself?

"What are your options on taxidermy?" Owen asks Gary Coons when they're seated in his office.

"Absolutely not." Alex waves Owen off, shoving a catalog across the table toward him. "I'm fine with any of the urns on page 5—pick one."

"But we got Penny stuffed," he argues, shoving the urn catalog back across the table toward her. "I think Mom would like it."

Alex ignores him, turning to smile at Gary Coons. She points to a sterling silver urn in the catalog with two doves flying eternally in a circle around the body of the urn. Just like her and Owen.

"We'll take two of these," she says. She doesn't know what she'll do with her own urn, exactly, but she doesn't want to visit a spot in the ground and she certainly doesn't want to encounter her mother's freeze-dried corpse next to their old cat, Penny, on the floor by the rocker in the living room if she comes back to visit Owen.

Still, when they leave the funeral home, Alex feels like they're making a mistake, although she's not sure what it is. Maybe she should have spent more time with her mother's body. After all, she'll never see it again. Maybe Owen's taxidermy idea isn't so kooky after all.

"Where are you going?" she asks when she notices him heading away from the house.

"I always get Taco Bell on Thursdays," he answers, taking a hard left into the drive-thru. He leans his head out the window to get a better look at the menu.

"Seriously, you're hungry right now?"

"I'm always hungry—do you not know me?" He arches an eyebrow. "What do you want?"

"Just a Diet Pepsi." If she eats anything, she might throw up. She roots in her purse for the bottle of the valium she'd snatched off her mother's bedside table before they left. A few years back, Alex had taken some maximum-strength ibuprofen from the medicine cabinet when she'd been home visiting for the weekend. Although the fuel of her mother's life had been disorganization, apparently, she knew down to the pill what she had in the house. The next day, when she went to take more, the cabinet was bare.

"Don't even try to look for them," her mother practically challenged her. "You'll never find them. You have a job; buy your own damn pills."

But when she'd come home the last time, when her mother was sidelined with what they thought was a back sprain, every bottle of pain medication in the house had migrated into one tight bunch on her bedtable. Some were even prescription meds, albeit harmless ones—valium, klonopin.

"Owen." She's studying the bottle as they wait at the drive-thru. She hadn't read the label before she grabbed it, recognizing the shape of the pills through the amber cylinder instead. "This prescription is made out to you—I didn't know you were taking valium."

"My doctor prescribed it once for anxiety, but I never took it." He turns away from her and leans out the window. "Two chicken gorditas, one soft taco, one bean burrito—are you sure you don't want anything?"

"Diet Coke," she repeats, gripping the prescription bottle tighter. A familiar sinking feeling settles into her stomach. "Did you give these to Mom?"

"Did you get all that?" Owen repeats to the order box.

"You got this valium for anxiety?" she asks when he's back in the car.

"Yeah." He shrugs. "I have trouble sleeping. Mom probably thought they were hers. She had some of her own too—legally."

He emphasizes the last word. When he turns and reaches for the bags from the drive-thru attendant, she taps one out and pops it in her mouth. She's not a prescription abuser, like her mother, so it's okay. Allowed even, under the circumstances. It dissolves, chalky and bitter on her tongue.

Owen drops the two bags, greasy and warm, in her lap, onto the folders from the funeral home.

"Jeez, Owen—careful." She pulls out the folders from under the bags and tucks them between her seat and the door. She supposes he could have gotten a prescription for insomnia. Hell, her doctor had written Alex a script after she'd told her about Kate.

"Oh, I got you a soft taco," he says, almost in apology.

"Thanks, I guess." She pats one of the bags like he'd given her a puppy. At the smell of the beef and cheddar, her stomach begins to gurgle in agitation.

"Remember the time when Mom drove through the Popeye's drive-thru and forgot the food?" Owen laughs as he puts the car in first.

"Oh my God, yes." Alex laughs too. "And she tried to back up to the window and make everyone else behind us back up, too? And her profanity, my God."

"I'd never heard the words 'fascist motherfucker' before that."

"So are you going to move out now?" she asks after a minute. "How many years has it been since you got your PhD?"

Alex figures Owen had an inkling of what was going on with their mother and Lewis, the insurance fraud stuff (and certainly the non-insurance fraud stuff that happened between Alex and Lewis). But the whole fraud thing had blown up the year before he'd graduated from college. She could understand him coming back and staying a little while, to make sure their mom was on the up and up (because Alex certainly wasn't going to). But not 10 years or whatever it's been.

"I think I want to sell," he answers. "Unless you and Kate want it?"

"Really?" A dull burn flares in her chest at the mention of Kate. "I mean, where would you go?"

As Owen slows down for a traffic light, Alex reaches into her shoulder bag and pulls out a small envelope. In it is a folded notecard the color of champagne, with Kate's monogram, KSL, engraved in rose gold. One weekend four months ago Alex went to visit her friend Lia in Boston. When she got home, everything of Kate's was gone from Alex's apartment, and the envelope had rested on the table: *Alex, I know this will probably come as a shock (maybe not), and I'm sorry. But I think we're at different places in our lives, and there's so much you need to do to open yourself up to vulnerability. I also don't want to be in a relationship in which I'm a third wheel to your past. Although I think you're wonderful and am grateful for the time we spent together, I know in my heart this is for the best. Love, Kate*

How is it the woman she'd been with for four whole years, with whom she hoped she'd spend the rest of her life, chose to break up with her via her stationary? She shoves the card back into her purse, ashamed she's kept it but unable to get rid of it either. She reads it at random times, as if she's Nancy Drew trying to decipher a code: *The Hidden Message in the Haughty Breakup Notecard.*

How had Alex been a different place in her life than Kate? She wanted to be successful at work; she wanted love. She possibly wanted to have children. And she was passable, she thought, as a successful, cultured person. Even though she came from a small town, she learned to love sushi and bibimbap bowls and espresso. She'd watched Fellini and Bergman movies and spent her summer vacation with Kate's extended family in their compound in Nantucket. She knew the difference between the Bordeaux and the Pinot and the Chardonnay glasses and had come to believe over time that the differences in those glasses were necessary.

Of course, as with anything involving her emotions, Alex managed to screw it all up somehow. *The only way you know what you're feeling is if you write it down—and even then, you'd edit the hell out of it,* Kate had accused her once. Kate, Upper East side-born, Vassar-grade, who appeared on Sunday morning network shows as a political commentator and repeated talking points she didn't even believe in. Who likened her job to selling Tabasco sauce to people who lived in hell—had accused Alex of being out of touch with *her* feelings.

"Do you think I'm out of touch with my feelings?" she asks Owen as the valium begins to turn the back of her head into wax.

"Your default setting is like, indignation," he answers as the light turns green. "If that's a feeling."

"I would like to be magnanimous," she explains, ignoring him. "When I'm here."

"Did Kate put you up to it?"

"Kate and I broke up." She grips the folder of her mother's things tightly.

"Oh." He pauses for a second. "You never told me that. I just thought she didn't come because she was busy or something. I'm sorry."

"It's okay," she answers. Maybe it is okay. She doesn't have to pretend anymore to be someone she isn't. But the more time she spends single, the more she's worried she'll become way too comfortable being herself.

"Wait—stop!" Alex cries so loud Owen slams on the brakes in the middle of the street.

"What?" He looks around, breathing hard, a dab of sweat near his ear. "Did I hit something?"

"There." Alex points at a building about thirty feet ahead on the left—the administrative offices of *The Shore Times*, the local newspaper. "I need to do something for the magazine article I'm writing. It'll only take a minute, I swear."

Chapter Five

"If you're not done by the time I'm finishing eating, I'm coming in there to get you," Owen warns as Alex climbs out of the Ninja Turtle car. He waves his hand toward his Dr. Who shirt, as if he knows it embarrasses her.

"So you're only giving me thirty seconds, then?" She smirks and slams the door.

The newspaper office is one-story, long, brick, dating back to the sixties, probably. Alex had visited once, when she was in high school, after she had written a scholarship-winning essay about the importance of civic duty. *It hasn't changed much*, she thinks as she sits in the waiting room with two chairs, both low-riding vinyl deals with wooden arms that makes her think Mary Tyler Moore will burst through the door from the newsroom at any minute. She picks up a copy of the paper from a row of them on the table. *Community Center Gets New Fitness Equipment; Sheriff Receives Honor; Bedbug Infestation at Local Hotel*. Award-winning reporting, for sure. She's folding the newspaper, as thin as its stories, when the door opens.

"Can I help you?" a woman asks. Her bobbed hair, the color of honey, cradles her face, soft and rounded, at the chin. Her eyes are green and large and welcoming.

"Yes," Alex answers absently. "I don't have an appointment, but I'm here to see, uh, Carolyn Pusey."

"That's me." The woman holds out as her hand as Alex jumps up, embarrassed.

"I'm sorry," Alex squeezes her hand a little too hard. "I'm Alex Maas, from the *Capitol Metropolitan*. Rowan, um, has told me so much about you."

"Well, that's so nice to hear—I've never met him in person." Carolyn leads her down the narrow, carpeted hallway into a room full of cubicles Alex recognizes as the newsroom. "I've read some of your work—online, and I enjoyed it."

"It's silly," Alex laughs, although secretly she's delighted her work has traveled across the Chesapeake Bay.

"I understand you're interviewing Juliette Sprigg." Carolyn leads her to a small office in the corner of the cube farm. A MacBook is on the desk, along with a bottle of water. A few framed stories line the walls, along with a bachelor's and master's diploma. It's impersonal in a way that pleases and slightly offends Alex—she had imagined there would be something dorky, like a Cathy office calendar or cat mug. There aren't even any pictures of family, she notes as Carolyn pulls something off the printer.

"We did a little profile a few years ago, when the restaurant changed hands—you've probably already read it, but I just wanted to pass it along in case you wanted any background information." Carolyn holds out the page.

Alex did read it, back on the bus, and thought it read more like an advertisement than a story, but she takes the sheet and holds it before her, pretending to scan it.

"Thank you," she says. "So Rowan said you knew a good photographer?"

"Yes." Carolyn leans against her desk. She's shorter than Alex, not by much, but definitely an embracer of sensible heels. No wedding ring. Alex wonders if all the men in town are like Owen, if there's something in the water. "Is that a problem?"

"It's just...do you mind if I look at the portfolios of the photographers you contract out to?" Alex looks up. "I think the sensibility of the photographer is just as important as the article."

"I can do that—I'll get them to you this afternoon, if that's okay." Carolyn nods, and Alex feels a little guilty. That it's too easy to run all over the editor of her hometown newspaper, who probably only makes a little more as editor than Alex does as a magazine writer in the city. Who maybe thinks maybe Alex is more sophisticated and educated or something and should be afforded respect, none of which is true.

"That's fantastic," Alex answers, her voice high and chirpy. "But even tomorrow, or the next day, is fine. You don't have to cater to me."

"Well, you'll let me know if you need anything else." Carolyn glances at the phone on her desk, which had not stopped ringing since they've been in the office.

"Of course." Alex folds the article and drops it in her shoulder bag. She tenses slightly as she imagines Owen wandering, like a newly hatched zombie monster, toward the entrance to the *Shore Times*. "I know you're very busy."

"Will you be in town long?" Carolyn does not move from where she leans against the desk.

"I...don't know," Alex answers. "My mother died yesterday, and I'm not sure...what I'm supposed to do. I mean, that didn't come out right. She's why I'm came home, to get things in order, and I just don't know—"

"I'm so sorry." Carolyn straightens up, arms folded. She meets Alex's eyes. "I didn't realize. Forgive me for not saying anything until now."

"You didn't know." Alex shakes her off. "How would you know? I knew Rowan wanted to do this story, and I just figured I'd do it while I was here."

"Well, that's very noble of you," Carolyn answers. "Considering what you must be going through."

"Not really," she answers. "I just don't want to be alone with my thoughts right now."

"There are a lot of times I feel that way," Carolyn laughs. It sounds as sensible as the heel on her shoes. "But you do what you have to get through, I know. Still, I'm so sorry."

Alex nods. She's embarrassed but doesn't know why. Maybe because she's been honest with a total stranger. No one who can hurt her in any way, she knows, but since Kate, she doesn't feel the need to be more open than necessary. At least not right now, when her emotions stab at her unexpectedly, like a sensitive tooth to coffee or ice cream.

"I'll let you get back to work now." Alex jingles Owen's keys, which she made sure to take with her. "Thanks so much for letting me stop by."

"Please." Carolyn untangles her arms and touches Alex's forearm. "Any time."

Alex nods again, patting Carolyn's hand before stepping back. "I can find my way out. You're busy."

She walks through the newsroom, its familiar clacker of keyboards oddly reassuring, grounding. It's the Morse code of her known life, regimented, predictable, and controlled. Outside in Owen's car it will be quiet, open, the sun burning through the windows and onto the pleather turtle shell seats. In such moments, a memory of her mother could rise to the surface, as quick as a beach ball held under water and let go.

She steps outside in the parking lot and flips on her sunglasses. She needs to keep skiing herself down this treacherous hill a little longer—next flag, Juliette Sprigg—before she completely wipes out into the dark woods below. She can take another valium, she figures, go to the restaurant that evening for dinner—maybe she can treat Owen—and get started on the article.

She strokes her forearm where Carolyn's hand had been as she glances at the cars in the parking lot. She wonders which one is Carolyn's. Her eyes rest on a sensible gold Corolla and, thinking she has filed away everything she needs to know about Carolyn Pusey, tosses the keys through the open driver's side window into Owen's lap.

"You're late," he says, ratcheting the seat up from a reclining position. "So I ate your soft taco too."

Chapter Six

"I need to call Aunt Johanna." Alex says to Owen in the kitchen as she pulls her phone out of the bowl of rice on the counter. She'd put it in it before they left for the funeral home, telling Owen she spilled coffee on it while on the bus, and to her relief, the screen reboots. But when she turns around, she realizes she's been talking to herself, that Owen's gone upstairs.

When he returns a minute later, he's carrying a box the size of an air conditioner. Tortoise sits on top of it.

"Maybe you can start going through these photos too." He drops it on the dining room table, Tortoise scrambling off.

"Jeez, you in a hurry to go through stuff?" Alex wraps her arms around herself. Maybe he's more organized, more motivated to sell the house than she thought. But why? The house is paid for; he can work his job at Staples the rest of his life and not worry about anything if he wants to.

"If you're only going to be here a few days, there's a lot to do," he answers before heading back upstairs. Alex shoos Tortoise away and grabs a handful of photos absently from the top, some in waxy photo packets and others, along with negatives, loose, and spreads them before her on the table.

She'd always thought, since her mother was an art teacher, she'd be a natural photographer as well. But there are no elegant black-and-white, artfully lit photos of Alex and Owen playing in the yard or sleeping in their strollers.

Instead, there's just volume. As if worried she would suddenly suffer amnesia, or short-term memory loss, or just didn't want to forget a single thing, their mother had taken photos and filled boxes and boxes of them, with no apparent organizational system, and no apparent regard for value. Every year their mother had taken a photo of the Christmas and Thanksgiving turkey, although it was not quite apparent, unless the date was stamped on the back from the photo lab to which she'd taken it, which years those Christmas and Thanksgiving turkeys were celebrating.

There are pictures, hundreds seemingly, of their old cat Penny, doing the things Penny did—sleeping, sitting in the bay window in the dining room, looking sour at the camera (when she actually looked at the camera). And did they even need those now, since she was still freaking here, stuffed, by the rocker? There's a picture of the dishwasher her mother had bought new fifteen years before. And pictures of Alex and Owen sleeping, drooling on the sofa, nodding off in the car, sprawled on the floor like victims of a massacre. Why had their mother been obsessed with taking pictures of them when they were at their most vulnerable?

"Because they're funny," she remembers her mother having explained one afternoon, when Alex confronted her with a picture from the latest pack. It was of Alex at fourteen, asleep on the sofa, her hair caught in a sofa cushion, wearing a nightgown with Garfield on it. "And I could always use the blackmail."

"I'm thinking of redecorating if we don't sell," Owen says as he returns with another box. "If that's okay with you."

"Fine with me." She shrugs, secretly relieved his plans to move have not progressed beyond the random-thoughts stage.

Still, it's hard for her to imagine Owen's decorating ideas. Or maybe it isn't. In his room there are two glass, climate-controlled cases of vintage action figures, a Cylon helmet from the original Battlestar Galactica television series, and a signed, framed poster of Carrie Fisher in her Return of the Jedi bikini. Their mother's scattered easels, unfinished sculptures of iron and glass bits, her treasured collection of *Vogue* magazines from the 1950s and 1960s, seems more appealing than whatever Owen had in mind.

She drops the photos back in the box. It might be easier to throw them all out than to rescue the two pictures she might actually want. She goes to the secretary instead and pulls out her mother's address book, flipping through the pages. Under the Ms, there is one listing: J. Maas.

Alex pauses. Shouldn't there be two? And which Maas is this—Jeffrey or Johanna? Probably Johanna. Still, she figures there'd at least be an old address for their father, scratched out or something. Unless—

As soon as she thinks it, though, she dismisses it off as a product of her overactive imagination. If she were writing a novel, maybe, her long-lost father would have transitioned to a woman. But those kinds of things never happen in real life—a father leaves his children because he isn't ready for the responsibility of family or doesn't want one. In real life, the father is usually a jerk.

And, since her mother never seemed to get over him, he probably was more than just a jerk. Alex dials the number listed under "J. Maas" and waits. It goes into voicemail.

"Leave me a sweet after the beep." A deep but feminine voice instructs.

"Johanna, it's Alex Maas," Alex speaks, relieved and disappointed at the same time. "I'm calling with some bad news—our mom died yesterday and, well, I just wanted you to know. I know you were close, and she always appreciated you, and we do too. If you wanted to call us back, that would be great."

She hangs up. *At least*, she thinks, *that's done*. Still, she wishes she'd gotten Johanna in person. Unlike her mother, Johanna is empathetic and warm, almost motherly. And, unfortunately, three-thousand miles away. She takes a few deep breaths and clenches her fists a few times until the feeling passes. Hearing herself say aloud that their mother is dead makes it more final, makes it more imperative than ever she and Owen drive back to the funeral home this minute and bring her home. And what, bring her back to life somehow?

And why did this this have to happen now, so soon after her breakup with Kate? Also, when had she actually *seen* her mother last? Had it really been almost a year ago? Should she have set a date for the Elsa Schiaparelli retrospective? Should she have followed through on her mother's back pain, urging her to make a doctor's appointment? Adeline Maas had been a heavy drinker, not in an always-obnoxious way, but still a drain-a-bottle-of-wine after dinner every night since Alex and Owen had been in high school. Surely, among other problems, it hadn't been kind to her liver.

And why hadn't Owen? What was so pressing in his life beyond his part-time job at Staples and comic books that he couldn't see whether their mother was having problems, health or otherwise? Of course, the otherwise had always been hard for Alex to get a read on, but why hadn't he done anything while their mother festered in bed, surrounded by pills, some of which were his own?

"I thought you were going through the photos." Owen peeks into her bedroom door a few minutes later. She is sitting on her bed, her laptop resting on her thighs.

"I thought I'd start working on the article instead," she explains.

When he's gone, however, she opens the top left drawer of her dresser and digs through her old socks until she finds an envelope containing a few more photos. She hadn't taken these with her to college, but she's never been able to get rid of them either. One is Juliette's senior photo and the other is four photos on a strip of Juliette and Alex together, taken at a photo booth in Ocean City. She studies Juliette's dark red hair, long and curling into ringlets on her shoulders, her heart-shaped lips, Juliette's fingertips resting on the side of Alex's neck in one of the photos, her face slightly turned toward her.

The last time she'd seen Juliette was high school graduation. They hadn't spoken for weeks, and their last names—Sprigg and Maas—ensured they'd be nowhere near each other in the audience of graduating seniors. Alex had told Owen and her mother to meet her in the parking lot after the ceremony. She had no intention of lingering in the high school gym, drinking fruit punch and eating sheet cake emblazoned with GO SENIORS and CONGRATULATIONS with the other kids who'd treated her like she was some highly contagious lesbian fungus.

She'd gotten through the first row of cars and spotted her mother in the fourth row, near the exit, leaning against their Subaru. Her mother wore Ray Bans and a black fedora, her arms crossed like she was the third Blues Brother or had materialized from some mid-80s new wave music video. As Alex raised her hand to wave to her, she felt another hand on her shoulder.

"Alex." It was Juliette's mother, Barbara Sprigg. She wore a floral print dress with a ruffled collar. A small crucifix hugged her thick neck. Her hair was red like Juliette's but her face ruddier, plastered with freckles. She smiled. "You're in a hurry! Congratulations!"

"Thanks." Alex glanced over Mrs. Sprigg's shoulder, saw Juliette, still in her graduation gown, lagging behind with her father and little sister. "My mom is taking us out to dinner."

"Oh, I won't keep you." Mrs. Sprigg said, clasping Alex's forearm as she did so. "You haven't been by the house for a long time—Juliette says you've been so busy getting ready for Swarthmore. I'm sure your mother is so proud."

"Uh huh." Alex nodded. "I know Juliette is excited to go to Eastern Shore State."

"Well, she's," Mrs. Sprigg glanced over her shoulder, "never been much of the academic type. I'm just glad I taught her to bake."

"It's a shame they didn't let you guys supply the cakes." Juliette's mother ran a bake shop in town. Even now, she smelled faintly of sugar and frosting.

"Well, they wanted some asinine discount," Mrs. Sprigg snorted. "Because Juliette is a student. Fine, but a 50% discount?"

"It was very nice to talk to you." Alex tugged her arm away gently. "But I've got to go."

"Is everything okay at home now, dear?" Mrs. Sprigg looked in the direction of the Subaru.

"Yes, why?" Alex glanced at Juliette again, her dark red hair, the few strands that stuck to her lip gloss. Alex wondered if the lip gloss smelled like mint, or strawberry. She wondered how Juliette's hair would feel splayed between her fingers at that moment.

"Okay. I'm glad." Mrs. Sprigg nodded, and Alex wondered what Juliette had told her. There was a lot, she thought, she could tell Mrs. Sprigg about Juliette.

They embraced, a half, light, back-patting hug, their cheeks brushing.

"Stay away from my daughter," Mrs. Sprigg murmured into Alex's ear. Then, as if nothing happened, Mrs. Sprigg waved vigorously and went to join the rest of the Spriggs. Stunned, Alex watched them walk toward their Buick. Before they reached it, Juliette turned her head, her mouth parted, her eyes searching Alex's. Alex wondered, for a moment, if she had been too hasty, too harsh, to Juliette, if there was something salvageable between them.

No, she decided. Her life after high school would be awesome, and she wouldn't remember Juliette any more than their high school mascot or her mom's boyfriend Lewis. She held up her hand to Juliette, as if to wave. Instead, she gave her the finger and joined Owen and her mother at the other side of the parking lot.

"Did you just flip someone off?" Her mother lowered her sunglasses. Her hazel eyes bored into Alex with an unwavering intensity of a gamma ray. "At graduation?"

"It was Juliette," Alex murmured, shaking her head. In her new life, she would be more mature. She felt fears in her eyes. "I shouldn't have. I just—"

"Are you kidding?" Her mother grabbed Alex by the shoulders and looked up at her. She grinned. Alex noted her mother had borrowed her lipstick. "I'm more proud of that than your stupid diploma."

Her mother pulled a pack of Benson & Hedges out of her dark cotton blazer with the rolled-up sleeves and tapped out a cigarette.

"Smoke?" She held out the pack to Alex. "You're almost eighteen."

Alex shook her head. "I don't want lung cancer."

"Your choice." Her mother shrugged, lighting hers. She took a drag, then exhaled with a flourish. "Welcome to adulthood."

*

"I don't like fancy stuff." Owen sits on the couch in his boxers. It's five o'clock in the afternoon and he looks in for the night.

"It's just dinner—my treat. I have to scope out Sprigg for the article." Alex kicks off her sneakers and touches her raw, skinned knee. Worried she'd gained a few pounds since Juliette had last seen her, she'd gone for a quick jog on the track of their old high school. Even though the kids on the surrounding fields—going through field hockey and soccer drills—were half her age, she felt every bit as young as them. Every bit as scrutinized. She sucked in her gut, picked up the pace, and tripped over her own feet. She'd cracked the screen on her iPod and shattered her dignity in front of an entire high school athletics program in fewer than ten steps.

"I don't know why you're even working on this story." He crosses his legs, feet on the coffee table. "Mom just died, and you're acting like nothing is wrong."

"That's not true—" she says over her shoulder as she went into the kitchen, although maybe he's a little right. "Oh, I called Aunt Johanna already, just so you know."

"Cool. What happened to you, anyway?" he asks as Alex comes back into the living room and sits on the edge of the coffee table. She pulls the backs of the bandage off and smooths it over her knee.

"I tripped over my own feet." She crunches the waxy tabs in her fist. "Something I like to do when I'm not putting them in my mouth."

"I have plans tonight," he answers. "So I can't go, anyway. Take my car though."

"You have all the time in the world to watch *The Rockford Files*." She rolls her eyes. "You have them all on DVD now. Besides, I can't drive—my license is expired."

"It's two miles to Sprigg—you can walk. Besides, I'm going out with my buddy from work." He stands up. "Sorry."

"Fine," she says after him, under her breath. "Have fun with your friends from Staples."

Immediately she regrets it. *Mag-nan-i-mous*, she reminds herself, spreading out the syllables as she says them like a mantra. In her bedroom she pulls two dresses out of her suitcase, smoothing the fabrics. She can just go by herself; it isn't a big deal. Hell, she'd gone to prom by herself.

"Why didn't you just ask someone?" her mother complained as she pinned Alex's hair in a French roll up-do. She wore a black peasant blouse and Levi's rolled up mid-calf. Pins hung out of the corner of her mouth. "Didn't you kids learn about Sadie Hawkins?"

"I wanted to." Alex blinked back tears. "But she's going with someone else."

"She?" Her mother stepped away. A few pins fell out of her mouth. "What do you mean? Are you coming out to me on prom night, Al-ex-an-dra?"

"No." Alex shook her head. "I mean, it doesn't matter now—we broke up."

Had she and Juliette actually been dating, Alex wondered, if no one knew it? Was something real if one of them could deny it?

"Jeez, does Owen know?" Her mother picked at a few loose curly tufts of Alex's hair. "Am I always the last person to know what's going on? I should have known this would happen to one of you, anyway. It's your father's fault."

"What do you mean, my father's fault?" Alex raised her eyebrows. Her mother never had a problem with gay people, as far as she knew.

"I mean your Aunt Johanna—the Maas genes," her mother explained dismissively. "Not that there's anything wrong with it. So, do I know the girl?"

"Of course, you do." She blinked back tears.

"It's Juliette, isn't it?" Her mother answered for her. "Juliette turned you down? That uptight little Christian bitch."

"It's not like that." Alex shrugged her mother's arm off her back. "I don't want to talk about it."

"Don't go." Her mom took Alex by the arms as she wept. She patted Alex's up-do as if it were a hamster. "Proms are stupid, sweetie. I never went to mine either—I went to see Yes in concert and tripped my ass off. Let's go out somewhere fancy, and we'll split a bottle of wine. We'll have our own coming-out party."

"Mom, I can't drink in public." Alex shook her head. "But thanks. Besides, I want to go."

The theme was something juvenile: enchantment under the sea or something calling for a lot of seashells—on the tables, etched on souvenir glasses and napkins. Alex sat alone and watched Juliette walk in with Scott Mueller, the varsity shortstop. Juliette wore all white, her hair loosely piled atop her head. Little emeralds dotted her earlobes. She glanced quickly at Alex before looking away.

Maybe her mother had been right. She watched Juliette dance with Scott. She had been accepted to Swarthmore on scholarship. She was never, ever coming back, if she could help it. Alex would work three jobs every summer in Philadelphia if she had to. She shouldn't have come here. But she walked over them on the dance floor, anyway.

"Alex, no." Juliette gripped Scott tighter as Alex approached.

"One dance." Alex put her hand on Juliette's bare shoulder. "Please? I'm so sorry."

"I swear if you don't go away, I'll never talk to you again." Juliette stared at her, her light green eyes seeming to crystalize to the same hardness as her emeralds.

"You're never going to talk to me again anyway." Alex tugged her arm.

"She said go away, you dyke," Scott said loudly, and, with all the diplomacy of a high school varsity shortstop, thrust himself between her and Juliette, almost knocking Alex on the floor. She teetered for a moment on one heel before righting herself. A circle of onlookers had opened up the dance floor around them. Alex looked toward the door; she felt like she'd fallen into a vat of ice water. But she couldn't leave; even if no one else knew what had happened between them, she wanted Juliette to never forget.

She wrapped her arms around herself and began to dance a few feet nearby to Simple Minds' "Don't You Forget About Me." But when they moved away, she didn't follow them. She closed her eyes and held herself tighter, humming to herself, trying to drown out the snickers and name calling. Les-bo. Dyke. Cunt muncher. When she opened her eyes, she saw Scott and Juliette were no longer dancing; they sat at a table in the front, near the prom queen and king, their eyes pierced, lips pursed, as they argued. At least, Alex had thought with some satisfaction, Juliette wasn't having a good time either.

She notices her prom dress, still hanging in its plastic wardrobe bag in the closet, as she pulls out the light blue sleeveless dress she hung up there earlier for dinner. Once, a few years ago, Alex had drunk stalked Juliette on Facebook, was smugly happy to find she had never made it out of town. But she had been a chef at a local upscale restaurant, nestled on the bend of the river. And, when the owner retired, she bought it and renamed it Sprigg. In a story meeting at the *Capitol Metropolitan*, the Marjorie, the food critic, had suggested a profile; Sprigg had championed the farm-to-table movement in a town that was literally built on farming. *Who goes all the way out there to eat?* Alex had wondered aloud. *Good food is the anchor of gentrification*, Marjorie shot back, *of suburban revival.*

Although Alex is happy in theory Juliette has done well for herself, she's a little disappointed she's done it without her, so much so she's now going to make Juliette grovel to her in return for a flattering article. But it's not that, if she's honest with herself. She's been looking (or at least daydreaming) for an excuse to see Juliette again after all these years, to find closure, and the excuse of death carried with it the least ulterior motives.

And a little sympathy too. She pulls off the light blue sleeveless and slips on a white linen sleeveless dress with a taupe belt she also brought along. She'll even borrow Owen's car—she'll just drive really slowly and park really, really far from the restaurant.

Her phone dings where it lies on the bed. Johanna, Alex thinks with relief as she scoops up her phone. But it's Carolyn Pusey, the editor of the newspaper, texting her the names of some photographers and their websites.

Sorry I'm just getting you these. Busy week so far. I hope you've been okay. Pls call me if you need anything.

Anything at all? Alex wonders. She certainly could use company. She picks up her phone.

Chapter Seven

The restaurant is crowded for a Tuesday night. Alex waits at the bar, nursing a blueberry acai mojito. She supposes if there is a place to hang out in this town, it would be Sprigg. The old restaurant had been dark, with lots of oak and equestrian memorabilia. Her mother had gone there because it was one of the last restaurants to allow smoking. Now, with its airy interiors, bamboo plants, its white marble bar and wall fountain behind it, its Café del Mar soundtrack, it seems to attract a young professional crowd.

"I'm sorry I'm late." She feels Carolyn's hand on her shoulder and turns a little too quickly, spilling a bit of her drink on the bar.

"No, you're fine." Alex moves her shoulder bag off the barstool next to her. "You look great."

"Thanks." Carolyn's wearing a loose muslin shirt and mint green Capri pants. "That's why I was late."

"You're so sweet to keep me company." Alex signals to the bartender. "What will you have?"

"Whatever you're having." Carolyn nods to Alex's mojito.

"I tried to get my brother Owen to come, but he's kind of a homebody," Alex explains, pressing open some edamame with her thumb. "Not that it's a terrible thing, I guess. But you don't meet people if you spend every night at home. I don't think he's ever had a girlfriend, and he's thirty-five."

"Maybe he's just not ready to meet people?" Carolyn picks up the mojito the bartender has set in front of her.

"He's not going to be young forever. My mom was alone most of her life, but at least she tried. It's just that she was kind of, I don't know, crazy."

"How many people are actually certified crazy?" Carolyn grins at her. "I mean, crazy is such an overused term these days."

She doesn't know why she's admitting to Carolyn all these things about her family. Probably because she's not looking to impress her. In some ways, it's a relief to open up to someone she'll never see again.

"I know my brother sounds like some kind of project, but he's not." Alex says more charitably after a minute. "I mean, he's really smart, and he's lived at home way too long. But he's kind and loves cats and he's great at computers and cars. If you know anyone in town who's single, well, they could do a whole lot worse."

"Sounds like you have a lot on your plate when you're home—your mother's estate, finding your brother a girlfriend, writing up Juliette Sprigg." Carolyn glances at her. "You don't seem to be leaving much time for your own grief."

Alex opens her mouth to answer, but she's at a loss for words. She looks up gratefully at the waiter who appears to take them to their table.

Juliette had always been interested in cooking. Her mother's bakery specialized in Smith Island cakes, an eight-layer cake with icing between each layer. *Diabetes cake*, Alex's mother had always chortled, but Alex thought it was kind of cool and would spend weekends at the Sprigg's house, watching Juliette and her mother making the thin layers of chocolate cream, banana cream, and strawberry. Juliette's mother was the opposite of Alex's own mother, who made elaborate dishes one night that would make Julia Child jealous and ate olives out of the jar the next, often leaving Alex and Owen on their own.

It was Alex's mother, though, who gave Juliette the greatest gift of all.

Baking is for moms, Alex's mother declared one day when Alex and Juliette were making brownies in the kitchen. They didn't mention to Alex's mother they had put hashish in them. Alex's mother went to the shelf over the sink that held her cookbooks. She pulled out *Helen Brown's West Coast Cookbook* and handed it to Juliette. *Here, take this. Everything you should know about the future of cooking is in here.*

Alex opens the menu the waiter has placed in front of her. In addition to Eastern Shore seafood, it's packed with Southern Californian cuisine: salmon, scallops, and Cioppino, salads of kale and heirloom tomatoes. Each entrée has a suggested wine pairing.

She glances up at Carolyn, who she realizes has been studying her instead of the menu. Carolyn looks away quickly, taking a sip of her drink. She has an unassuming, nonjudgmental face; the kind you could tell anything but also didn't think twice about. Alex figures it probably gives Carolyn an edge as a journalist.

"Did you always want to be a writer?" Alex asks, closing her menu.

"I love discovering things and explaining them," Carolyn answers. "I guess it helps me to understand them myself."

"Me too—I always feel a little out of place and being someone who people want to talk to gives me the upper hand." She glances around the restaurant. Would Juliette be here tonight? She knows from her research Juliette hired another chef last year to free her up to scout a second location, and she spends time procuring ingredients with vendors, doing publicity. She's purportedly in talks for her own reality show on cable.

Alex wonders suddenly if Juliette will think she and Carolyn are dating if she sees them here together. But why would it matter if she did? After all, Juliette is married. Still, Alex picks up the leather-bound menu again and opens it, lowering her head.

"Like now?" Carolyn laughs as she watches Alex try to squeeze herself behind the pages.

"I'm just doing reconnaissance tonight," she explains. "I haven't even contacted Juliette yet."

"Would she know you?" Carolyn raises an eyebrow.

"She knows *you*," Alex answers quickly. She thinks, for a second, Carolyn has somehow figured out her history with Juliette. But, of course, she couldn't have. Alex smiles conspiratorially. "Don't blow my cover."

"I'll try not to." Carolyn sets her menu upright and dips her head down, too, her eyes peering out at Alex over the top. Alex can see, from the squint in her eyes, she's smiling.

"My mother loved to cook," Alex scoops up a handful of edamame and tosses it in her mouth. "I just love to eat. She's the one who told me all about Sprigg."

"That's kind of a nice touch for your article," Carolyn remarks. "Your family."

"I tend to leave my family out of my work," she says, and then added, even though it's a lie: "to preserve their privacy."

"So, what did your mother like to cook?" Carolyn asks after the waiter takes their orders: Alex a goat cheese salad and artichoke ravioli and Carolyn the scallops.

"Everything—she was the kind of person who could throw together whatever was on hand—she told me all I ever needed on hand was a little garlic, a little olive oil, and a little wine. Of course, she drank most of the wine while cooking, but some of it made its way in the meal." Alex stirs her glass in the air in thought. "She didn't really fit in here, in this town. I didn't either."

"High school was tough," Carolyn agrees. "But, coming back here, I found most of the people who stayed left all the cliquey stuff behind them. There was this girl at Southside who was just the bitchiest little cheerleader when we were seniors. Never looked at me back then. Yet, when I ran into her at the library the other day, she talked my ear off for fifteen minutes, invited me to join her book group."

"Did you?"

"No." Carolyn shakes her head, smiling a little. "It was—I mean, I applaud her literacy, but..."

"Chick lit?" Alex nods knowingly.

"Actually, *Game of Thrones*—who'd have thought?" Carolyn looks at her empty glass. Alex signals the waiter to their table for a fresh round of drinks.

"Do you plan on...." Alex glances at the ceiling as she tries to think of the right words. "I mean, is this your forever home? Wait—I'm sorry, that's not what I meant."

"No, I like it." Carolyn laughs. She laughs easy and open, not forced, the way Alex does. "Like shelter pets, we're all in need of rescue sometimes, a forever home to call our own."

"I don't know how you can stay here." Alex rolls her eyes. "Rural living—I would go insane. I've been on my own since I was eighteen. And the damsel in distress thing—totally not my bag either."

"Well, sometimes situations can be out of your control." Carolyn picks up her napkin off her lap and smooths it. "And you just play the cards you're dealt."

"I'm sorry." Alex puts her palm on the table. "I didn't mean to sound so dismissive. Or cavalier."

"No, it's okay." Carolyn smiles. "There really isn't much here for me anymore—I just get cold feet thinking about what my next move in life will be."

But she did kind of mean it, Alex thinks to herself. There's no reason for Carolyn to languish here, in a place as inhospitable to her as the desert is to a dolphin. As the waiter serves them a second round of drinks, Alex studies the other diners. A mix of older, professional couples—the doctors and lawyers who run the town. Some younger male-female couples. A couple of middle-aged women with amorphously shaped print blouses and colorful reading glasses. Alex and Carolyn.

And Juliette. Alex perks up before cowering in fright as she watches her emerge from the kitchen. Her hair's short now, bobbed around her ears, her curls tight around her face. She stops at the first table to her right, leaning over and touching the shoulder of a salt-and-pepper haired man. Even from this distance, Alex can see the large-karat engagement ring above Juliette's wedding band.

Alex's heart is clicking like a metronome in her ears. She's not ready to talk to Juliette yet. Maybe not ever. She glances quickly toward the restrooms, trying to calculate whether she can slip across the room without Juliette seeing her. Her path's obstructed by other tables and, in one aisle, a folded-out serving table, from which a waiter is transferring ravioli and lamb dishes to the middle-aged woman.

"She's here—I need to hide." She looks at Carolyn. Juliette's now two tables away from them.

"Too bad the waiter took our menus," Carolyn laughs. Alex scoots her chair away from the table. When Juliette moves again, one table away, Alex bends as far as she can underneath the table, opening her purse. She watches a pair of chef's clogs appear near her face.

"How is everything this evening?" Juliette's voice is deeper, more honied. Alex wonders if she plays it up as part of her Southern roots.

"Everything's fine, thank you," she hears Carolyn say.

"I'm so glad," she hears Juliette responds, followed by a pause. "Is everything okay here?"

"Yes," Carolyn answers. "Just... looking for a contact."

"Oh." Juliette sounds concerned. "We can turn the lights up. I can signal over to our staff—"

"Found it." Alex pipes up from under the table, not moving. "Everything's fine."

"Oh, I'm so glad." She can almost see Juliette smiling, the one slightly crooked upper tooth that sometimes grazes her lip. Once, it nipped her when they were making out in Alex's room. "Contacts are the worst sometimes."

Alex's neck hurts. She grabs the base of the table for support, rocking it. Is Juliette going to wait there until she crawls out? With her other hand she squeezes the toe of Carolyn's espadrille, urging her to do something. But what? Carolyn shakes her hand off.

"Well." She hears Juliette say finally. "I should get back to the kitchen. Let me know if everything is to your liking. Thanks so much for coming to see us."

"Of course," Carolyn replies. Alex watches the clogs disappear, counts to five, and then slowly extricates herself from under the table.

"You take your reconnaissance seriously at *Capitol Metropolitan*." Carolyn looks bemused. "Maybe we can find you a Deep Throat working in the kitchen."

"My neck is killing me." Alex rubs her neck as she glances toward the kitchen door, making sure Juliette has really left. "For a second, I was worried she was going to crawl under the table."

"It was hard to think of something on the spot," Carolyn laughs. "But I thought the contact bit was brilliant."

"Let's not get carried away." Alex laughs too, picking up her fork. "Brilliant would have been David Blaine-ing me into the bathroom."

"You're hard to impress." Carolyn looks into space. "Most of you city girls are."

Alex opens her mouth to say something but shuts it. Carolyn's comment seems not directed to Alex, but someone else. If Carolyn were her friend, Alex might interrogate her with the intensity of Detective Benson on the television show *Law & Order: SVU*, but she has sense enough to know her natural aggressiveness is off-putting to strangers.

"I'm an Eastern Shore girl at heart," she says instead, smiling. She raises her refilled mojito. "To teamwork— thanks."

Carolyn eyes her over her mojito glass. Alex feels her gaze on the top of her forearms, the back of her neck. Chemistry? She assumes most people she knows aren't gay, only because no one ever seems to think Alex is. She has a sort of reverse gaydar: when she used to go to gay-friendly bars in the city, she'd wind up hitting on the only straight woman there—the woman who had tagged along with a group of lesbians or was hanging out with her gay brother or coworker.

Or women like Carolyn, who had only genuine interest in people and their welfare, interest Alex often misconstrued as romantic.

She digs into the ravioli, which is unfolded, like little tortillas, showcasing its ingredients—artichokes, toma-toes, parmesan, parsley. It's delicate and light, creamy, but not too overpowering. A taste that made you hungrier, but not in a gluttonous way. Instead, like a wine, its delicacy reveals different accents—like zests of parsley, a dash of lemon, the rich tartness of the parmesan—with each bite. She regrets not ordering a Sauvignon Blanc to compliment it.

"Are you up for dessert?" Alex askes after she trades her last bite of ravioli for Carolyn's last scallop.

"Only if you want to split something," Carolyn answers, stranding up. "I have to go to the ladies' room. Pick whatever you'd like, if the waiter comes back."

Alex digs in her purse for her phone. Her mother always called her on Wednesdays, although she didn't always answer. It seems strange to reflexively pick up her phone for a call she logically knows will not be coming. She opens her mother's contact information and stares at her mother staring back at her. In the picture Alex chose, her mother wears a pork pie hat (she loved hats, particularly men's, which she picked up by the half dozen at the thrift store); a few locks of hair, as dark as licorice, fall over her left eye. The realization she's dead keeps coming in waves, the way the sun peeks out of clouds at random intervals. She blinks as she shuts off her phone, trying to keep herself in the clouds a little longer.

"You were trying to hide from me, pretty lady?"

Alex feels a hand on her shoulder. Her body stiffens at the sound of Juliette's voice. She turns. In Juliette's other hand is a plate holding two hot beignets. "I brought these over for you and your date."

"Thanks, but she's not...." Alex shakes her head, looking in panic toward the hallway that houses the restrooms.

"So what brings you to town?" Juliette continues. If she's still mad at her after all these years, she doesn't show it. The dimples caused by her smile crease deep into her face. Alex notices the lighter fan of laugh lines around her brown eyes.

"Is there somewhere private?" Alex stands up suddenly, almost into Juliette's arms. "Where we can talk?"

Juliette nods toward the outside deck. Sprigg sits on the bend of the river, and a dock holds 8-10 tables outside. She ushers Alex into a little serving station dressed up as a Tiki bar. Alex squeezes behind one of the support beams and glances back at the restaurant. Satisfied she's hidden from view from Carolyn (but can see whether she returns), she looks at Juliette.

"My mom died," she explains. "And I came to profile you for the *Capitol Metropolitan.*"

Juliette blinks twice, presumably for each revelation. She grasps Alex's forearm. Alex closes her eyes again, savoring her touch.

"Oh, Alex," Juliette says simply. "I'm so sorry. When?"

"Yesterday." Alex opens her eyes and looks at Juliette's hand, still grasping her forearm. "And while I was here, I told my editor I'd do this story."

"And that's why you were hiding under my table?" Juliette raises an eyebrow, grinning.

"No—I just wanted to check it out on my own, before I saw you." Alex glances back at the restaurant. "Get a feel for the place."

"So who's your friend?" Juliette moves closer. Alex can smell traces of garlic and mint on her breath, a little wine.

"She's the editor at *The Shore Times*—Carolyn Pusey." Alex can see through the windows Carolyn has returned. "She's hooking me up with a photographer for the article."

"Oh—I thought she looked familiar, but I meet so many people now, it's hard to remember them all," Juliette answers. "But you and I will meet again, is what you're saying? For an interview?"

"Here." Alex places her phone into Juliette's open hand. "Give me your number."

"I'm really sorry, Alex," Juliette says again as she types in her digits. "About your mother. She was...one of a kind. I can't imagine what you're going through."

Juliette presses the phone back into Alex's hand. Then, she leans over and kisses Alex's cheek.

"I have to get back to the kitchen." Juliette moves toward the entranceway of the tiki bar. "Call me tomorrow?"

Alex nods as Juliette slips away. She touches her face where Juliette has kissed it. Had all that just happened? What was Juliette's angle? Alex doesn't believe in sincerity, that people are forgiving because of maturity, or time, or introspection. There's always something in it for them. For Juliette, Alex presumes, it's the article.

Still, she hadn't known about the article when she came up to the table. She looks at her phone, Juliette's name staring back at her. Then she remembers Carolyn, who's probably wondering whether Alex has skipped out on her.

"I'm sorry." Alex slinks back into her chair at the table. "I left something in my car."

"I'm glad you ordered the beignets." Carolyn motions to the plate. "They're my favorite too."

Alex nods. She feels guilty but doesn't know why. There'd be no harm in telling Carolyn about her knowing Juliette. If she had done it sooner. Now her lie of omission has begun to sprout, little green buds poking out of the soil.

But she's not going to see Carolyn again. Now that she has the names of photographers, there's really no need to.

"I'll get this." Alex pulls out her credit card when the waiter leaves the check. "I'm sure the magazine will comp me."

"Can I make it up to the magazine somehow?" Carolyn smiles at her. "By having one of their best writers over for tea?"

"I'd love to, if I have time." Alex looks apologetic. "We have so much to go through at the house—we haven't started, really." Has she only been here twelve hours?

"Of course." Carolyn nods, resting her palm on the table. "If you need any help, you'll let me know?"

Alex nods too. She glances toward the kitchen, wondering what Juliette is doing, if she's watching. She wonders if Juliette's jealous of Carolyn, if it's advantageous in any way to make her. She reaches across the table and clasps Carolyn's hand lightly.

"You're sweet," she says to her suddenly. "I may take you up on it."

As they leave the restaurant, Alex puts her hand on the small of Carolyn's back while opening the door for her. Carolyn seems surprised and pleased by Alex's chivalry. *You can leave high school*, Alex thinks as she glances back toward the kitchen, *but high school never actually leaves you.*

Chapter Eight

Alex wakes up on the couch, her head throbbing. She doesn't remember deciding to sleep here. She wasn't drunk when she parted ways with Carolyn at the restaurant, but she had plucked a half-empty bottle of prosecco her mother had left behind in the fridge and continued drinking in the living room at home, staring at her cell phone and wondering what she would say to Juliette.

She rolls over and presses her face into the couch cushion, trying to constrict the flow of blood to the left side of her head. She doesn't know how her mother did this every night. Alex never thought their mother was an alcoholic; she thought alcoholics drank from the moment they got up in the morning to the time they passed out at night. They drank whiskey, or vodka, or gin. Having a bottle at dinner, on the other hand, seemed normal, even if their mother was the only one drinking it.

"You were really drunk last night," Owen says when he appears in the living at 12:30, Tortoise curled around his shoulders like he's Siegfried or Roy. Alex is still on the couch, but in a semi-upright position, at least. She listens to him open a can of Fancy Feast in the kitchen.

"You came home really late," she says after she joins him. "Intense game of Magic: The Gathering?"

Owen ignores her as he scoops the cat food onto a plate, which has a picture of a Himalayan cat on it with the words ALL MINE underneath. She knows Owen had bought it. It was the kind of thing that would give her mother, who crowed for a week about a nearly complete vintage Heinrich china set she'd gotten from the Goodwill for a mere hundred dollars, hives.

"You hungry?" He offers her the box of Lucky Charms. Alex is hung over enough to want it. She pours the milk—relieved it's at least 2% milk fat. Owen would never switch to almond, or cashew, or even soy, because he didn't see the point in complicating what he liked.

She arranges herself at the dining table, relocating one of the boxes of pictures that's still there onto the floor, when Owen puts Tortoise's heaping bowl of smelly ocean whitefish across from her. She sighs, gets up, and takes her bowl back over to the couch. She picks up her cell phone and rests it on her thigh next to her cereal bowl. It's then she notices the text from Carolyn.

> *I had a great time last night-I should get out more. I was wondering if you had time to check out a movie while you're here? My Night at Maud's is playing on Thursday at Summer Revival Night at the university. No worries if you're too busy with everything/not up to it. C*

Alex frowns. She feels bad that Carolyn seems lonely and, identifying Alex (incorrectly) as perhaps a sophisticated urbanite, has decided to cling to her like some buoy in a sea of cultural hee-haw. But Carolyn can move to the city. She isn't stuck here, like their mother was, having to raise two kids. Nor is she unemployable, or socially awkward like Owen. *In fact*, Alex thinks with a smile, *she's surprisingly quite nice.*

But Alex doesn't have time for a project. Not another one anyway.

"Owen, will you get that?" The sound of Alex's own voice gives her a headache as she calls out to him in the kitchen to answer the phone.

"It's probably just a telemarketer," he says. "Or a bill collector."

"Jesus." She vaults herself off the couch to get to the phone before it goes into voicemail, forgetting her cereal bowl's still in her lap. It spills onto her favorite pair of J Crew chinos and milk drips down to her mother's oriental rug.

"Crap—look what you made me do." She glances up. But Owen is gone, up to his room. She grabs the phone off the hook.

"Oh, Alex, honey, I'm so glad I caught you. It's Johanna. Oh Alex, your poor mother—how?"

"O-overdose," she chokes out. "Accidental."

"Oh god—I can't say I'm surprised, but I'm still in shock." Alex hears a sniffle. "You poor little girl—how are you and Owen holding up?"

"We're doing okay," she answers. *If doing okay,* she thinks, *means walking around like zombies and bickering.* "We went to the funeral home and made arrangements for cremation. We need to go through the house, but Owen still lives here, so it doesn't have to be done right away."

"Well, sweetie, I just wanted to let you know I bought my ticket, and I'll be there tomorrow."

"What ticket?"

"My plane ticket. Can somebody pick me up tomorrow at the airport? My plane arrives at 12:30."

"You're coming here?" Alex repeats in surprise.

"Alex, sweetheart, your mother just died. My best friend in the whole world just died. Of course, I'm coming. I can't wait to see how you've grown. We have so much to talk about."

"Wait—did you get in touch with...our father?" Alex grips the phone.

"He knows—I'll tell you everything when I get there. Oh, Alex, I can't wait to see you. Even under these circumstances. 12:30 Delta, honey. Here's my cell number."

Alex grabs a pen from the secretary and scrawls down Johanna's cell phone number. As she hangs up, she's relieved. A woman she can talk to who knew her mother and also wasn't her mother. And someone who knew her mother somewhat intimately, who might be able to outline the method of her madness. Although Johanna had only visited once, Alex remembers her mother getting letters from her, the both of them talking on the phone sometimes after Alex had gone to bed. Although she'd strained to hear her father's name in conversation, neither seemed to mention him. They talked about the best leg wax and mascara and the trail of shitty men who seemed to move through their lives like ticker tape.

Johanna had sent Alex a letter during her freshman year at Swarthmore. It said all the things a relative might say to someone on their own for the first time (although, unlike most relatives, Johanna had also thrown several condoms in her envelope). Alex remembered her own polite response—about how excited she was to be in college, how grown up and cute all the boys were (she hadn't been ready to out herself as a lesbian to semi-strangers, even if they were relatives). She didn't write how miserable she was, how much she missed Juliette. That, after Lewis, she was barely on speaking terms with her own family.

She retrieves her cereal bowl from the living room floor and notices Owen has left his bowl on the table, along with Tortoise's plate. She picks them up, making a face at the disgusting flaky gravy pieces Tortoise didn't finish before she followed Owen upstairs. She considers breaking the plate in the sink but thinks pretending it was an accident would look cowardly. Plus, it's something she shouldn't be so angry over.

But why is she so angry? She remembers someone telling her once that being upset and being angry were shades of the same emotion. She's grieving, she decides, and seems to have to be ambitious even about that.

She gets a rag and a spray bottle of cleaner and kneels on the rug, blotting the droplets of milk, feeling it stick to her thighs through her wet pants.

But she could just be angry too.

I'm not going to be mad at you, honey. Her mother slurred into the phone. Beside Alex in bed, Kate wore an expression that changed from concern to fury the longer spent Alex on the phone. *Just tell me the truth. You're a lesbian, for Christ's sake. You didn't even like Lewis— were you just trying to get back at me for something? The time I stole your Percocets after you got your wisdom teeth out? The time I forgot to pick you up after your class trip?*

I don't know why you just don't tell her, Kate said after she hung up, studying her as she tucked her pillow under her chin.

I already told her. Alex left the phone receiver off its cradle. She didn't believe me the first time.

Alex smells the damp rug, which she's blotted and sprayed with carpet cleaner and blotted again. She thinks she can still smell the milk faintly. She worries it will be a small thing Owen won't notice, the way he never notices anything important, until it turns sour, and then maybe Tortoise will bother with it. She sprays the area again, rubbing this time. After a while, with the added layer of disinfectant burning into her nostrils, she can't tell anymore.

Still, she's convinced the smallest stain is still there, one that will fester.

You should see a therapist. Kate lay on her back, staring at the ceiling. She should have been asleep, would have been asleep, hours ago, if not for Alex's mother. In three hours, she'd have to head to work. The phone, still off the hook, beeped on the floor by the bed beside them, but neither of them heard it anymore. It became white noise, beeping frantically in direct proportion to the unspoken words growing like moss between them.

I hate therapists. Alex shook her head. She'll forget about it in the morning. My mother is an unreliable narrator.

But you won't forget about it, Kate said, her eyes closed. And I won't either. I'm already pretty sick of it.

Alex pushes the coffee table across the room. Then, she rolls up the rug and puts it outside next to the trash can. She paces back and forth on the hardwood, wondering if she should call Kate. But she doesn't know what that will solve, or what point she's even trying to make. That Kate had been right?

Tortoise has returned and now stands before the spot on the hardwood where she had spilled the milk.

She shoos Tortoise with her hand and kneels back on the floor, her nose close to the hardwood. She wonders whether there are spores of mold sprouting out of the wood right this moment, whether she will contract something like Legionnaires', and should she really stay here?

And what about Johanna? Will she want to stay here? Will Owen want her to? She's technically family. *But not even family*, she thinks as she glances around the living room (did her mother attempt to install a hammock inside, by the front window?) *should be made to stay in this house*, in which a nude mannequin painted purple and named Candy Darling stares outside one of the front windows, spooking mail deliverers, Jehovah's witnesses, and candidates for city council since 1989, and a clawfoot tub sits opposite the couch in the living room filled with dirt and housing two lemon trees, lemons her mother used to make cocktails.

She picks up her phone off the coffee table.

> *I had a good time last night too.* She texts Carolyn back. *So, do you know a good hotel?*

Shouldn't we get to know each other a little better first? Carolyn responds a second later.

Alex pauses, taken aback. She decides Carolyn's just making a joke. Isn't she? It would be totally like Alex to misread a straight woman's intentions.

*Our aunt is coming tomorrow—*She types—*And the house is a mess.*

After a minute, Carolyn's reply pops up.

I'm sorry. It was a stupid joke

It's okay. Alex answers, but she's a little disappointed *it was just a joke. Don't worry about it.*

Can I make it up to you somehow? I'm working from home today.

Probably not a good idea. I'm a little hungover from last night.

I'll make ginger tea. It'll help?

Upstairs Alex peels off her wet, stained pants in her bedroom; she thinks she hears Owen snoring. How can eating breakfast make someone want to go back to sleep?

She should start going through her mother's things; it'll be easier without Owen standing over her shoulder. But when she glances across the hallway to her mother's room, she's exhausted. It's only stuff, she reminds herself.

And not much of it not any use to her.

Instead, she picks up her phone again.

How can I refuse such an offer? She texts Carolyn.

She'll only be an hour, she promises herself. And then she'll start going through things, straightening up the house as much as she can for Johanna. She sets an alarm on her phone to make sure she gets the car back in time for when Owen's supposed to go to work (just this once, and she'll never drive again) and, before she can lecture herself about responsibility, slips out the door.

Chapter Nine

Ten minutes later, she pulls up in front of a small bungalow on a street of three houses, each separated by large swaths. They boast the seeds of rural sprawl: bright yellow plastic Tyco playsets, tricycles, rusting motorboats, beaten-up sheds. Only Carolyn's has a fenced-in yard. The porch is enclosed by tulips, daffodils, and daisies.

"Was it hard to find?" Carolyn opens the door before Alex's foot reaches the top step of the porch. She's wearing jeans and a faded denim shirt with the top buttons open, sleeves rolled up. She looks as genuine in real life as she does at the office, although, when Alex gets closer, she can tell, by the wet tips of Carolyn's hair, she's recently showered.

"I just looked for the one without—" Alex points to the pickup truck parked at the bungalow down the street. "That." Then to the orange plastic play slide abandoned in the driveway of the other. "Or that."

"Guilty." Carolyn opens the door wider. Alex glances at her own clothes, workout clothes she'd put on after she finished cleaning up the milk. She hasn't even showered and probably smells like hangover. She bends down to pull off her Asics and leave them by the door, surreptitiously sniffing at her armpits, smoothing her thin running pullover down her arms.

"Is that your car?" Carolyn's still standing at the door, looking at the green Miata. "I saw it in the parking lot of Sprigg last night. It's, uh, something."

"Oh God, no—it's my brother's," she answers, folding her arms and looking around the living room. "Your place is nice."

It *is* nice, in a cozy way: an overstuffed armchair by built-in bookcases along one wall, neutral colors, framed prints of photos Alex assumes are from the newspaper, judging by their content: a sunset over a marsh, fishermen hauling in a catch, the beach in winter. It's a place she could see herself living in.

"Do you take honey with your tea?" Carolyn moves past her, brushing her elbow with her hand.

"Sure—whatever you're having," Alex shrugs. She's not much of a tea person, veering between coffee, vitamin water, and vodka martinis, depending on the time of day.

"Why don't you sit?" Carolyn motions toward the armchair as Alex makes to follow her. Alex sits down and lets her eyes move over the rows of titles on the bookshelves. Doris Lessing. Simone de Beauvoir. Adrienne Rich. bell hooks. Jeanette Winterson. Carolyn's feminist streak isn't surprising as much as the copious lesbian writers tossed in the mix. But everyone Alex knew at Swarthmore, even the straight girls, half of whom she'd unsuccessfully hit on, had taken Women's Studies in college, so she's careful not to jump to any conclusions. She leans back in the chair with Carolyn's copy of Adrienne Rich's *Diving into the Wreck*.

"That's one of my favorites." Carolyn says of the book when she reappears with a tray of tea. She places a teacup in front of Alex and sits across from her on the sofa, tucking a leg underneath.

"Yeah," Alex answers. "I read it a lot when..."

Carolyn raises her eyes as she waits for Alex to finish.

"When I was in college," Alex finishes. She had begun to say when she and Kate had broken up but decides against it.

"I don't read poetry much anymore," Carolyn agrees. "I read a lot of nonfiction now—something I heard about on NPR, usually."

"You seem very educated." Alex picks up her cup as carefully, she hopes, as her words this time. "To be living here."

"I grew up here and went away for school. Like you." Carolyn cradles her teacup in her hands, leaning back. Had Alex told her that? She supposes it wouldn't have been too hard to find out. "But I came back. I hadn't planned to stay, but I guess nothing ever happens the way we think it will."

"Why?" Alex lets the tea touch her lip. It's too hot. She holds the cup like an anchor on her lap.

"Why did I stay, or why does nothing ever happen the way we think it will?"

"Either—I'm guessing the answer's the same."

Carolyn looks off to a spot to the left of Alex. When she glances over to see what it is, her eyes fall on the mantel. On it rests a black and white picture of a young girl in silver frame.

"Your mother?" Alex guesses.

"Yes." Carolyn seems grateful, almost, for Alex's answer. As if there's more. If she, like Alex, is deciding what's worth throwing away into conversation with a stranger and what's worth keeping close to the vest. "She got sick. She was in a home for a few years before she died, and I came back to be close by before she did. We lived on a farm—my parents and me—a few miles south of here. I sold it to Perdue to pay for her assisted living."

"You lived on a farm?" Alex smiles. "You had farm animals and stuff?"

"Yes, we had farm animals and stuff." Carolyn smiles back. "And I was really popular in school, let me tell you—always smelling like chickens and pigs. The smell gets into everything. Sometimes I think I still smell it."

"Smells fine in here." Alex makes an exaggerated sniffing smell. "Smells like tea and candles."

"That's good to know." Carolyn nods. "I guess that's not the reason I'm still single, then. Hey, do you want to meet Billie?"

Carolyn's already standing. Alex follows her into the dining room, where Carolyn draws back one of the curtains by the window. Inside the wooden fence Alex had seen from the road is a small coop, and in the yard, one brown chicken, pecking some seed just inside the coop.

"I took her from the farm when I moved," Carolyn explains. "She doesn't lay eggs anymore, but I couldn't bear to kill her."

"Is she named after Billie Holliday?" Alex wonders aloud. "No, of course not. That's stupid."

"It's not stupid." She can feel Carolyn's elbow touching hers, but she doesn't move away. Carolyn continues to look through the window. "I love Billie Holiday."

"Me too," Alex thinks of the song she and Kate used to dance to—*"Girls Were Made to Take Care of Boys"*—although they always referred to it as *"Girls Were Made to Take Care of Girls."* She knows at this very minute Kate's probably in yoga class in Bethesda. She thinks of Kate's hair piled on her head, arms tee-peed over her head in Vriksasana.

And in the next second, she thinks of Owen. She can introduce Owen to Carolyn. Carolyn would be a great girlfriend. Alex turns to her.

"This is so incredible, your chicken, Billie, I mean—I want to introduce you to my brother, Owen. The one I told you about. He lives across town and has this thing about his cat, Tortoise."

"You mean set me up?" Carolyn frowns. "I don't think so."

"I know he drives a car that looks like a ninja turtle, but he has a PhD in applied mathematics. There probably aren't many single men our age of his caliber in this town. Not there aren't great guys, I'm sure. I'm sorry—that sounded elitist."

"It's not elitist." Carolyn lets the curtain fall back. "But I'm not interested."

"You should think about it," Alex touches Carolyn's forearm.

They go back to the living room. Alex had wanted to be helpful. She often said things, borderline cruel, without thinking, but she didn't think this was one of them. But how to explain, then, the dampened mood between them?

"I'm single too," Alex says by way of apology, before taking a gulp of now-lukewarm tea. "I'm more career-focused right now anyway."

"How are you getting on everything?" Carolyn rakes her hand through her hair. "Speaking of why you're also here."

"It's been hard," Alex says vaguely. "Although it was never easy."

"Were you close?"

"We weren't, well, on bad terms all of the time," Alex explains noncommittally. "In fact, my mother had been dying to be friends with me for years. But she did some shitty stuff when Owen and I were growing up that she never apologized for, and I wasn't interested in making up. But it doesn't make it any easier now, because there are so many things I still wanted to talk about. It doesn't feel like closure."

"No one said death was closure." Carolyn looks at her. She smiles over her teacup. "Look at us—two adult women who live in their heads trying to talk about their emotions."

Alex laughs. It seems like the most hilarious thing ever, and she keeps laughing. She keeps laughing until she's crying.

And then she's just crying, crying, crying like a dumb baby. She covers her face and bends over, ashamed it's happening at a time when it shouldn't be. She hears Carolyn stand up and walk over, bend down before her.

"I'm so sorry," she hears her say, feels her hand on her shoulder, rubbing it.

"You didn't say anything wrong," Alex chokes out. She straightens up and nods. "I'm okay."

"Are you sure?" Carolyn's palm hovers near Alex's face but doesn't touch it. Why had Kate left her a few months ago—how could she not sense then Alex would need her so much right now? Why is she losing it at a complete stranger's house—is there really no one in her life she can turn to?

"The thing I came for: the wreck and not the story of the wreck/the thing itself and not the myth," she says finally.

"I thought you only read Adrienne Rich in college." Carolyn smiles faintly.

Alex leans back in the seat, rubbing her face. She sighs. "I probably should go back to the city soon. It's just that Juliette..."

Carolyn sits back on her haunches, her expression blank. "Juliette what?"

"I'm just not finished with Juliette yet," Alex closes her eyes, wiping away her tears. That much is true.

"What do you think of her?" Carolyn asks, neutrally. Neutrally in a way, Alex thinks, that's not.

"She seems to have done well for herself," Alex answers just as neutrally.

"She's a big fish in a little pond here." Carolyn stands up and goes to the mantel instead of the sofa. "Some people like that."

"Do you?"

"You mistake me for a big fish," Carolyn says, running her fingers along the mantel.

"You're a bigger fish than you think," Alex replies. "At least, I think so."

Carolyn looks at her, as if to say something. But she doesn't. She looks so vulnerable there, in space, one cuff of her denim shirt unraveling, that Alex wants to hug her. She scoots forward on her chair.

The alarm on her phone goes off. She stands quickly up and, instead of going toward Carolyn, makes for the door.

"Thanks so much for the tea. And the company. It was great to get out of the house, meet Billie. I gotta run—"

"Do you still need that recommendation for a hotel?" Carolyn walks over. "Or to talk?"

"Oh, no—I'll find something," Alex laughs, a little forced. "Like I said, our aunt is flying in from Seattle, and I want to make sure I get her into a good hotel in case our place is too much of a mess for her. But there's probably still only one hotel here though, right? I guess I've lived in the city too long."

"Choices?" Carolyn forces a smile. "I should move to the city, then."

"Don't." Alex pats her lightly on the shoulder. "It's no place for chickens. I meant Billie—not you. You're not a chicken. Oh God, I'm sorry."

"Stop apologizing," At the door, Carolyn grasps Alex's arm lightly. "Don't worry about it—you're allowed back. Come back."

"Thanks. Okay." Alex fumbles with her sneakers. She gives a mortified a little wave as she steps through the doorway, not looking back. Carolyn's probably the nicest, most sane person in this town. Someone Alex would even want to be friends with, if she lived here.

But she doesn't live here. In the car, she glances at Carolyn, still on the porch, waving. Alex waves and backs up the street with all the dignity someone who hasn't really driven a stick shift much in two years can muster. When she runs over something plastic and hard as she's trying to navigate the pedals, she keeps going. It's only when she stops at the Royal Farms to get gas, she discovers a baby doll stroller trapped in Owen's wheel well. After she pries it out, pays for coffee and gas, and sits in the driver's seat, she checks her notifications on Facebook. Carolyn, despite witnessing that oblivious and cavalier display of toy carnage, despite the fact that Alex is cruising around town in a car that looks like a ninja turtle and believes the proper way to avoid someone in public is to crawl under a table, has still decided to send her a friend request.

Chapter Ten

"Is there anything I can just throw away?" Alex asks Owen as he comes down the stairs for work. Instead of his Staples polo and khakis, he's wearing cargo shorts and an anime T-shirt.

"I don't know." He scratches the top of his head, belching softly with his mouth closed. "Like, you know, obvious trash you can throw away, and whatever you want to take— whatever you want."

"I came on the bus." She shakes open a trash bag. "What am I going to take—the wardrobe? And why aren't you dressed for work?"

"I'll change at the store," he answers, although he isn't carrying any other clothes. "It's embarrassing to go out in public like that."

"You know what the solution to that is?" She frowns at him. "Get a job you're not embarrassed by."

"Oh, we can't all be overachieving know-it-alls like you," he answers, going into the kitchen.

"You got a scholarship to school too," she says. "Don't act like you didn't have any opportunities."

She listens to him drink out of the orange juice container before returning, keys in hand.

"I'll be home at eleven," he says. "But you don't have to wait up if you don't want to."

"I'm picking up Aunt Johanna tomorrow," she says as he opens the door.

"What?" He closes it and looks at her, wide awake. "She's coming here?"

"That's what she said—that's why I'm cleaning."

Owen stands in the hallway, working out what appears to be a complex mathematical equation in his head.

"Um, okay," he says after he's finished, and opens the door. "But keep this door closed at all times—Tortoise safety."

"Oh, I thought I'd leave it open like a barn," she calls out as he closes it behind him. But she knows what he means. She's already found Tortoise preening herself in her half-unpacked suitcase, getting fur all over everything, and she will try to eat or lap up anything you leave unattended—she's already found a whisker in her coffee mug.

She sits on the sofa with the opened trash bag and looks around. She figures she should start here, since it'll be the first room Johanna will see when she arrives tomorrow. It isn't quite like the houses on that cable show about hoarders, but it's close. Just the magazines are enough to make Alex want to cry: piles of vintage *Vanity Fair*, *Harper's Bazaar*, *Artforum*, *Art in America*, *Interview*, *Rolling Stone*, *Cooking Illustrated*, Alex and

Owen's old *Highlights Magazine* and *Ranger Rick* from the nineties. They sit in piles of ten or twenty on either side of the sofa, under the end table, atop the end table, atop the entertainment center.

At least, she thinks, *I can get rid of these and the VHS tapes.* As far as she can tell, Owen and her mother no longer have a VHS machine, anyway. She opens the doors to the entertainment center and begins to pull out dusty cassettes: *Annie Hall, Dr. Strangelove. Harold and Maude.* Movies she might like to own if they weren't on outdated media. Behind the VHS tapes an uneven stack of children's books has been shoved—*Where the Wild Things Are* and *Make Way for Ducklings.* She doesn't remember her mother reading them to her. However, she remembers reading them to Owen, back when they were in the cloakroom.

The Cloakroom Days, she and Owen always referred to them jokingly in their teens. When their mother would yell at them for biting their fingernails or wondered where their table manners went or didn't put their clothes in the hamper, they'd respond, *We must have picked it up during the Cloakroom Days.*

You kids act like I kept you in fucking Auschwitz or something, their mother would snort in a huff. But she usually left them alone after that.

Not that the cloakroom days were completely terrible and actually absolutely necessary. Unable to afford childcare, their mother would set them up with coloring books and drawing paper in the unused cloakroom in her art room at the elementary school, warning them under no condition to come out unless one of them was dying.

Pretend you're ghosts, like Casper. She would order them before pulling closed the curtains. Once in a while Alex would peek out of the curtains and watch the other children, angry their mother leaned over their shoulders, helping them to mold their clay bowls or bend pipe cleaners into people, that she was too tired to do the same for her and Owen at night at home. But mostly Alex liked the chalky, moldy smell of the cloakroom. At five, she was reading regularly and had been trying to teach Owen, who was four. They could spend hours poring over picture books, sometimes copying the illustrations on the construction paper their mother had given them. Their mother had set up a "go" bucket in the corner of the cloakroom for emergencies, although Alex never wanted to go because she hated the smell of it there, in the corner. Owen was afraid someone would hear him peeing and come to investigate, even though their mother had lined the bottom with industrial paper towels (it was a problem, peeing in public, that plagued him for years after). So they learned to wait until her mother's planning period or held it in until they thought they would pass out from the abdominal pains.

That's child abuse, Kate had widened and narrowed her eyes as she stood at the stove, reducing ingredients for a consommé. Her hair, so blond it was almost white, was pulled back in a ponytail. *Did you tell anyone?*

We did what we had to do. Alex shrugged, slicing tomatoes for salad. Kate had gone to private schools all her life, even had a nanny as a child. *My mother needed that job.*

You were four and five years old. Kate shook her head. And unsupervised. What if a shelf had fallen on you? What if you found some turpentine and drank it?

Kids our age picked peaches during the Depression. Alex laughed. And worked in factories at the turn of the century. We just had to be quiet for a few hours.

It sounded like something her mom would say, and probably had said to her, but she didn't have any nightmares about those days in the cloakroom. She would rather be there, with her books, and Owen with his Star Wars figures, than at daycare with a bunch of other children. But she often wondered if it affected Owen. He didn't know any children his own age, or any other children at all, until he entered kindergarten. By then, like Alex, he'd grown accustomed to retreating into his own, imaginary world. Unlike her, he seemed content on never leaving it.

She takes the books upstairs with her, leaving the VHS tapes scattered on the living room floor, and draws a bath. Maybe it wasn't child abuse—Kate was always so dramatic—but maybe it wasn't smart. One thing she's learned in life is that everyone has a blind spot. Some people's blind spots are much, much bigger than others, but everyone has one fault to which they are completely blind. Alex has a few theories about her own blind spots— the belief she's absolutely right about everything and knows the best for everyone. It was the only way she made it through college, and then graduate school, living on her own in a strange city juggling jobs and less-than-ideal living situations. Indecisiveness cost her money, gigs, and opportunities. And if she was wrong, she didn't ever really feel wrong because whatever happened, short of her own death, was a learning opportunity.

Of course, her life philosophies haven't made her the most popular employee or classmate, and she can be a real shit to live with, if her epic battles with Kate about how to organize Kate's spice rack, which way to put the toilet paper on the roll, or the fastest way to get to Eastern Market on a Saturday morning were any indication. And yet, she had never quite made a stand about her mother remaining in or out of her life. Sure, she'd only been home a handful of times in the past fifteen years, but she'd never changed her phone number like Kate insisted (she figured Owen would give any new number to their mother anyway) or even stopped answering the phone when her mother called. She sent Owen and her mother holiday and birthday cards and occasionally small gifts. She didn't know if it was guilt or holding out for her mother to become the mother she'd always wanted.

And if Alex's blind spot was being a know-it-all, what was her mother's blind spot? That she hadn't hurt Alex through the years? That she was harder on her than Owen, making Alex fight for the tiniest compliment, compliments that were usually laden with her mother's own sense of self-importance?

You'll be fine, her mother always used to say when Alex got upset about something—a B+ on a chemistry test, a bad dream, being passed over for a promotion at work, her mother stealing her favorite pair leggings and accidentally burning a hole in them with her cigarette.

But she isn't fine. Maybe compared to her mother and brother she is—but compared to someone like Kate, she's a complete failure. She has no friends, at least not since college. And even then, at some point when acquaintances turned into friends, when they shared their fears and their histories and their trust, Alex had always stayed on the surface. Her friends at school came from good families. They went to Europe or did internships over summer break and didn't wait tables on the graveyard shift at iHop or take shitty temp jobs at office parks in suburban Philly. They didn't have to find places to crash over winter and spring break, when the dorms were closed and then lie to their mother that they were staying at their friend's house because they were never going home again, not if they could help it.

When she gets out of the tub, there's no toilet paper on the roll. She sighs and squats before the vanity under the sink, pulling one from of a packet of eight. Everything underneath the sink is covered with a thick layer of dust, as if it had stopped being needed back in 1994. Because Owen's mind is organized like a desktop, mostly everything he uses—toilet paper, shaving cream, razor, soap, toothbrush, and toothpaste—lies scattered and damp across the top, within his sightline. And who knows where all her mother's toiletries are scattered, like pollen across a meadow: she once found a bottle of Summer's Eve douche in the map pocket of her mother's Subaru.

Alex smiles as she extracts, like an anthropologist, a half-filled bottle of Dep hair gel she used in high school, before she could afford better hair products. She inhales its fruity overtones with a heavy undertone of alcohol as she notices something else in the right back corner: a container of Lewis's Right Guard deodorant.

When she was sixteen, in order to buy the Subaru (their old Chevette was held together, their mother used to joke, by duct tape and black magic), her mother had taken a part-time job in the evenings and weekends working for Lewis, a divorced psychiatrist who was twelve years younger. She submitted insurance claims, made appointment reminder calls, and did light clerical work.

She even finagled Owen some free counseling appointments with Lewis because she was worried, since he spent hours in his room playing *Call of Duty*, he'd become a "kid in a bell tower."

Of course, any man who strayed into her mother's orbit also became, by seduction, coercion, or persistent nagging, a boyfriend.

One night, when she came home from her job at the mall, her mother stood just inside the front door, as if she'd been waiting for her. She circled Alex's bicep with one hand and pulled her to one side, her finger to her lips, and pointed upstairs.

They're bonding, she whispered to Alex.

Who? All she heard was the sound of machine gun fire coming from Owen's bedroom. *Owen has a friend?*

Lewis. Her mother grinned manically. *Lewis stopped by after work.*

I thought you were afraid Owen was going to be a psychopath because he played video games. Alex arched an eyebrow as she started up the stairs.

Lewis is a psychiatrist—he knows what he's doing. Now shh! Her mom hissed after her, like Lewis and Owen were rabbits in the backyard and Alex was going to spook them. She stood outside Owen's room and peered into the doorway crack. Inside, Lewis and Owen were huddled over Owen's computer monitor, mowing down enemy soldiers of indeterminate racial origin.

There's one in the corner, Owen said to Lewis above the din of a chopper and the clatter of their fingers on the controls.

Got him, Lewis answered. Lewis looked young enough, in his V-neck sweater, corduroys, and docksiders, to be in high school himself. It was hard to understand how her mother was even dating him, but she'd dated worse—like Rod, the carpenter who blasted Lynyrd Skynyrd and drank a case of Bud in their driveway while he had dutifully kept their mother's Chevette running each week. In fact, each boyfriend seemed picked to solve a pressing problem in her mother's life. Once the Chevette was beyond repair, her mother next found the man, Lewis, who would produce the down payment for the Subaru.

Lewis turned and looked at her through the crack, as if he knew she'd been staring at him. He winked at her. She paused, and then winked back. She thought, at the time, they were winking about the same thing—his stewardship of her little brother. In fact, at the time, Alex felt almost as sorry for Lewis as she did Owen. She figured, like her mother's other boyfriends, he'd be no match for her. That she'd be demanding, critical, clingy, and bat-shit crazy all at once and chew him up faster than an African leopard did a rabbit.

She stands up and tosses the Right Guard into the trash. Shows what she knows.

How could she tell her friends at college, and then her coworkers, that her mother's boyfriend was a creep? That her mother had been indicted, along with Lewis, for billing patients' insurance companies and Medicaid for sessions they'd never scheduled, diagnoses they never had, and drugs they never used? That her mother had stolen a prescription pad from Lewis and wrote herself prescriptions, that she owned a copy of *The Physician's*

Desk Reference and paged through it during the evenings on the couch the way a real mother might leaf through a cookbook? That she'd become a cooperating witness in the insurance fraud case against Lewis and had her sentence reduced to community service? That even though she didn't have a felony on her record, her mother had lost her job as an art teacher and spent the last few years before early retirement working as a waitress at Denny's and buying and selling antiques and other bric-a-brac on Etsy?

Jesus, Al-ex-an-dra, her mother would roll her eyes. You act like my sole purpose on this earth is to make your life miserable. Not everything's about you.

Thank God for Juliette, Alex thinks as she pops another of Owen's/her mother's/the family valium in front of the bathroom mirror. If she didn't have Juliette in high school, she doesn't know what she would have done.

Can you meet me tomorrow?

She texts Juliette when she goes back downstairs. Although if she's too chicken to even call her and set up a time, how the hell is she even supposed to get through the interview?

Can you come over to me at ten?

Juliette responds immediately, and Alex feels a flutter in her stomach as she grabs her laptop.

At Sprigg?

She shouldn't have been hungover, wasted time over at Carolyn's today, as she steps over the VHS tapes and magazines lying all over the living room floor and heads back upstairs. There's so much to do. Everything she's done since she's been here has been so sloppy, so emotionally wrought, so out of character.

My house. Juliette texts back. *Just you and me, okay?*

She sits on her bed and closes the lid of her laptop. Juliette's husband will probably be at the hospital, where he's a surgeon. There isn't anything wrong with meeting a woman in the privacy of her own home. Alex has done it before; it just wasn't her ex-girlfriend who she was meeting.

She lies back on her bed and slips her hand beneath her underwear as she remembers the first time she kissed Juliette. Juliette's parents and sister were away visiting relatives in another state. Juliette had lied and said she had a big chemistry test on Monday so she could stay home, and there'd been elaborate plans exchanged between Juliette and her stoner friends David and Alex about having a monster party. David's friend Tyrone's jam band was going to play in the yard, and David was going to get couple of sheets of acid from some girl at the University of Delaware. But then David's cousin at University of Maryland was having his own massive party, and the plan was scrapped in favor of driving out to College Park.

You want to go? Juliette asked. They lay on Juliette's bed, sharing a joint. A box fan hummed in Juliette's window, pulling out the smoke, and a stick of incense burned in front of the bedroom door, covering whatever smoke remained. "Box of Rain" by the Grateful Dead was playing on Juliette's stereo. Alex propped up her head on her elbow and studied Juliette, the way her curly hair splayed across the pillow as she touched her tongue to the strawberry she was eating. A crucifix was nailed above Juliette's bed; her Bible lay open on her desk.

They'd been friends for just that past year, after they'd been assigned a project together in English class on *The Glass Menagerie* a few months earlier. Alex had chosen the play, finding it to mirror her family in some ways, and was surprised Juliette was as interested it in as she was. That Juliette wasn't another pretty, vapid, Christian girl at school who tormented Alex while pretending to be a model student.

And she was gorgeous. Juliette had soft, curly, pre-Raphaelite features: hair the color of wine, pale, unfreckled skin, almond-shaped eyes, round cheekbones, heart-shaped lips. She was busty but thin, albeit not on the athletic side. She spoke softly and thoughtfully and, even though a step detached from everyone else, had intersectionality and acceptance among all the cliques. Although Alex had never thought of Juliette as available in any way, Alex indulged herself, like a chocolate bar hidden under the mattress, bits of her fledgling crush.

I'm sure there'll be lots of hot guys there, Alex answered. She took a long draw on the joint, letting the strong, skunky smell settle in her lungs. She had learned to say things like that, about guys, even though there was no feeling behind them. She didn't consider it lying, exactly. Words, she had convinced herself, could sometimes be clouds, a layer of subterfuge. Protection. Only those really interested in knowing the truth would fight their way through the haze.

What about David? Juliette asked. Sometimes, when Alex and Juliette were together, Juliette would touch Alex, weaving her hand through the back of her wavy dark hair, touching her hip, her shoulder. Boundaries over which Alex wouldn't have let just anyone cross. Now, Juliette brought up the palm of her hand and pressed it against Alex's collarbone.

I'm supposed to like David, right? Alex thought aloud. In the corner, Jerry Garcia sang, 'What do you want me to do/to do for you, to see you through?'

Do you, or don't you? Juliette laughed. One night when Alex's mom had been away, she went to an off-campus party at Eastern Shore State with David and Juliette. David sat with her in the back of Juliette's Datsun, his arm slung atop the seat, above her shoulders. But Alex had spent most of her time at the party sitting on the steps outside the white farmhouse and talking to Juliette as they watched David play hacky sack by the fire with a bunch of college boys. She had convinced herself she was too shy to talk to David, but she really rather would have stayed with Juliette, anyway, their knees touching, Juliette's head resting on her shoulder.

Honestly, I could give two craps right now. Alex let her head fall into the pillow next to Juliette's. For Alex, being high was a convenient, easy way to surrender one's agency, or opinions, about most things.

She laid the roach of the joint in the ashtray by the bed and slung her arm around Juliette. If Juliette looked uncomfortable, Alex decided she would roll away, get up, and get ready to meet David in the parking lot of the Shore Stop for the two-hour drive to College Park.

But instead Juliette nestled closer.

What am I going to do when you go away to Swarthmore? she whined. Juliette never talked much about boys either, only about food. What she was cooking, wanted to cook. The places she wanted to travel—Paris, Lisbon, San Francisco—to sample their food cultures. The places she and Alex could rent an apartment after college and live together as roommates, Alex getting a job at a newspaper or teaching, Juliette a chef at a restaurant.

Live in Paris and make a mean crème brulee? Alex kissed her forehead. Think of me when you eat it?

Why don't you study abroad and live with me? Juliette lifted her lips to Alex's. I'll make all the sweetness in the world for you.

You already do, Alex said softly. She waited for Juliette to move away, but she didn't. She began to count to five. At three, she pressed her lips to Juliette's. At five, Juliette's tongue, tangy with strawberries, filled Alex's mouth.

They didn't go to the party. They didn't even go the Shore Stop to tell David they weren't going. That weekend, they barely got out of bed at all. It seemed so organic, Juliette's body, naked, pressed to hers, as they kissed and touched every part of each other. There was no awkwardness in knowing what to do, whether it was a sin. There was no discussion of what would happen next, or even what was happening in that moment. It was quiet and perfect. At the time, Alex wondered whether it was love.

Of course, she would mess it up back then with Juliette. Like right now, even, masturbating instead of getting interview questions together. But after her orgasm and the valium conspire to keep her trapped in bed for the foreseeable future, the questions she really wants to ask Juliette would never appear in a magazine, anyway.

Chapter Eleven

"I ran into her once, at the gas station, maybe last year," Owen says. He's eating Chef Boyardee Beef-A-Roni and orange juice for breakfast. "She asked me how you were, and I said you wrote for the *Capitol Metropolitan*. That you'd were dating a political correspondent we'd never met."

"Why didn't you tell me you ran into Juliette?" Alex's hands shake, probably because she's on her third cup of coffee. She didn't sleep well the night before for a number of reasons, one of which was her interview with Juliette. What she'd say. How to give off the perfect amount of *I don't give a crap about you anymore but I'm also kind of available, even though you appear to be married.* How she'd actually wind up acting—talking too fast, laughing too much, suddenly very aware of her hands, what to do with them.

"You said you hated her—I didn't think you'd care." He shrugs. "You didn't even tell me you were going."

"You didn't get home until early this morning." She frowns. His shift at Staples ended at 11; yet she'd heard him let himself in a little after 2:30 am. She worried he was secretive about his "friends." Maybe he was gay too—

not that it would bother her—or going to the strip club a few miles out of town, The Cat's Meow, a name that had all the subtlety of a nuclear bomb. Or, worse yet, maybe he was really into a Dungeons and Dragons, or Magic: The Gathering cult.

"Still, the house is a mess." He takes a gulp of his orange juice. "Why did you leave the living room like that, tapes everywhere?"

"I, uh, checked with the Hampton Inn—there's availability if Johanna can't deal with all of—this." She makes a sweeping gesture of the dining room—their mother's easels, unfinished paintings, guitar and amplifier, piles of magazines, newspapers, and fabric she'd collected for collages.

Owen pushes the bowl, which has a thin layer of tomato broth at the bottom, toward Tortoise, who sits on the table next to him. They both watch as she begins to lap up the broth.

"Is that good for her?" Alex asks after a minute.

"She's been eating it for years," Owen answers. "Couldn't you just have told your editor your mom died, and you have no interest in interviewing the girl who broke your heart?"

"She didn't break my heart," Alex snorts. Still, she's a little shaky. "I didn't even know what love was then. I'm not sure I even do now."

She runs back upstairs to grab another valium, just in case. Last night, she had leaned into the room and put the bottle back on her mother's night table, figuring she would be less likely to take them again if she had to go in there. She reaches in the doorway again and picks up what she thinks is the same bottle, trying not to look around the room. But when she turns the label to look at it in the hallway, it's Ativan, not Valium.

And this one also has Owen's name on it.

She scoops up all the pill bottles and takes them to her room, dropping them on the bed. She then picks up each and examines the labels: Ambien – Owen Maas. Adderall – Owen Maas. Xanax – Owen Maas.

That her brother is a pill head would be the biggest plot twist ever, one likely to make her stop watching whatever television show had the gall to suggest it. That Owen pill shopped for their mother—one thousand times more likely, although still not a good look. Especially now that she's dead.

Why does she have to think about this now, right before her meeting with Juliette? Maybe there is a more innocent explanation Owen can offer. In the hallway downstairs, she stuffs the bottles in her purse and wanders back into the dining room, where Owen is still sitting, staring into space.

"I have to pick up Johanna afterward," she says, choosing to ignore the subject completely for now. "So make sure your dishes are washed."

Juliette offered to come get Alex, but Alex doesn't want her to see the house. And that's saying something, since she'll have to illegally drive Owen's ninja turtle car once again and park it in Juliette's driveway. As she waits at the traffic light, highlights (or maybe lowlights) of their relationship flicker through Alex's memory.

I love you, Juliette said before slipping her class ring onto Alex's finger. They were at the beach. It was late

March, the wind still bitter and slicing at times and heavy with condensation. But they sat in the sand, huddled together in their hooded sweatshirts, an old Indian print blanket wrapped around their legs, watching the waves, holding hands under the blanket.

Alex had worn Juliette's ring for approximately an hour before Juliette had gotten nervous about her mother noticing it was missing and asked for it back. *You can wear it when we're alone*, she explained.

You're such a coward, Alex had accused. Alex wasn't particularly a trailblazer, but she honestly hadn't cared enough about the people at her school to be worried about any retribution for coming out. Although she'd begun to be popular, probably because she was hanging out with Juliette, it wasn't awfully exciting. Most of the popular kids were dumb. She was unable to hold a conversation with them in the cafeteria at lunch or at parties. None of them had read Edith Wharton or seen any Hitchcock films, subjects that were required reading/viewing for Alex and her mother. Being unpopular again for the last month of high school, she reasoned, was no great loss. But Juliette wasn't going out of state to college. Her parents were active in their church. She had a sister in the eighth grade in the same school. She had so much more to lose.

Alex read once that adulthood is about coming to see stories in which you thought you were the starring character from the perspective of other characters. And she understands now, and is even more forgiving of, what she saw back then as Juliette's faults.

On the other hand, if she were adult Juliette, she'd want absolutely nothing to do with Alex Maas.

Juliette has done well for herself, Alex thinks as she pulls into the driveway next to a pewter-colored BMW. She and her husband, an orthopedic surgeon with privileges at the local hospital, live on the other end of the river from Sprigg, in a wooded, gated community. She walks up the driveway to the slate-colored Craftsman house.

"Alex Maas." Juliette opens the door holding a glass of mimosa, even though it's 10 a.m. on a weekday, which she presses into Alex's hand before she even makes it inside. Juliette wears a light blue scoop neck shirt and white jeans. Her hair is pushed back from her face with a headband that matches her shirt. "It's been too long."

"Yes," Alex manages to say. She feels the muscles in her body begin to twitch as she holds on to the mimosa with two hands. She's never been nervous about interviewing people for the magazine; after all, she wielded the power of the pen. But this time, she feels like the one subject to scrutiny. She glances at a hanging wedding photo in the wall of the foyer, trying to calm herself. "Congratulations...on all this."

"You act as if you haven't been so successful yourself." Juliette laces her arm through Alex's and leads her to the kitchen. "I don't want to bore you with a tour—it's so pretentious, a house tour, and unless you need it for the article, I'd prefer to sit in here, if you don't mind. It's where I do most of my thinking."

"Whatever you'd like." The kitchen is airy and white. Half of Alex's apartment can fit into it. A large white counter island stands in the middle, flanked by four chairs. It overlooks a double sink, which rests underneath three windows overlooking the yard. Beyond the patio,

Alex can see the river glittering in the early morning sun. Juliette pulls out a chair for Alex and moves to the other side of the counter, picking up the bottle of champagne and repositioning it in the bucket of ice.

"Tell me what happened with your mother." Juliette reaches across the island and takes Alex's hands. Icy water drips into Alex's palms. "Please?"

"She died in her sleep," Alex says simply. It's technically true, although stripped of its more important details. Juliette gets up and goes to a small bookshelf by the stove. There's a larger one, almost floor to ceiling, to the right of Alex, filled with hundreds of cookbooks. But the small shelf holds smaller, more beaten, and presumably more used cookbooks. She returns back with one and places it in front of Alex. It's the copy of *Helen Brown's West Coast Cookbook* Alex's own mother had given her years ago.

"I still refer to this often." Juliette's hand rests on the cover. "It was one of the greatest gifts I ever got from anyone."

"I'm sure she would have been happy to know," Alex answers. Her mother had been perversely proud and irritated Juliette had opened Sprigg. *You think she'd offer me a job*, her mother grumbled once during her nighttime phone calls. *That spicy olive bread recipe is practically mine.*

"You're going to put that in the article, aren't you?" Juliette looks encouraged. "About your mother giving me this cookbook?"

"No." Alex shakes her head. "I want to remain impartial."

Juliette raises an eyebrow at Alex. They stare at each other for a few minutes. Alex silently dares her to bring it up, or, rather, bring them up.

"Owen said you met a really nice woman," Juliette says finally, playing with the locket she's wearing.

"I see you met a very nice fella," Alex answers, nodding back toward the foyer.

"So I guess things worked out okay for both of us," Juliette murmurs. She rubs her forefinger into the cookbook. *Any harder*, Alex thinks, *she might set it on fire.*

"Would it matter if it didn't?" Alex takes a sip, bigger than she anticipated, of the mimosa. "Are you going to talk to me about Sprigg?"

"We haven't spoken for over fifteen years, Alex." Juliette pours herself a glass as well. "Excuse me if there's a few minutes of awkwardness."

"It was high school." Alex shrugs. She gave it her best *I don't give a crap* look. "We were kids. It doesn't matter."

"It mattered to me." Juliette looks at her, her lips parted, heavy with other words she doesn't give voice to.

"I'm sorry," Alex says finally, drawing a line in the condensation of her mimosa glass. "It...wasn't that it wasn't important. It's just that it was a long time ago, and we have our own, different lives now."

"Don't apologize." Juliette opens the cookbook, flipping absently through the pages. "You don't have anything to apologize for. I'm just glad you're happy."

"My girlfriend moved out." Alex looks up. She ignores a sharp pain under her ribcage. "I wasn't expecting it."

"Oh." Juliette looks up, then repeats. "Oh."

After a beat, Alex digs into her purse, pulling out her portable digital tape recorder, a notepad, and pen. She cues up the recorder. She has nothing going for her in her life—A breakup she hadn't wanted to see coming. A mother whose actions she barely understood who was now completely inaccessible to her. A brother she understands even less. But what had back happened then was very simple, she knows. A high school crush between two girls, one who was merely curious, not gay. She doesn't know why she's been making it out to be something more since she's been home. Why she even got into contact with Juliette, thought Juliette would still be interested in her. *At least*, she thinks charitably, *with Owen what you see is what you get*. With her, it's a funhouse of mirrors.

"I'm glad you're doing what you really love, by the way." Alex glances up at Juliette. "I guess you could say I'm proud of you."

"Thanks." Juliette smiles. She comes around the counter island. Alex straightens as Juliette wraps her arms around her from behind, lets her chin fall on Alex's shoulder. "You were always the person I wanted to be."

"I know you have to be super nice to me because of the article." Alex glances back at Juliette. Flattery of any kind makes her suspicious. "But why were you nice to me before, at Sprigg?"

"I was excited to see you." Juliette holds on to her. "I mean, I don't hate you. At least not anymore."

"I didn't realize you hated me then," Alex says. But she knows she'd made things hard for Juliette at school.

The popular girls shunned Alex after prom immediately, but they kept Juliette on, albeit at arm's length. *Wasn't it so terrible, her coming on to you like that?* Chrissie Spangler whispered to Juliette at the lockers one day, loud enough for Alex to hear. But another time, in biology class, she overheard Hallie Johnson and Michele Wooten talking at their lab table. *Do you think she is?* Hallie asked Michele. *I don't know.* Michele heated the Bunsen burner. *It wouldn't surprise me if Juliette was. She was always so touchy with Alex. It wouldn't surprise me at all if they were licking each other.*

"I guess I didn't hate you," Juliette answers. "Obviously, I liked you."

"You know, I was a jerk to you," Alex says, tapping her pen against the countertop, white and quartz, shiny but opaque. Had Juliette put truth serum in the mimosa? This isn't going the way she planned it. "Because I was scared. I'm sorry."

Juliette straightens, her hand resting on Alex's shoulder briefly before she takes the bar seat next to Alex.

"What did I tell you about apologizing?" She smiles. "Now, what would you like to ask me about Sprigg?"

Alex positions the recorder between them. Even though she's inadvertently spilled her guts, it doesn't feel like closure. In fact, it feels disappointing, embarrassing, and yet also anticlimactic, but she knows she's an adult now, and it will have to be good enough. It's enough, she figures, to get through the interview today, to bang it out on her MacBook later, to e-mail a few follow-up questions, and move on with her life for good.

"So what was your idea to transform Sprigg into?" Alex scribbles in the margin of her notepad. She pauses, marveling how much her own handwriting looks like her mother's. She thinks of her mother, teaching her when she was five how to write cursive, the pointy top of the A in Alex, like a mountain, the curling river at the bottom of the mountain: A. She swallows, focusing and unfocusing her eyes. She wonders whether this had been a good idea after all, trying to work when suddenly she wants to be curled in a fetal position the corner of her bedroom. Her mother would want her to be here, she reasons, and not at home feeling sorry for herself. She takes a sip of her drink and clears her throat.

"You know, we are primarily an agricultural-based community, and yet none of the restaurants were serving farm-to-table food," Juliette explains. "I grew up having a little garden in the back of our house, and most of our meals featured something from that garden. And they were the most delicious meals I ever had. I guess, in a way, I'm recreating my youth."

You can never go home again, Alex thinks. And what if you've spent years running away from it, only to decide, after your mother has died, what you wanted more than anything was to come back, to have her back?

"Are you all right?" She feels Juliette's hand on her forearm.

"I'm fine." Alex nods, clearing her throat again. "That's nice, what you said, wanting to go home again."

"Are you sure you're okay?" Juliette squeezes a little, as Alex feels her eyes go glassy.

"Maybe we could do this another time?" Alex sighs. "I'm just feeling very distracted right now, and I want to give you my undivided attention."

"Of course, you're distracted," Juliette laughs as if Alex is crazy. "Your mother just died. I understand."

"I'm very sorry." Alex clicks off the recorder and shoves it into her purse. Why is it all coming apart now, when she needs to be calm and collected the most? "This is completely unprofessional of me."

"Are you free for dinner Friday?" Juliette walks her to the door. "Jack is out of town at a conference for a few days. I'd love to cook for you."

"You don't have to do that." Alex slings her purse over her shoulder. The sight, the smell, the pressure of Juliette's fingers on her arm, is all too much. Maybe it's just human contact she's craving. But maybe, she thinks again as she glances up at Juliette's tight red curls, the way one curl's caught on her silver hoop earrings, *I'm really, really still craving Juliette.*

"I want to," Juliette reassures. "I'll make something I thought of for the restaurant, based on a recipe of my mom's that included vegetables from our garden. It'll be perfect for the article. And then, if you're up to it, we can talk about what you've been going through with your mom. Okay?"

Alex nods, glancing around the walls, the wedding photos, perfectly staged shots of Juliette and Jack on a sailboat, hiking. She puts her hand on the doorknob, but before she opens it Juliette takes her in her arms and holds her. Alex exhales, letting her chin touch Juliette's shoulder. After a moment Juliette pulls away and puts her hands on Alex's cheeks, her eyes soft. It's then Alex notices, out of the corner of her eye, Juliette's wearing the sterling silver bracelet Alex had given her in high school. It's just a bangle, really, with a simple floral etching that has been rubbed down a little over time. She'd bought it at one of the antiques shops her mother liked to drag her to on the weekends. It wasn't expensive, but her mother had estimated it to be from the 1930s, which had impressed Alex at the time.

Juliette could have planned to wear it, to curry favor with Alex during the interview, but the fact she's kept it all these years, when she probably has more expensive, more tasteful, jewelry, makes Alex's heart leap a little. She meets Juliette's eyes for a moment, soaking in the cottony silence between them, feeling a dizzying rush of blood to her head, before she puts her hands atop Juliette's and squeezes lightly.

"Seven?" she suggests, breaking free, taking a step toward the door. "What wine should I bring? Or dessert?"

"Just bring yourself." Juliette smiles. "Leave the menu up to the professional."

Outside Alex slides into Owen's car and stares back at Juliette's house. It's grand, the home, more than anything Alex could have given her. *If this*, Alex thinks angrily, *is what Juliette wants—a safe, cushy life with some guy she probably doesn't even love.* Had Juliette mentioned Jack at all, except to say he'd be out of town?

Sure, Juliette had been a deadhead, had smoked pot, in high school. But it was cool back then, not cutting edge. Cutting edge would have been acknowledging their relationship. The last few months of senior year Alex was at turns angry and heartsick. She wanted Juliette to think for herself, make her own choices and not be bullied by her family or the other kids at school. She figured, if Juliette really cared for her, she would choose her over everything. But she hadn't.

Although once she had. Alex always leaves that part conveniently out of her narrative of martyrdom.

Alex hadn't thought then that maybe she'd been every bit a bully as everyone else. Maybe it hadn't been her call to demand what Juliette choose for herself, then or now. And maybe Juliette was happy, really in love with her husband. And Alex should be okay with that.

And if Alex isn't happy, that's her own damn fault and not Juliette's. She starts the car and backs slowly out of the driveway. *Maybe people are capable of introspection and change,* she thinks, as she makes it safely back to the main road and heads toward the airport. Maybe she's even one of them.

Chapter Twelve

The route to the airport mapped out by her phone takes her along the main street. The old movie house that once stood on the corner was torn down when the multiplex at the mall opened her senior year. And the office on the opposite corner also has a new, makeshift sign: *Shore Tax Services*. Before, it had been *Lewis Mahoney, MD*.

Alex pulls into a space along the sidewalk. She gets out and stands in front of the office window. The inside hasn't changed, only the clientele. Instead of sullen teenagers and nervous-looking women, a man in a service uniform sits in a chair, holding a folder full of receipts. TAXES FOR AS LOW AS $20 reads a poster behind the reception desk. Alex touches the window with her fingertips, lightly tracing what Juliette had scrawled there one night with her lipstick: ASSHOLE CREEP CHILD MOLESTOR.

She turns away, touching her stomach, which feels like it holds an undigested shoe. Lewis was sentenced to two years for insurance fraud. Of course, he'd be out by now. Could she run into him at the Wawa, getting gas? The Starbucks? It's not like it's a huge metropolis here. Of course, the last place she'd want to be after she was released from prison for insurance fraud and having her medical license revoked would be the town in which she got caught.

It's crazy enough that this backwater even has an airport. It had opened sometime in the sixties and, like the newspaper office, seemingly hasn't been remodeled since then. At least, she thinks, as she walks through the sliding doors, it's the size of a 7-eleven. Not that she'll have trouble finding Johanna. She stands by the Delta gate and opens her cell phone.

> *Been thinking about you.* Carolyn has texted her. *I have an assignment later today I think you'd enjoy, if you need a break & want to tag along.*

Why has Carolyn been thinking about her? Probably, Alex thinks, because that's what nice people do. Nice people actually think about other people than themselves.

She starts to text back "I'm at the airport" but realizes her hands are sweating. As she wipes her right palm on her skirt, she drops her phone on the floor. Just then she sees Johanna come off the tarmac. She's taller than Owen, and wears her trademark chiffon headscarf, although her hair is blonder now, less sandy, and cut in choppy bangs. She spots Alex and waves excitedly.

Alex's chest opens up, but in a different way than when she thinks of her mother. She's relieved. And, even though Johanna's only...an aunt, one she hasn't seen in over twenty years, Alex is connected to her in a way she doesn't expect to be. Because she looks like Owen, she rationalizes, and familiarity breeds comfort. As she bends to pick up her phone, she keeps her eyes on Johanna, on the long scoop-neck white T-shirt and skin-tight white jeans, her multicolored woven basket purse.

Alex doesn't realize her own purse clasp is open. As she reaches forward to grab her phone, Owen's pill bottles tumble out onto the old linoleum floor, along with her tape recorder. She gapes in horror as several of the bottles open (stupid child-proof caps) and pills of every shape and color scatter and roll in different directions.

"Oh, dear." Johanna's before her now. With her wedge sandal, she pushes a pill bottle toward Alex's hand.

"They're not mine," Alex explains, glancing around and catching the eyes of other travelers. She watches one pill get crushed under the roller of an older man's suitcase as he stops and bends to pick up a bottle in front of him. She squats and gathers the pills in her hands, throwing different pills in the same bottles.

"I'm not one to judge," Johanna says as Alex stuffs the cylinders back in her purse and buttons the clasp this time. "I knew it was you the minute I saw you—you look gorgeous."

"So do you," Alex answers as Johanna takes her by the arms. In fact, it's uncanny how much Johanna looks like Owen, down to their curved noses and hazel eyes. Uncharacteristically, Alex hugs Johanna. Surprisingly, Johanna's sturdy but soft at the same time. She smells like freesia and baby powder.

"Oh, Alex," Johanna murmurs. She plays with Alex's hair. "I can't believe how grown up you are. I wish I'd come more often, to see you more. I've missed so much of your life."

"It's okay—you're here now." Alex still holds on to her. This time, as she starts to cry, she lets herself. She knows Johanna will protect her. Or, at least, people will give them a wide berth.

"Did Owen come?" Johanna cranes her neck around the airport as Alex dabs at her eyes with a tissue.

"He's at home," Alex explains, grabbing the handle of Johanna's suitcase. "I had an assignment this morning—I work for a magazine—so I borrowed his car. I apologize in advance for that, by the way. My license, uh, expired—I just take the metro everywhere when I'm home. I guess we could rent a car under your name?"

"The happiest day of my life was when I got my new passport and license," Johanna says as they walk through the automatic doors outside. "With the correct *everything* on them—even my weight! And I needed them—I've been living out of my car the last year. Not literally—it's just that I'm at the winery so much."

"What do you do at the winery?" Alex asks as they walk through the parking lot.

"I own it, dear heart," Johanna responds. "Tiresias Vineyard."

"After the Greek somebody?" Alex's knowledge of mythology is thin, at best.

"Yes, a prophet—Hera changed him into a woman." Johanna grabs Alex's arm above her elbow. Alex wonders if Johanna's pleased Alex has guessed correctly and feels a little pleased herself. But then she realizes Johanna is gaping at Owen's car.

"Oh my God." Johanna stops walking and squeezes Alex's arm tighter. "*This* is your car?"

"It's not mine," Alex explains for the second time in two days. "It's Owen's."

Johanna walks slowly around it. "It is supposed to be an alien?"

"It's a ninja turtle." Alex opens the trunk.

"What on earth is a ninja turtle?" Johanna lowers her sunglasses and gives Alex a cockeyed glance.

"It's a comic book character—a children's toy." Alex slams the trunk shut. "And that's pretty much all you need to know about Owen."

In the car, Johanna moves the passenger seat all the way back. Still, her feet press against the front of the wheel well with such force Alex worries she might accidentally eject herself through the rear window.

"So what's new?" Johanna asks as she flips down the sun visor and puckers her lips.

"About Owen?" Alex raised her eyebrows, confused. "About Mom? About the house?"

"Or about you." Johanna pats Alex's thigh lightly. "I want to make time for girl talk before we get down into the muck-muck."

"Want to get a drink?"

"It's one o'clock in the afternoon."

"Is that a problem?"

"No." Johanna traces her lips with a coral-colored lipstick. "I'm still on West Coast time, but when in Rome or home, right? Where can we get a BLT and a good rosé?"

There is literally nowhere to go in this town, she thinks, *that isn't the Walmart of restaurants*. Except Sprigg, which is the last place she wants to be right now.

But she doesn't want to take Johanna to the Cracker Barrel, so she heads over.

"My ex-girlfriend owns this place," Alex explains to Johanna at Sprigg as they get settled at the bar. Would Juliette even be here yet? Alex prays she isn't.

Alex digs her phone out of her purse. She thinks about texting Juliette she's here, just to warn her, but she also doesn't want to look too eager. Especially after she's already fled from her today in tears.

"Let me try your best rosé." Johanna says as the bartender arrives. "And a BLT, white bread. Heavy on the mayo and pepper."

"I'll have a vodka tonic," Alex pipes in. "And a garden salad, dressing on the side."

"She'll have a rosé too," Johanna says to bartender before turning to Alex. "Sweetheart, you're carrying a Walgreens in your purse and drinking vodka in the middle of the day. I know your mother just died, but I don't want to have to do an intervention while I'm here, okay?"

"It's not like that." Alex opens her purse and scoops out all the bottles. She shows one to Johanna. "These are all Owen's, see?"

"Oh my goodness—your brother's a drug addict?" Johanna's mouth opens. "Adeline said he was just a homebody."

"I think he was pill-shopping for Mom," Alex explains.

"I was worried it would come to this." Johanna picks up the glass the bartender put in front of her and swirls it.

"I should have come sooner. I'd wanted to come years ago, but your mother didn't want me to."

"Why you?" Alex regrets it as soon as she says it. Why does she have such a knack for being insulting? "I mean, why not Dad?"

"It's complicated." Johanna sips her rosé.

"You mean, it gets weirder?" Alex picks up her own rosé and gulps it.

"Not weirder." Johanna pats her arm. "At least, I don't think so. Just complicated."

"What do you know about Lewis?" Alex signals the bartender for another glass.

"Adeline's narcissistic, criminal ex-boyfriend?" Johanna sighs. "What has he done now?"

"Nothing." Alex shakes her head. It's probably not the best time to bring up her own emotional trauma, in the middle of her ex-girlfriend's restaurant. But when will she have the chance again?

"I'm just glad she got out of that situation." Johanna punctuates each word with a period as she speaks. She squeezes Alex's hand. "But I want you to know, as much as a bitch your mother was sometimes, she loved you. She loved you, she really did."

"Look." Alex picks up her fork. "I appreciate what you're trying to do, and I'm not saying my mother had no redeemable qualities whatsoever, but I'm just here because she died. Because I need to sign a few documents and get probate started. That part of my life is over."

"Oh, honey." Johanna grabs her forearm like she's going to flip her over the bar. "You never divorce your family—they're always in you."

"Like a genetic predisposition to cancer?" Alex rolls her eyes.

"No—you come from your family. You are your family." Johanna lets go of her forearm as the bartender slides her BLT toward her. She takes one half of the sandwich in both hands and holds it up to her lips, as if examining a crown jewel, before taking a small bite. She continues to speak while chewing. "The only way you can know yourself is to learn who your family is."

"I know who my family is," Alex answers. "My brother has a PhD and works at Staples. My mother was the Cookie Monster of impulse control."

"And you're the star. At least, according to your mother."

"I wouldn't say that." Alex frowns. She's able to keep plants alive in her small apartment in Adams Morgan and meet deadlines for the magazine, but everything else seems amorphous and vague, crammed deep inside, like an M&M in a car seat. And if it threatened to pop up, she signed on for another assignment, another happy hour after work, another spin class on the weekend.

"Well, you certainly did well for yourself," Alex changes the subject. "A whole winery!"

"You have to love what you do, honey." Johanna holds up her empty glass as the bartender refills it. "When I was little, I knew I wanted to be either Leslie Gore or a bacchanal goddess. Of course, bacchanal goddess when I was little meant I wanted to be like my mother, who made her first martini at two after she came back from the hairdresser and her last at eleven, with my father before bed. But being a wife never happened for me, and when I needed money for my hormones, I took work as a tasting attendant at one of the other wineries outside Seattle. Are you getting all this? Because I'm hiring you to ghostwrite my memoir, *The Grapes of Maas*."

"It's funny." Alex stares at the bottom of her now-empty glass. "I'll probably wind up knowing more about you than I ever will my own father."

"No, you won't," Johanna says quickly, gulping her wine down as well.

"Why?" Alex asks. "Is he going to feature prominently in this memoir as well?"

"Look." Johanna taps the bar with the bottom of her glass, signaling the bartender again. "There'll never be the right time for this, but there was a reason I wanted to talk to you first."

"About what?" Alex feels a chill pass over her as the bartender arrives with the bottle of rosé. "Is that your third glass?"

"Yes, it is my third glass," Johanna answers as the bartender pours. "And yes, I am your father. Was your father. I'm your *parent*. Co-parent. Other parent...?"

"I'll have one too." Alex practically knocks Johanna's glass away from the bottle with her own. Her whole body screams like pins and needles. It makes so much sense now, who Johanna is, theoretically, but it *feels* so weird. So surreal. Like another death, but with a resurrection.

"I'm sorry I had to tell you here." Johanna touches Alex's elbow again. "But I wanted to test it out before I got to Owen. Is parent okay? You like parent?"

"It's fine." Alex takes a generous sip of wine. Some of the rosé spills over the lip of the glass and onto her chin.

Some of it makes her choke a little. "I mean, the terminology."

"What about the rest of it?" Johanna asks. Her voice lilts; for the first time since she's arrived, she sounds nervous.

"Well." Alex stretches the syllable out as long as she can. "I'm not totally surprised. But I'm a little upset that you waited this long."

"Well, I didn't want to blurt it out over the phone. I wasn't even sure I was going to tell you just now. I mean, your mother just died—you need someone to be there for you, not tie up last season's cliffhanger."

"Actually, any year before this one would have been fine." Alex stares at her. "You've had like thirty of them."

"I didn't know if you wanted that," Johanna explains. "I know your mother didn't. She never accepted my transition—she was devastated, and she mourned a long time. She said it was if as I killed Jeffrey."

"But you came out to see us—"

"And that was the last time." Johanna grips the stem of her glass. "All Adeline did was cry. And I don't blame her. It was hard, even for me. Anyway, I didn't want you to feel the same way—that I killed your father, so when your mother said not to come back, I didn't argue."

"You could have just asked," Alex rolls her eyes. "It's not as if anyone in our family is capable of subtlety."

"Well." Johanna takes a deep breath. "Do you accept me?"

"I guess." Alex shrugs. "This is all so unexpected. I mean, you wrote me some nice letters in college. You sent some beautiful holiday cards over the years—I really loved keeping up with the adventures of your parakeet Bono. But did you ever think, all those years, just a little line— oh yeah, I made you, Alex Maas? Hey, Alex, is your mom driving you crazy? Talk to me about it. Or, hey, Alex, you seem to be having a hard time in your personal life— anything on your mind?"

"First off, the phone works both ways—"

"Easier for you to say when you know I'm your daughter! I mean, at least you knew how important I was to you." Alex widens her eyes. "I mean, am I important to you?"

"I've been a bit of a coward, I know. But I was scared." Johanna puts her arm around Alex's shoulder. "I still am—scared and a coward."

Alex glances at her phone, which is buzzing in her purse. She draws in a breath, hoping it's Juliette.

It's Owen instead.

Where are you?

"We should get going." Alex pulls out her credit card as she texts back *Home soon* "I hope this was the practice run you wanted for Owen."

"Let me." Johanna blocks her hand and pushes her Amex Gold card across the bar. "I'll expense it. Oh, and I'll ask the bartender to get you two ice-cold spoons before we leave. It'll shrink those bags under your eyes to nothing."

Alex touches the skin above her cheeks as she pulls out her sunglasses. She didn't even consider, after breaking down in tears twice today, she looks like absolute shit. She considers going to the ladies' room to touch up her makeup instead but figures there's no point, now they're heading home.

She looks up at a patron entering the restaurant before turning toward Johanna.

"Oh Jesus hell—it's Barbara Sprigg," she whispers into Johanna's shoulder. She'd know that wardrobe anywhere—solids in nonpareil colors with paisley scarfs, like some sort of bizarro-world Prince. "What's she doing now?"

"Waiting by the kitchen doors," Johanna answers, loudly enough, Alex is sure, for Barbara to hear. Then, as if to confirm her suspicions, "Now she's looking at us. Oh please don't say that's your ex-girlfriend because I'm really going to have to question your judgment."

"It's her mother." Alex taps Johanna's thigh. "Will you please stop talking? Just stop. Stop."

"Turn around, turn around, they're coming over." Johanna tries to shrug Alex off, but Alex clings to her arm like ballast in the sea.

"What do you mean, *they're*?" Alex murmurs into Johanna's shoulder.

"Alex," she hears Juliette's voice. She closes her eyes, wishing her away, and wonders what her mother would have done in this situation. Go on the offensive, definitely. Alex clenches her teeth and extricates her head from Johanna's armpit.

"Alex is a little fragile right now," Johanna explains before she has a chance to embarrass herself.

"I know," Juliette answers. "I was just telling my mother about how charitable Alex is, agreeing to interview me for the *Capitol Metropolitan* when her mother just passed away. I don't know if I could do it."

Juliette and her mother are standing a few feet from them, Juliette looking at Alex, her lips curled into a smile, Barbara looking at Johanna, a smile so forced her eyes are almost squinted shut.

"This is my...this is Johanna," Alex says to Juliette. "She flew in from Seattle. To help with...things."

"Alex tells me you own this chic little restaurant." Johanna holds out her business card. "I may be able to help you with some wines."

"Oh, I don't think Juliette's in the market for any new wines," Barbara answers as Juliette examines Johanna's card. She takes it out of Juliette's hand before she has a chance to respond and drops it into her old-lady Dooney & Burke purse. "She sources a lot of local wineries here in Maryland. Not *foreigners*."

Alex growls under her breath as Juliette looks away from her mother in embarrassment. What does Barbara think Johanna is, exactly?

"*De acuerdo entonces*," Johanna says, as if she knows what Alex is thinking too, and stands up. She gives Barbara a smile that says *I will tear out your tongue if you speak again*. "I'll be around. If you have any questions, you have my cell."

"I'm so sorry about your mother, dear." Barbara smiles at Alex as she walks past her. "I know she's home now, with the Lord."

Alex nods. If her mother was at home with the Lord, she must've gotten lost on the way to somewhere else.

As Alex passes Juliette, she feels Juliette's hand brush hers, squeeze her pinky. Her index finger trails the length of Alex's palm. Alex gives her a glance, a little smile. She wants to take Juliette into a closet in the back and devour her like one of Barbara Sprigg's Smith Island Cakes.

"I want to shove a cork up that woman's nostril." Outside, Johanna glares back at the restaurant. "Prissy old hag."

"Did you have to do a sales pitch?" Alex shakes her head. "I could have asked Juliette about the wine—I'm having dinner with her Friday. Although I'm not even sure that's ethical, since I'm writing this article."

"Oh please—it's just business." Johanna stops in the middle of the parking lot. "Business never takes bereavement days. Now, where is that bitch's car?"

"Probably that one." Alex points at a champagne-colored Buick across from them with a bumper sticker that says DON'T FOLLOW ME—FOLLOW JESUS!

"I've got a steel nail file that would look great in her rear tire." Johanna opens her basket purse and roots around in it.

"No, you won't." Alex tugs Johanna's arm. "I don't even know how you got that through the airport."

"TSA usually is so busy worrying about who's going to have to pat me down that they never even get to my purse." Johanna holds up the nail file.

"There's people around." Alex nods toward an elderly couple getting out of a Ford Grand Marquis, the luxury liner of retiree cars. "I think they could easily remember to tell the police they saw two women riding around in a ninja turtle car leave the premises."

"Oh, Alex." Johanna touches her arm and laughs so loudly the retirees stare at them anyway. "I'm just playing with you."

"Good." Alex exhales as she unlocks Owen's car. "Because then I was really going to have to question *your* judgment."

"Although I do hate that Barbara Sprigg bitch." Johanna slides awkwardly again into the passenger seat. "As much as I hate this car."

"I guess we are related, then." Alex touches her puffy eyes with her fingers and smiles.

Chapter Thirteen

Owen has straightened up, kind of. There are vacuum streaks in the Oriental rug in the living room (that he has rescued from the trash) but dust bunnies and cat hair crowd the corners and underneath the furniture that he's not bothered to move. His Mountain Dew bottles are in the recycling bin, along with the various scraps of aluminum foil their mother had been saving for art projects. The cat vomit, although not completely scrubbed from the couch cushions, has at least been picked up. Some of their mother's sandalwood incense has been recently burned, gray wisps of clouds snaking through the hallway.

"Oh." Johanna stands just inside the doorway, inhaling deeply. "Your mother and her sandalwood."

"Hey, Aunt Johanna." Owen walks across the living room, wiping his hand with a dishtowel before holding it out. He's wearing Wolverine T-shirt today and cargo shorts. "Thanks for coming."

"Oh my Lord, Owen." Johanna drops her purse on the floor and takes Owen in her arms. "You were so small when I saw last you."

"Have you been drinking?" Owen looks at Alex over Johanna's shoulder. "You smell like a winery."

"We had lunch," Alex answers. "There's no food in the house. I mean, food we'd want to eat."

"Oh." Johanna has released Owen now and strides into the living room, as if hitting a mark on stage. "Oh. Your mother's essence is all over this place."

"I, uh, changed the sheets in Mom's room," Owen says, after a beat. He bends and picks up one of Johanna's bags. "I'll take up your things."

"I'll help you." Before he can pick up the other, Alex grabs it. She needs to warn him, or something, about what is coming. But how? In the bedroom, Owen has scooped up all the junk on their mother's bed—more magazines, a coffee cup, crushed cigarette packs, a shower towel with some blood on it—and thrown it in the laundry basket.

"Can you put this in your room?" He picks up the basket and holds it out toward her.

"Can't you put it in your room?" She believes she spots, poking out from underneath the towel, a pink dildo.

"Tortoise will get into it." He pushes it against her chest until she grasps it.

"All this stuff could've gone right into a trash bag," she complains. "I really don't know about you sometimes. And what about the pills, Owen?"

"What pills?"

"All the pill bottles around this house that have your name on them," she hisses.

"Do we have to talk about this now?" he whispers, pointing at the floor, to presumably Johanna below them.

"Should we not talk about it like we don't talk about anything else? Like Lewis?"

Suddenly Johanna is like at the door, hands on either side of the doorframe. Owen and Alex both stare at her, stunned at her stealth-ness. Alex concentrates on the laundry basket, trying to destroy the offensive objects with the power of her mind.

"This is nice." Johanna scans the room. "Much cleaner then I remembered."

"We can get a hotel for you—" Alex starts as Johanna waves her off.

"No-no-no. This is fine." Johanna enters and sits at the edge of the bed, smoothing the bedspread with her hands. She looks up at them with an expression of pride. "The last time I saw you, you hadn't even gone through the changes. Adeline sent me pictures over the years, but I always wondered what you sounded like, what you felt and smelled like. And now you're the age Adeline was back then. I know she was as proud of you as I am."

Owen and Alex look at each other, knowing what the other is thinking—that Johanna is full of crap. That their mother was the only thing tethering their lives and, now that she's gone, they are floating through space like astronauts in their own darkness.

"Did you tell our father that Mom died?" Owen asks. Alex's arm shoots up reflexively, like a lie detector. She pulls it down with the other as Johanna gives her a look. The look, as far as Alex can tell, is absolute terror.

"He knows." Johanna nods. "And he's here, in spirit. One hundred percent."

"Really, that's it?" Owen arches an eyebrow. "Well, I guess he's totally done with us, then."

"It's been thirty years, Owen," Alex says before she realizes it's unhelpful. "I mean, well, a lot has changed, right, Johanna?"

"He cares very much about you." Johanna plays with a turquoise ring on her index finger. "It's just your 'father' can't be here."

"Is he disabled?" Owen asks. "In prison? Institutionalized?"

"No." Johanna draws out "no" to four beats. "It's just that he's, well—"

"A secret agent?" Owen continues. "In witness protecttion?"

"No-no-no." Johanna sits up straight. She closes her eyes and breathes deeply, her fingers curling and uncurling, all serenity now, the gloss of her French manicure catching the light. Her lips move, but no sound comes out. Finally, she looks at Alex. "It's just that, well, he's scared."

"Oh." Owen exhales forcefully. "Well, you could've just said so."

"But surely you've told our father we wouldn't judge him if he came to see us?" Alex presses. She can't believe Johanna's chickening out on Owen after just blurting it out to her in the middle of Sprigg.

"I have." Johanna nods. She keeps nodding, as if she's got clamshell headphones on and is listening to a chill track. "And, if, you know, he changes his mind, I'll be as thrilled as you."

Alex stares at Johanna so hard she expects her to catch on fire.

"It just would be nice to see him, just once." Owen rubs the back of his neck. He looks a little sad now. Or maybe gassy. "I bet we wouldn't even recognize him."

"You wouldn't." Johanna is still nodding. She folds her hands under her thighs and stares at the floor. Suddenly, she looks up, as if she has a great idea. "But he gave me something to give to you."

She scoots up off the bed and opens her suitcase. Alex and Owen stare at the pairs of thongs, lacey bras, and a toiletry bag that would make Kim Kardashian jealous, before Johanna finds what she's looking for.

"It's old, but it still works." Johanna holds out a man's watch to Owen. "It's your father's Rolex. He wants you to have it."

"Wow." Owen lays it out over his forearm, like they do the prizes on a game show. He looks up at Johanna. "It's pretty cool, but he doesn't have to buy me off or anything."

"No, of course not." Johanna waves him off. "Put it on, let's see it."

"So our father *does* have money." Alex narrows her eyes at Johanna as Owen attaches the clasp. "Just not any for us growing up, or Mom? Or maybe he came into money, like after starting a business?"

"Well, the truth is." Johanna picks up her toiletry bag and cradles it absently in her arms, like a baby. After a moment, she looks at Alex. "I gave your father that Rolex. It was a gift from me that he's now decided to give to you."

"Johanna owns a winery." Alex explains, and suddenly Johanna is a blabbermouth, telling Alex and Owen about the flavors, aromatics, and tannins of her grapes. Alex studies Owen, who listens politely (he's much more a microbrew person), stealing glances at the Rolex now and then. *I get the truth*, Alex thinks, *and Owen gets a nice freaking watch.*

"Why didn't you tell him?" Alex hisses under her breath when Owen goes downstairs. Johanna begins hanging up her dresses in Adeline's closet.

"Eww—did your mother ever quit smoking?" Johanna makes a face as she pushes some of Adeline's old blazers off to the side. "It smells like a VFW hall in here."

"Seriously, I'm not keeping this secret from Owen." Alex inserts herself between Johanna and the clothing. "I'm having enough trouble processing it myself."

"Is it a bad thing that I told you?" Johanna's face falls. She brings a sundress close to her breast and hugs it. "This is exactly what I was scared of."

"No, you need to tell him." Alex grabs her by the arms. "He may react differently. He's much nicer than I am."

"But he's my son, and boys aren't wired the same." Johanna's eyes roll to the ceiling. "Believe me, I *know*. I had such trouble with my emotions. And a temper to boot."

"Valium helps." Alex nods knowingly.

"I know." Johanna nods knowingly too. "And lots of therapy."

"Well, not for me." Alex turns to leave.

"You've *never* had therapy?" Johanna catches her shoulder and spins her around. "No wonder you're tighter than a champagne cork."

"Lewis was a therapist," Alex mutters. "And he ruined my life."

Something inside her is closing down, like the aperture on a camera. Maybe it's the wine, but it's probably not. It's probably other things, like emotions. How she is going to deal with them. She closes her eyes and pretends she's home, in DC, if not working, then maybe at the Target in Columbia Heights meandering the aisles, wondering whether a new packet of leggings or a Keurig coffee maker would be the thing, the missing piece in the jigsaw of her life (as if there weren't entire pockets of the puzzle undone, gaping holes in the upper corner where the sky should be, floating islands of pieces in the middle, grasping for the edges, for something). She wants to be at Kate's house, watching an old Bergman film, her legs woven between Kate's. She wants to tell Kate she still loves her and that it wasn't Kate, it's her. She's never been able to get close to anyone, always afraid if she trusts someone, they'll disappoint her. Anything to be somewhere rather than here.

But she's still here, in her mother's bedroom, with Johanna. A stranger. Owen's not a stranger, and she doesn't even know him anymore either. Not like when they were eleven and ten, left at the mall for hours by their mother, sharing a single Orange Julius shake or huddled on the carpet in the corner of the children's section at Waldenbooks, trying to solve Encyclopedia Brown mysteries. They probably didn't know then that they would have bigger mysteries to solve as adults, ones without answers, even. Ones that weighed heavy, wet, between them, like the sound of Tortoise licking her hoo-haw by the bed, and how did she even get in here and think that now was the time for preening her privates?

Something bad is about to happen inside her, and she needs a safe distance from which to analyze. She needs to get out here. She needs to get out of here fast.

"Anyway," Alex says. "You need to tell Owen. Like, by tonight. If it's too hard with me here, I'll leave or something."

She feels for her phone in her skirt pocket and hurriedly texts Carolyn back.

> *If you haven't hit your assignment yet, I'd love to go.*

"Besides, I need to meet with the photographer," Alex lies. She feigns apology. "I'm sorry; I forgot. I'll be gone for just a little bit. You're going to tell him, right?"

"I will." Johanna stretches her arms over her head. "But I'm a little jetlagged. And I probably shouldn't have had a third glass of rosé. This has been emotionally difficult for all of us. I'm going to take a nap. Wake me for dinner."

Chapter Fourteen

"I'm sorry my ride isn't as pimped-out as Owen's," Carolyn remarks as she backs away from Alex's mother's house.

"*Thank you.*" Alex squeezes Carolyn's hand in an exaggerated fashion. "For letting me ride in anonymity for once."

Carolyn glances at Alex as she releases her hand. Alex takes inventory of the car interior, bare and clean, like she imagines her own would be, aware Carolyn's attention hasn't completely left her but not sure what to do about it. Should she tell Carolyn about Johanna? She hasn't even given herself time to process it. She never wanted anything from her. And Johanna didn't seem to want anything from them either. Until their mom died. Is she really here for emotional support, or something else?

And when will she tell Owen? Alex is jittery, like she's had way too much coffee. A vein in her neck pulses with such force she flips down Carolyn's mirror visor to make sure it's not going to hemorrhage out of her skin like the alien from Sigourney Weaver's stomach.

"Are you sure I'm not taking you away from anything?" Carolyn asks after a minute. "I felt bad the minute I texted you. I mean, I know you're not here to socialize."

"No, it's okay," Alex insists. And then, to make her feel better, "You're one of the only nice surprises about this trip home."

"Your aunt got here okay, uh, then?" Carolyn clears her throat.

"Yep." Alex plays with the door handle. "She, uh... she's okay."

"And did you meet up with Juliette?"

"I did." Alex touches the back of her neck, feeling her heart there too. "She's cooking me dinner at her house tomorrow. Just the two of us."

"Oh." The word is innocuous, but the way Carolyn says it isn't. A little too casual and too curious at the same time. Carolyn picks up the coffee mug but puts it back in the holder before she even drinks from it. "That's awfully generous of her."

"It's for the article—to sample one of her dishes." Alex folds her hands in her lap. "I had started to interview her the other day, but, I don't know—I just wasn't feeling up to it, so we rescheduled."

After Carolyn doesn't respond, Alex wonders if Carolyn thinks she's being unprofessional by accepting dinner. She worries, as she thinks of Juliette brushing her fingers earlier today at Sprigg, that she could be more unprofessional still.

"How much longer do you think you'll stay?" Carolyn asks finally.

"I don't know," she answers. A trip to the probate lawyer and slipping a few mementos into her suitcase has ballooned into so much else. "Now that Johanna is here, everything has gotten kind of weird all of the sudden."

"Well, hopefully not to add to the weirdness, but—surprise!" Carolyn smiles as she pulls up into the parking lot.

"Your assignment's at the zoo?" Alex looks at the pictures of turtles, bison, and owls on the log-framed sign at the entrance.

"I thought it might cheer you up," Carolyn explains as she gets out of the car. "I hope you didn't wear nice shoes."

Alex follows Carolyn to the entrance. It isn't the National Zoo, with its pandas, lemurs, and black howler monkeys. It isn't even the state fair; still, she's never been to the zoo in her own hometown, so she gives Carolyn points for novelty. "What are you covering?"

"Bella, the sloth, had a baby," Carolyn answers. Inside the entrance awaits a man in his fifties, wearing a khaki shirt and shorts. He's slightly husky, clean shaven, with ruddy cheeks, like a big child, and a sheen of perspiration covers the hair on his arms, as if he's just been picked off the produce shelf at the supermarket.

"Hey Carolyn." He leans over and gave her a hug. "You've come to witness the miracle of birth, or the after birth, I guess."

"Jim, this is Alex." Carolyn motions to Alex, who immediately holds out her hand, in case Jim is an indiscriminate hugger.

"Carolyn and I went to high school together." Jim glances at Carolyn and winks. "Go Tigers."

"Jim was one of my only friends." Carolyn touches Jim's sweaty forearm. "We went to prom together."

"I find that hard to believe," Alex says as they walked toward a thicket of tall trees cordoned off by a log fence.

"What, that Carolyn asked me to the prom?" Jim glances back and laughs. "It's true, I'm not her type. Although she's not mine either."

"No—I meant that you were Carolyn's only friend," Alex explains. Did Jim just openly admit Carolyn isn't his type? Of course a man would say something so insensitive. She frowns. "She's so sweet. I'm sure she had thousands of friends."

"I'm sure *you* had thousands of friends," Carolyn brushes her arm with hers. "Speaking of modest."

"I went to prom by myself," Alex answers.

"I find *that* hard to believe," Carolyn laughs as they follow Jim. "You're beautiful."

Alex freezes, but Carolyn and Jim don't seem to notice her, walking ahead. It would be just like her to take Carolyn's compliment completely out of proportion. Alex can analyze for days one random gesture made by a friend at dinner, only to find from the friend later it meant absolutely nothing. She hurries to catch up with them.

"Now that we've relived the halcyon days of high school, may I present Bella and her daughter, Nelly." Jim holds out his hand with a flourish. The small wooden enclosure is walled off on three sides. Inside, nestled in hay, a little brown ball burrows into Bella's chest, the most serene creature Alex's ever seen. She looks like a sock puppet with fur.

"Oh my God, they're adorable." Alex leans forward. "Were you able to witness the birth?"

"Actually, we didn't even know Bella was pregnant," Jim explains. "One of the zookeepers found Nelly when they were cleaning out the enclosure last month."

"Oh." Alex eyes Carolyn, as if to say, *some operation they're running here.* "You just found her? Did you find the deadbeat male sloth who knocked her up, too?"

"You mean Pat? Of course—I know I said it was a miracle, but not the biblical kind." Jim tilts his head and laughs. "Do you want to hold her?"

"You should." Alex nudges Carolyn. "It's your assignment."

"We could both hold her," Carolyn suggests, putting her purse on the ground as Jim reaches into the enclosure.

"Together, like proud parents?" Alex grins. "If you thought we were moving fast before, we've just hit warp speed."

Carolyn's eyes widen. Alex digs into her purse for her phone, anything not to look at her. *Just stop talking.*

"They like to hold on to tree trunks," Jim explains as he transfers the ball of fur onto Carolyn's upper arm with a gentle facility Alex doesn't think a large, sweaty man would have. "They spend most of their lives hanging upside down."

"I'll take your picture." Alex opens the camera on her iPhone, still not looking at Carolyn. "And post it on your Facebook."

"Get in there." Jim practically rips Alex's phone from her hand and pushes her toward Carolyn. "When's the next time you're going to be holding a baby sloth? They don't have these at PetSmart."

Alex sidles up stiffy next to Carolyn and puts her hand on Nelly's butt, above the bend of Carolyn's elbow.

"Closer," Jim commands from behind Alex's iPhone. "I'm not taking a landscape."

Carolyn leans her head toward Alex's as Alex touches Carolyn's back with the tips of her fingers.

"I don't want to look," Carolyn says as Jim hands the phone back to Alex. "I always look awful."

"You look great." Alex studies the photo. *It would be a good couple photo*, she thinks, *if we were one*. Carolyn looks relaxed and happy. Surprisingly, Alex thinks, so does she.

A message pops up on her phone. From Juliette.

"Excuse me for a minute," Alex says, walking a few feet away from the enclosure.

> *Thinking about you a lot today. Was hard seeing you hurting.*

She reads the message a few times. She wants to tell Juliette everything, like she did when they were teenagers. She wants to feel Juliette's arm gripping her waist, her head nestled in her shoulder. She wants the future with her she didn't dare to dream about in high school.

Of course, *it's just a text*, she thinks in the next minute. She's probably said equally heart-warming things to people she's cared less about.

> *Thanks.* She types back. *I'm really glad we've reconnected.*

"She's *cute*." She hears Jim say. When she glances up at Carolyn and Jim, their faces are pointed in her direction, although they aren't looking at her directly. She puts her phone back in her purse, not even wanting to consider whether she's Jim's type, whether he thinks she's his, that she's interested in him.

"Everything all right?" Carolyn asks in the parking lot. Alex barely said goodbye to Jim or thanked him for the tour; in fact, she realizes she may have even scowled at him on the way out.

"What were you two talking about?" Alex asks as they get into Carolyn's car. She knows she's about to pick a fight with Carolyn and push her away, but she doesn't know why.

"What do you mean?" Carolyn takes a sip from her coffee mug, not looking at her.

"Who's cute?" Alex continues.

"The sloth," Carolyn answers, blinking. "We were talking about Bella."

"I can't believe Jim said you weren't his type." She shakes her head. "What a jerk."

"Well, he's gay—so he was just being honest." Carolyn reaches over and touches the top of her hand. "Alex, I feel like I did something wrong and I don't know what it is. Will you tell me?"

Alex pulls her hand away, trying to keep from crying. Now she just feels stupid. Of course, Jim is gay. How could she not see that? But she's still sure Jim was talking about her, not Bella. She feels her neurons firing up, close to connecting.

"Everything's fine," Alex says, right before she bursts into tears. She feels Carolyn touch her shoulder as she bends over, trying to make herself disappear. If she had never answered Owen's phone call a few days ago, none of this would be happening. At least she wouldn't be a hysterical mess every time she's in the presence of Carolyn Pusey. Carolyn Pusey, who's thinking about her and always wants to see her and why she hasn't run away yet in alarm after witnessing the beginnings of Alex's nervous breakdown is anyone's guess.

"I'm sorry," Alex chokes out. "I'm not upset about the sloths—really. That was a lovely present. I'm not upset about Jim either."

"No—I'm the one who's sorry," Carolyn sighs. "I've been so selfish. You're grieving, and I've been acting like..."

You like me, Alex thinks as her synapses finally spark. Of course, Carolyn's a lesbian too—the lesbian literature, the way she looked at Alex at the restaurant, the texts, her offense at Alex trying to set up her with Owen. And she knows Alex is as well. Alex still has old pictures of Kate on her Facebook, even though her status is set to single—she doesn't announce her sexuality to everyone she meets, but she doesn't keep it a secret either.

She needs to process this new development. She needs to get out of here. She needs to get out of here fast. Alex closes her eyes tight. She pretends she's in Target again, looking at candles. They smell like vanilla and bamboo and sandalwood and juniper. Maybe she needs a shower curtain, or a soap dish. So many nice, inert things she can put in the empty spaces in her apartment, the empty parts of her. She feels Carolyn place her hand on the side of her face, and it feels good to be touched. She puts her hand atop Carolyn's and squeezes it, imagining, for a second, what it might be like to date Carolyn— coming to visit her in DC, seeing a revival movie at the theater in Silver Spring, listening to the National Symphony Orchestra, eating Italian ices at the Cherry Blossom Festival.

Her phone dings. She peeks into the opening of her purse and sees, with a jolt, Juliette has texted her back.

Me too. I've wanted to see you for a *long* time.

"You're not acting like anything," Alex says to Carolyn as she pushes her purse shut with her foot. "You're acting like any person— a friend—would. Thanks for being a good friend. I really need one right now."

Carolyn moves her hand away from Alex's face.

"I have to get back to work," she explains, starting the car.

"Of course." Alex nods. She wonders, now Carolyn has gotten the hint, if she'll ever see her again. It's for the best, Alex thinks, and, once Carolyn has a few hours to think about it, about Alex and her United Nations of red flags, she'll probably agree.

"Thanks for taking me to the zoo," Alex says as Carolyn idles in front of Alex's mother's house. "It was nice to escape the one here at home, at least for a little while."

"You're welcome," Carolyn says quietly, looking through the windshield. There's an awkwardness, heaviness, between them. In unison, they lean over the middle console and hug.

"Take care of yourself," Alex says, not looking at Carolyn, before she gets out and closes the door. She leans against it, wondering if she's made a mistake. She turns and pulls at the handle on the Corolla, but Carolyn has already locked it.

"Did you forget something?" Carolyn rolls down the window. She's put on her sunglasses, her eyes hidden behind the tinted frames, and it's hard for Alex to tell what's she's thinking.

"No." Alex lets go of the locked handle. She figures it's a sign. She thinks of another couplet in *Diving into the Wreck*: *And now: it is easy to forget/what I came here for*.

You came to explore the wreck, she tells herself, not looking back, walking up the broken flagstones to her mother's house as Carolyn pulls away. Not check out the mermaids.

Chapter Fifteen

Inside, it looks like a bomb has gone off in their living room. Even Tortoise appears stunned, weaving around stacked boxes with her mother's beaded scarves and hats hanging out of them. Her mother's canvases are stacked against the wall; her unfinished sculptures crowd the coffee table. Johanna must've powered napped for all of five minutes to have gotten so much done. Alex looks up as Johanna comes down the stairs with another box.

"Did you tell him?" Alex asks as Johanna brings another box into the living room.

"Not yet—he went to work. We're going to have to rent a truck, by the way," Johanna says as she places the box next to the others.

"So we can take all this stuff to Goodwill?" Alex rubs the back of her neck. She's only half listening, still thinking about Carolyn's hand on her cheek.

"No, to the post office." Johanna pulls out one of the long, beaded scarves and ties it loosely around her neck. "Your mother had such incredible taste, and I can't take all this home with me on the plane."

"Oh, yeah, sure." Alex drops her purse on the hallway table and goes to the kitchen. She should be happy

Johanna is attacking the clutter she herself has done nothing but run away from. Still, she's a little offended their house suddenly has turned into an estate sale.

"Owen said he was probably going to get rid of everything, and that you wouldn't want much, that I could take what I wanted." Johanna says from the living, as if reading her thoughts. "Is that okay with you?"

"That's fine." She waves her hand, distracted, opening the refrigerator. She pulls out the orange juice but then remembers she saw Owen drink from it earlier. She finds a bottle of water in one of the crispers. It's already been opened, but it's easier to drink, not knowing whose lips touched it last.

"Are you okay, sweetie?" Johanna comes into the kitchen and cups Alex's shoulder. "I know I dropped a big bomb on you earlier."

"I'm still a little in shock." Alex admits, drinking the water. "You're here, Mom's not. I'm still expecting her to wake up from her afternoon nap and wonder what the hell we're all doing here."

"I know." Johanna sighs, her hands on Alex's shoulders. "Owen seems to be taking my being here pretty well."

"I wonder how well he'll take it when his dad shows suddenly shows up." She puts the half-full water back in the fridge. *Like the valium*, she thinks, *it's the family water now.*

"He did bring up your father again—before he left for work."

"What did he say?" Alex straightens up. Perhaps Owen isn't so dense after all.

"He wanted to know what your father does, so I told him I gave him a job at the winery."

"What do you mean, you told him you gave him a job?" Alex turns. She's confused again. "Why didn't you just take that opportunity to tell him the truth?"

"Because I realized I wanted you there." Johanna puts her hand on her heart. "For moral support. Not to say anything—and I mean anything—just moral support."

"Fine." Alex closes the refrigerator and goes over to the makeshift bar. She opens one of her mother's rail vodkas, the kind you can get three for twenty dollars at the liquor store for frat punch. The vodka will at least kill Owen's germs from the orange juice she's going to mix it with. "But you're telling him tonight. You're just making it worse. Owen will be totally fine with it. I promise. I mean, he'd never keep a secret from you—he's an open book."

Johanna pours the rest of the vodka in the sink. "Okay, but as long as I stay here, we're not going to drink this. We need some Stoli or something."

"Owen's at work," Alex says. "We can't go anywhere unless we get an Uber."

"He left that thing he calls his car." Johanna tosses the empty bottle in the recycle bin. "An older woman, a co-worker of his—Shelley? Do you know her? Anyway, she picked him up so we could use it."

"My license is expired, remember?" Alex says as Johanna walks past her. "I shouldn't have even picked you up this morning."

"I don't care—I don't drive stick," she answers over her shoulder.

Johanna goes upstairs to freshen up. In the living room, Alex picks through the boxes Johanna has set aside for shipping. Her mother's jewelry box is in there, as well as an expensive tea set of French white china. She wonders whether Johanna plans to sell them online, and whether she plans on sharing the profits with Alex and Owen. Alex doesn't care about the money (although a little extra for her grad school loans would be nice), and doesn't know why, if Johanna is giving away Rolexes, she does, either, but it's the principle of the thing. These are her mom's memories, all that's left of her mom. And she doesn't know if she's ready to let her go—all the infuriating imperfections of her—yet.

She glances up and sees her mother's purse—a vintage Chanel shoulder bag—hanging on one of the dining room chairs and grabs it. Again, it's not the money but what could be inside. Small fragments of her mother's life, clues, answers. Alex takes it into the kitchen and stuffs it into one of the cabinets above the stove, where her mother had stored an ancient oil popcorn popper before waiting by the door for Johanna.

One thing Alex notices while they're out running errands: Johanna is like her own Teenage Mutant Ninja Turtle car. Although people don't honk at them in the grocery store, she feels the eyes of every shopper as they move through the aisles; Johanna is tall and she is a chatterbox, if not to Alex, then to herself or to the person who happens to be standing the closest to her.

"How are the pork cutlets in this store?" she demands of a man in the meat department, who only has a can of Pringles and a case of Budweiser in his cart. "I'm thinking Cuban tonight."

Alex guesses it make sense; if you know you're going to be looked at, take the lead and control what people see.

"What was it like for you...before you transitioned?" she asks Johanna as they squeeze avocados in the produce section.

"Depressing as hell," she answers, dropping one in a bag. "It was like I was watching myself from outside my body trapped inside my body. I never identified as queer—at least not how you identify as lesbian. It wasn't even about wanting to sleep with men, per se. It was wanting to be on the outside what I was inside."

Alex looks up at an older woman. She's standing by the onions, frowning at them in that way. As if they don't belong here, in this quaint little, economically depressed, God-fearing town, Johanna specifically.

"Is there a problem we can help you with?" Alex raises her eyes at her, and the woman walks away. "You see, Johanna, this why I never, ever come back to this place."

"I appreciate your sticking up for me." Johanna lightly touches Alex's forearm. "But it's a full-time job and exhausting. I just ignore them. Besides, it happens just as much in Seattle, too, believe it or not."

"It's just so...stupid." Alex shakes her head. "What business is it of theirs anyway?"

"It can certainly be life-changing, not just for the one who transitioned, but their family and friends." Johanna lets her fingers trail over the cloves of garlic. "What if your mother had decided she wanted to transition? Would you have been okay with it—not having a 'mother' anymore?"

"I don't know." Alex glances at the woman who gave them a look. She's over by the meats now, studying a package of ground beef. "I mean, it would be really weird, but if it made her happy, I think I would be happy for her. Geez, it might even be a blessing, since she was so bitter at the world most of the time, specifically you."

"How so?" Johanna's hand stops mid-trail.

"Being abandoned. Being broke. Being single. Being left with me and Owen." Alex looks back at Johanna. "Seriously—I'm not telling you anything you don't know?"

"I felt terribly about leaving you two." Johanna pushes the cart toward the front of the store. "It's bothered me for years."

"It bothered you so much you never tried to do anything about it." Alex rolls her eyes. "Mom had her moments, but at least she fed and clothed us. She could have transitioned into a unicorn for all I care."

As they wait in the checkout line, Alex stares at Johanna, who is flipping through an issue of *Vanity Fair*. Maybe Alex shouldn't have been so short with her. *But it's a big deal.* All this time she assumed her father was just someone who couldn't be bothered with family. It happened often in society—it was something she could, if not understand, at least live with. But having a parent alive all these years and who wanted to see them but didn't because of fear, because of their mother, because she felt it was better for them? And if any of that is true, then why now?

She guesses now is better than never. But she's not ready to award Johanna a medal for it.

"This is a really shitty nail polish." Johanna plucks out the $5 bottle of pale pink polish Alex has placed in the top of the cart and holds away from her like it's a cat turd.

"You need three coats of it and it still chips off after a day. I have a better one at home in nearly the same color that you can have."

She stuffs it on the shelf above the conveyer belt that houses gum and picks up a package of Ferrero Rocher chocolates.

"Did your mother teach you anything about beauty products?" Johanna shakes her head, putting the chocolates on the conveyor belt. "I'm going to go through your makeup bag when we get home. Some of that stuff is just terrible for your skin. Believe me, I know—I've spent the last several years trying everything on the market."

In fact, Alex is so engrossed in Johanna's recount of her journey to finding a matte, full-coverage foundation that doesn't make her face look cakey she forgets until they're outside to see whether they're picked everything up on their grocery list.

"I forgot the trash bags—we need to go to Staples," she says to Johanna when they're in the car. They can use Owen's Staples discount. At least there's that. Then she remembers the other thing that's been bugging her since Johanna arrived. "What did my mother tell you about me?"

"Oh, goodness, I don't remember exactly now." Johann unwraps a ball of the Ferrero Rocher chocolate and pops it in her mouth. "Oh, oh—wait. That you were too smart for your own good. Something once about her checking account balance."

"Oh Jesus." Alex rolls her eyes. "Really? She should have been thankful I kept an eye on her accounts—it's how I found out about the insurance fraud."

But she's a little taken back, hurt, even, that her mother complained to her non-parenting parent about Alex taking over the family's finances. Or that her non-parenting parent would even be privy to them.

Where is all this money coming from? Alex pushed the printout of her mother's checking account balance across the table.

I worked overtime for Lewis. Her mother glanced up at her. She was wearing her readers, working on a psychedelic-themed jigsaw puzzle. *I thought you'd be happy—no bouncy-bouncy.*

Well, of course, but. Alex pointed at the numbers. How much overtime are you working? All this money—you're working the equivalent of two full-time jobs here.

Well, Lewis is generous. Her mother pushed a pile of purplish pieces toward her. *Here, make yourself useful.*

He runs a private psychiatry practice and pays alimony and malpractice insurance, I'm assuming. How can he afford to pay you so much? Alex stared at the jigsaw pieces, the innies and outies on them. She and her mother, she thought, were pieces with all outies.

Well, he's, you know, contributing toward our household expenses. Her mother lit a cigarette. He does spend the night here now.

Alex let her eyes go slack, watching the purples morph and slide together. There'd been no announcement when Lewis had started staying over. And yet, she'd been startled awake twice in the previous two weeks by someone standing outside her door, hovering in the hallway, just as she'd done that night when Lewis and

Owen were playing video games. Once she swore he was actually in her room, standing at the end of her bed. She'd told herself it was a joke he was playing on her. Still, at night she stared at the small square of her room, wondering how to rearrange the furniture so her bed wasn't in the sightline of the hallway.

"Your mother appreciated your help," Johanna says.

"I appreciate your diplomacy," Alex answers. "But at this point, I value your honesty. I mean, for all I know, she painted us as horrible monsters, and I can maybe see why you'd never come home to see us."

"Your mother didn't badmouth you to me—she was proud of you. And she told me she reached out to you an awful lot over the years." Johanna wraps up the rest of the chocolate. "Do you think if she didn't like you, she would have done that?"

"She knows what I wanted to hear from her." Alex pulls into the parking lot of Staples a little too sharply. "An apology. It's not my fault she never gave one."

The phone calls followed a pattern: always late at night, always when her mother had had too much to drink. They started with her mother whining she was lonely, wanting Alex to visit, or proposing she visit Alex. They reached a crescendo with her mother accusing her of hating her (not quite true), or being ashamed of her for committing insurance fraud (kind of true), or being unable to put Lewis behind them (definitely true)—to which Alex always pointed out that her mother was the one who had brought him up, not her. They ended with Kate whispering to Alex *hang up, just hang up* or one of them leaving the bedroom. The calls from her mother were a stalemate that were tolerable only for their consistency; her weekly reminder that her mother was alive.

"I'll see if I can find Owen, and you get the trash bags," Alex instructs inside Staples, as Johanna wanders toward a display of cell phone covers. Maybe she'll get an extra second or two alone with Owen, and she can ask him what else Johanna told him while she was with Carolyn.

At the back of the store, at the double doors that lead to the warehouse, where Owen works, she stands on her tiptoes and peeps through the window.

"Can I help you find something?"

She whirls around to find a young blonde employee, whose name tag spells the name Renee in a way she's never seen: R-A-N-A-E. Her hair's pulled very tight into a ponytail, as if she's trying to give herself a DIY facelift, and Alex wonders whether the restricted blood flow to Ranae's head is responsible for her seemingly preternatural happiness.

"I was, uh, looking for my brother, Owen," Alex explains. "Is he back there?"

"Owen Maas?" Ranae looks stumped. "Owen doesn't work here anymore."

"What?" Alex looks at Ranae as if she's opened a box of thumbtacks and thrown them at her. "What do you mean?"

"He got fired." She shrugs. Suddenly, Johanna is beside them holding not only a box of trash bags but a three count of disinfecting wipes, unassembled packing boxes, and a roll of bubble wrap. Her presence seems to trigger a reset in in Ranae's programming. She turns to

Johanna and repeats herself. "Can I help you find anything else, uh, ma'am?"

"Fired?" Alex interrupts her. "You know our mother died this week, right? You know he's grieving, right?"

"Oh, that's not why he got fired." If Ranae senses any aggression coming from Alex, she doesn't show it. "He got fired for insubordination."

"Insubordination?" Johanna repeats. She looks as if Ranae has thrown thumbtacks at her as well.

"It's when..." Ranae starts.

"We know what it is." Alex flicks her hand dismissively. "We're leaving now."

"Wait." Johanna grabs Alex's arm and looks at Ranae. "Where's Shelley? Does she still work here?"

"Oh, yeah." Ranae seems nonplussed about their intimate knowledge of Staples' employee roster. "It's her day off. She's the one who fired Owen."

Now Alex and Johanna are the ones who are stumped.

"Can I help you find anything else?" Ranae asks after a minute.

Chapter Sixteen

Alex remembers Johanna buying the Ketel One at the liquor store on the way home, and she remembers having a cocktail before dinner, maybe two, and texting Owen regarding his whereabouts. But now it's morning and she's in her bed, Tortoise lying on her chest. And she's pretty sure something crashed downstairs a minute a before, which is the only reason she's awake.

"There she is." Owen peeps his head in the doorway of her bedroom.

"Where else would I be?" Alex murmurs, struggling to sit up.

"Not you—Tortoise." Owen takes a step into her room. "We thought she might have had slipped outside while we were moving stuff."

"Moving stuff where?" Alex's head feels like there's a crowbar embedded in it. "And what about your job, Owen—what the hell!"

But Owen's gone back downstairs. As she grabs her towel and heads across the hall to the shower, she peers into her mother's room. It seems bigger, airier. And missing a lot of things, including the three-legged wardrobe that indirectly was responsible for this whole situation.

"Where are you taking all this stuff?" Downstairs, Alex, now dressed, stares through the front window at U-Haul truck in front of the house. She turns to looks at Johanna, who's wrapping a lamp in bubble wrap.

"Some of it to Goodwill, and some of it to the post office," she answers. "We're getting ready to head out, if you want to come."

When Johanna carries the lamp outside, Alex heads to the kitchen and pulls her mother's bag out of the cabinet above the stove. She transfers her cell phone and her wallet into it and heads outside with them.

"Are you on board with all of this?" Alex whispers to Owen near the driver's door of the truck. "You haven't even gone through all this stuff."

"I've lived with this *stuff* for over ten years," he answers, getting into the driver's seat. "I thought you'd be happy it was moving along so quickly."

"Do you know what's she's keeping for herself?" Alex says. "A lot of expensive pieces, that's what."

"You're the one who invited her," Owen says, starting the engine.

"I didn't invite her—she invited herself." Alex glances back at the house. "And what did she tell you about 'Dad,' exactly?"

"That he's very handsome and looks a lot like me," Owen answers, adjusting the rearview mirror.

"She hasn't told you yet?" Alex looks at him incredulously.

"Told me what?"

Just then Johanna comes back outside. She sashays lightly down the sidewalk, her purse anchored to the inside of her bent elbow, and points Alex into the truck with the flick of her wrist. Alex obeys without responding. Inside the cabin smells faintly like cigarette smoke and vomit and whatever industrial chemical they used in an attempt to cover it all up. She squeezes in the middle between Owen and Johanna as Johann turns on the radio.

"Hungover." Alex puts her hands on either side of her temples as Johanna searches through the stations.

"I warned you about drinking in the middle of the day," Johanna says. She turns the volume down exactly one notch.

Alex really needs coffee, or she's going to look and sound even bitchier than she already does. She points, like a mute, at the Starbucks, making a moaning sound like a distressed sea lion until Owen squeezes the U-Haul into the drive-thru.

"I love this song." Johanna turns up the radio.

"Get me an iced coffee with soy milk," Alex says, pulling her wallet of her mother's purse. "Do you want anything, Owen? I'll pay for it, since you don't have a *job*."

Owen gives her a dirty look as he leans out the window. The cab of the truck is moving along with Johanna, who's shaking her fists and bouncing in the seat to Elton John. "*Shine the light/shine the light*."

"We went to Staples yesterday, and Ranae told us everything," Alex continues. "You know, your former coworker, Ranae?"

"Oh, this is gorgeous." Johanna runs her palm over Alex's mother's Chanel purse as Alex opens it. "Did you just get this?"

"Kind of," Alex answers, pulling out her wallet. "I need something with a stronger clasp. Something that'll keep all of Owen's pills from falling out."

She holds the ten toward him, which he snatches away before he shoves the cold coffee into her palm.

"Yeah, there's the job, the pills, your boss, Shelley." Alex takes a sip. "So much to cover today."

"First of all, Shelley asked *me* out." Owen's eyes bulge. "Not the other way around."

"Wait, what?" Alex chugs too much coffee, which spills over into her trachea. As she leans over and coughs, Johanna whacks her back a little too hard, and she hits her head on the dashboard.

"Oh goodness, I'm sorry." Johanna massages the back of Alex's head, even though it's the front that made contact. "I'm such a klutz."

"It's okay." *Mag-nani-mous.* She reaches for the radio knob and turns it off. "What were we talking about?"

"Shelley, Owen's much older boss, asking him out." Johanna is still massaging her head. "Didn't she fire you, by the way, for being insubordinate?"

"It's not like that." The U-Haul lurches over the curb on the way out of the drive-thru, and some of Alex's coffee spills on her leg. "She didn't fire me for bad performance, but conflict of interest."

"What conflict of interest would you have working together at Staples?" Alex is upright again, one eye shut, head pounding.

"I was going to tell you eventually." Owen pulls into the back of the Goodwill Center, where the drop-off is located. "I proposed to her. At the store. She fired me because it would be conflict of interest to work under her."

"Oh my God, why does it keep getting stranger?" Alex presses the cold coffee against her left temple. "Can't you just say you got fired for stealing a packet of post-it notes?"

"So you'd rather me be a thief than be engaged? That's very touching of you." Owen cuts the motor and slides out of the truck, slamming the door. Johanna and Alex sit in silence.

"You could be a little more delicate," Johanna says after a minute before opening the passenger door. "I'm going inside to get a receipt."

Alex sighs—why does being the responsible one always make her the bad guy? It must be her presentation. She sulks for a minute before joining Owen at the back of the truck.

"I'm sorry," she mutters, testing the weight of a box near the door as Owen pulls out an old dresser. "So, you're engaged, huh? To your boss? How come I'm just hearing of this?"

"Because you never want to hear about anything." His face flushes as he leans backward with the dresser.

"I don't want to hear about Tortoise." She puts her hands on the other side of the dresser, steadying it. "In fact, I'd be less surprised if you were engaged to her."

"At least I'm not single." He backs up and Alex goes with him. "I can't imagine anyone wanting to listen to you criticize them all day."

"I don't need to criticize the people I date." Alex leans her head against the back of the dresser. "They're adults."

"Let it go," Owen says.

"Let go of what? You're the one who dropped the engagement bomb."

"No—the dresser." The dresser dips suddenly, and Alex must squat to keep her balance. It lands with a thud on the floor of the drop-off center. She follows Owen back to the truck.

"Like I said, you've never wanted a relationship with me since I came back and stayed with Mom—at least someone did." Owen pulls out some trash bags with clothing.

"It's one thing to make sure someone's okay—it's another entirely to pill shop for them." Alex grabs a box of old school supplies. "I mean, she overdosed! Did you not think that was going to happen?"

"You act like I got those all in a week—those are like six bottles over a year or two." Owen glares at her. "None of those are habit-forming, and Mom was such a paranoid crank, I was *happy* to get them filled for her. Believe, me, I'd rather her take a valium once in a while than freak out all night thinking Lewis was going to hire some thugs to rough her up."

"And Lewis!" Alex tosses the art supplies next to the dresser. "Thanks for freaking supporting me there, Owen. And you wonder why I can barely bring myself to respond to your phone calls?"

"I don't know what happened between you and Lewis, but I swear to you, I never saw anything."

"You never saw anything?!?" Alex is shaking. "You were standing at my bedroom door when it happened."

"I wasn't there." Owen knits his brows and sighs in exasperation. "I told you—I wasn't there. You probably just saw a shadow. And your door never closes—it probably just opened because you were moving around. I mean, Jesus—don't you think if I saw something, I would have said something?"

"I don't know—you and Lewis were pretty close." Alex wraps her arms around herself.

"You're just freaking insulting." Owen looks at her in disgust. "Of course, I would believe you over Lewis."

"Are you sure? Even if you didn't see anything, you could have believed me. You could have defended me against Mom." Alex moves toward the door that leads out onto the show floor. "What the hell is taking Johanna so long?"

She steps through the door and finds herself in the houseware section. Rows of old coffee makers, mismatched plates, souvenir mugs. Even here, the smell of mothballs is overpowering. She remembers the Saturdays her mother dragged her here as a preteen, looking for hats or glassware or gowns with fabrics she could use to make scarves. She was the type of girl, she thought, that would love being a thrift rat. But her mother, her perpetual 16-year-old sister, had ruined even that for her.

She stiffens as Owen pops up next to her, sweaty and panting from moving the dresser.

"I did take your side—I keep calling you, don't I?" he argues. But he's had a few minutes to think about it. And, even now, as he stops and picks up a promotional glass from Burger King with Han Solo it, he's already distracted from defending his argument.

"We're getting rid of stuff, not taking it home." Alex redirects his hand and glass back toward the shelf. "Besides, you would just call and talk about nothing. I don't call that being supportive."

"Jesus, can't anyone do anything right by you?" Owen calls after her as she takes a short cut through the sporting goods, looking for Johanna's scarfed head over the aisle shelves. "No wonder Kate is gone."

"You have no idea what happened between me and Kate." She whirls around. "So don't even go there."

"I don't even know why you came home." Owen is holding the Han Solo glass again. "And I'm getting this—you're not my mother."

"Yeah, you're just going to marry her instead," Alex mumbles. "Where the hell is Johanna? She was just supposed to get a receipt."

Just then, Alex sees her headed toward the dressing room, a stack of clothes hanging over her arm. As she notices Alex, she sighs and speeds up, trying to get into the dressing room before Alex catches up with her.

"I thought I heard you two bickering." Johanna shakes her head when Alex intercepts her. "Can you take your differences outside and not embarrass me in the middle of Goodwill?"

"What are you doing?" Alex gestures toward the clothes. "You were supposed to get a receipt."

"Do you know how hard it is to find clothing in my size?" Johanna frowns at her. "No, of course, you don't. You're a perfect little size four. How was I supposed to know some large-boned, tall woman decided to let go of her perfectly good blouses?"

"Weren't you supposed to be getting a receipt?" Owen joins them. In addition to the glass, he's holding an old Nintendo console and a box of cartridges.

"I was just telling Alex I'm pretending to not know either of you." Johanna opens the door of the dressing room. "Now, do you want to come inside and tell me how I look, or do you want to resume your episode of *The Real Housewives of the Eastern Shore*?"

"I'll be in the truck." Alex wanders through the store. She wonders how many things in here are the result of people dying. Could the whole store be a repository of dead people's things? It seems sad to her, that one minute someone's clothes, all their things, are minding their own business in the house and the next they are whisked off and separated, never to be together again, an Oxford button-up never brushing against its favorite blouse in the closet, an afghan sweater in the dresser never pressed against its neighboring friend the cardigan. If they're lucky, they'll wind up in new homes, but even then, the life, the person they know and love, is long gone.

And now they're subjecting their mother's clothes to the same lonely fate. She's totally not ready to let her mother's things go into the wardrobe of anonymity. She's not ready to let her mother go, period. It all seems too soon, too unexpected. Unfair. Extremely inconvenient. But isn't that the nature of death?

As she walks back through the drop-off area, she squats and picks up a trash bag that contains some of her mother's sweaters and T-shirts.

"Hey, you can't take that," an employee who's already sorting through their mother's shoes calls over to her.

"I just dropped these off." She backs up, toward the exit, still holding the trash bag. "I changed my mind."

"You can't take those," he says again, standing up.

"They're mine." She glares at him, and, not sure if that's enough, turns around and runs outside with the trash bag. She runs past the truck and cuts through an alley that runs along the side of the store. As she comes out the other side, she walks through the strip mall adjacent to the Goodwill. Running with the bag of clothes has wiped her out, so she leans against the little brick ledge outside the Subway and catches her breath. She wishes her mother was here; it's this kind of craziness she would've appreciated (although usually the kind of crazy-making of which her mother was the chief architect). If her mother called her phone right now, she would answer. Alex would come home and visit, make peace somehow. She realizes she has no friends, no one she's close to. Not even Owen. She needs a few allies in her life, she realizes as she wipes her eyes, even if it one of them is her mother.

She looks up as a mother and her daughter, who looks about five, come out of the Subway. When Alex was that young, she didn't know her mother was different than other moms—she still thought of her mother as someone who had all the answers, who could protect her, who was judicious and wise, and, yes, beautiful, in kind of a mean pixie way.

"Here." She looks up. The little girl from Subway is standing before her, holding a five-dollar bill.

"Did you want to get something to eat?" The girl's mother, not frumpy and cranky like Barbara Sprigg but definitely Christian, explains. "We can watch your things if you want to go inside and order."

"Oh, no." Alex stands and heaves up the trash bag. "No, I'm not homeless. Thank you—I'm just taking these things over to Goodwill, and I got tired."

"Are you sure?" The woman blinks. The little girl holds the bill higher, as if Alex doesn't see it.

"Yes, thank you." Alex smiles with all the dignity she can muster. She holds up her mother's handbag as she stands up and backs away. "See? It's Chanel. I'm not homeless."

She hurries back through the alley with the trash bag, and when she gets to the curb, she's stunned to find the U-Haul gone. She walks around in a circle, looking around, wondering if Owen moved it into a space, since Johanna apparently thinks they're on a shopping expedition. But no, it's totally disappeared.

She thinks about going back inside but doesn't want to be harassed by the Goodwill employee about the trash bag again. This time, she sits on the curb, far away from the loading dock and away from any other businesses and shelter, and texts Juliette.

> *I'm so sorry. I'm in a bit of a bind and I need someone to pick me up.*

She closes her eyes against the bright sun as she waits for Juliette to reply.

What's wrong? Juliette stopped. They were in the back seat of Juliette's Datsun, parked on the dead-end road off Route 50. Sometimes Juliette would pick Alex up when she got off work and drive her home, even though it was only a fifteen-minute walk from Alex's house to the mall. Most of the time, Juliette drove to the dead end first, where they were hidden from the highway by the dense thicket of elms.

Nothing. Underneath Juliette, Alex pulled up her jeans. She pressed her face into the Juliette's shoulder, smelled the traces of fabric softener on Juliette's crewneck sweater. "It's okay."

Is it me? Juliette cradled Alex's head with her hand.

No, of course not. If she closed her eyes, she saw him, Lewis, hovering over her. The same way he had been the afternoon before. She'd been taking a nap after school, when she felt someone touch her beneath her stomach, in the space between her hips, smelled the sharp, spicy notes of aftershave.

His longish bangs hung suspended between them as he looked at her. She drew in a breath, feeling her body lock, rigid, into place. His corduroys were opened, his dick bobbing outside of the zipper like a fishhook. She noticed, on the end of her bed, her mother's keys. Had he taken them from the office so she couldn't leave work, discover him here, jacking off over her daughter? And where was Owen, Owen who had no girlfriend or after-school job to keep him away from home?

As soon as Lewis lifted his left leg toward the bed, and presumably to climb over her, every muscle in her exploded, a fire-hot charge of rage and survival as she sat up, knocking her forehead against his in the process.

Get the hell out of here. She pushed at his chest, drawing her knees up. *I said, get out!*"

Just over his shoulder, she noticed her bedroom door close. It didn't have the deadbolt then. Just a cylinder so slippery you could open and close it without even turning the knob. It was how Lewis slipped in without waking her.

Owen. She was relieved he'd seen them, angry he hadn't done a damn thing. Still, it was enough. Owen had seen them. She scrambled off the bed as Lewis zipped himself up.

Don't ever fucking come back here. Alex stood opened her door and stood in the hallway. Owen's door was open, but he wasn't inside. She ran down the stairs, blood screaming through the veins, and checked the kitchen, the dining room, and the living room. Through the front window, she saw Lewis's Volvo parked in front of their house.

I couldn't have been dreaming, she thought as she went into the back yard and sat on the deck, shaking. Someone had closed the door. Someone had seen them before closing it. She stood up, aware Lewis was still in the house, and walked around their development, trying to breathe and also trying not to think. Did he have a key to their house now? Could he let himself in any time he wanted? When she came back to the house fifteen minutes later, the Volvo was gone.

That's how, Alex remembers, she and Juliette wound up that night in front of Lewis's office. She remembers in the Datsun telling Juliette what had happened with Lewis, Juliette climbing off her and starting up the car, screeching back onto the road. She wondered whether Juliette was going to confront him, hoped she wouldn't, but wouldn't stop her if she did. In front of Lewis's closed office, Juliette got out of the car and stood before the storefront window that overlooked the darkened waiting room. Alex watched as Juliette rifled through her purse and pulled out a tube of lipstick. Then, she leaned on the glass and began to write.

Alex opens her eyes and looks at her phone. Juliette still hasn't responded. She absently shifts through the shirts at the top of the trash bag. About three shirts in there's a screened T-shirt her mother had probably gotten at the Goodwill herself. Atop the marbled red cotton are the words HOT CHICKEN CAPITAL OF THE WORLD, NASHVILLE, TENNESEE, along with a chicken on the bottom right. It looks like Carolyn's chicken, Billie.

Carolyn. She shouldn't, but it's hot out here. Her nose is starting to burn in the early afternoon sun. She picks up her phone again and texts Carolyn this time.

Can you pick me up? I'm stranded at Goodwill.

I'm in an editorial meeting until two. Carolyn replies a second later.

No worries. She types back, embarrassed. *Sorry to bother you. I can get an Uber.*

Carolyn texts her back a second later. *Don't. I'll come get you.*

Chapter Seventeen

"Should I ask what happened?" The inside of Carolyn's Corolla is cool. Alex holds Carolyn's briefcase in her lap. In the back seat the trash bag of her mother's things slouches to one side.

"No," Alex laughs. She blots her face with a napkin. "I'd rather not get into it. Thanks for coming to get me."

"Well, am I taking you home?" Carolyn asks as she pulls out of the Goodwill parking lot.

"I don't know," Alex answers. "Maybe somewhere air-conditioned where I can hang out with this trash bag without questioning, like the library?"

"Well, I could work the rest of the day from home," Carolyn suggests, then adds: "If you want to hang out with me."

"No—I've been such a pain already," Alex sighs. "I shouldn't have even texted you."

"Then why did you?" She feels Carolyn glance at her.

"I wanted to give you a shirt," Alex lies. "I'm sorry for pulling you out of your meeting—you're not my personal chauffer. You have every right to be angry with me."

"I'm not angry," Carolyn answers. "I made the decision to leave and come get you."

"You're very kind," Alex says as Carolyn flips on her turn signal and makes the turn out of town, toward her own house. Alex decides not to argue. "I wasn't sure if you were mad at me about yesterday."

"Why would I be mad at you?" Carolyn glances at her.

"I don't know." Alex drums her fingers on the arm rest. An awkward silence, colder than the air conditioning, weighs between them as the car bounces over the railroad tracks toward the outskirts of town.

"So let's see this shirt." Carolyn says as she cuts off the engine in her driveway. Alex, as if sprung from prison, lurches over into the back seat and pulls it out of the trash bag.

"It's kind of dumb, but it made me think of you." Alex holds it out toward her.

"Thanks," Carolyn says as she spreads it out over the steering wheel. "But I'm sure it's too small. You could probably fit into it though."

"It's not really my style anymore." Alex takes the shirt and folds it up carefully. "My mother dressed like she was a sixteen-year-old punk."

"Well, at least that's kind of cool." Carolyn smiles. "I didn't even need to go through my mother's clothes when I got rid of them, they were so dowdy."

"What was she like?" Alex asks.

"Do you really want to know about my mother?" Carolyn frowns, staring through the windshield.

"Yes, I would." Alex tosses the shirt into the back seat, missing the trash bag. Although it seems stupid to amass information about someone she'll probably never see again, she realizes she wants to know about Carolyn, honor her experiences, her feelings. She wonders if this is what caring feels like.

"My mother disowned me after I told her about Carrie," Carolyn says after a minute.

"Your...ex-girlfriend?" Alex confirms, and Carolyn nods.

"But when my father died, I knew my mother couldn't take care of herself. She'd been diagnosed with Alzheimer's a few years before. I resigned from my job at Drexel—I was an assistant professor of journalism—moved back home and found a job at the newspaper here."

"Oh my God." Alex blinks. "I had no idea you left so much behind in Philly. How advanced was your mother's Alzheimer's?"

"For the first year or so she knew me, and I had her in adult daycare while I worked. But then she started leaving the oven on when I was home or wandering outside or leaving the front door open." Carolyn takes off her sunglasses and dabs her eye with her pinky. "Even though I rarely went out at night or weekends, it was too overwhelming trying to monitor her all the time. So I moved her into a facility and sold the house."

"I'm so sorry," Alex says simply. "It must have been so hard, being solely responsible for your mother." She suddenly feels a little bad for Owen staying home with their own mother.

"Do you want to know what the hardest thing was?" Carolyn looks at Alex. "It wasn't watching my mother slowly lose her entire identity. It was that she was nicer to me after she didn't remember who I was than when she still did."

Alex reaches over and touches Carolyn's shoulder.

"We had the best year of our lives together when I was a complete stranger to her," Carolyn continues. "And maybe I should be grateful for that, but it seems like a complete lie. Maybe because it was."

"It wasn't a lie," Alex says. "Some part of her—her cells—knew it was you. Her cells are in you."

She reaches over the console and hugs Carolyn. She wants to give Carolyn something, some reassurance she's okay, a whole person, but what business does she have trying to give her that? Alex, who's been carrying grudges half her life (rightfully so), thinking she was alone in her search for the white whale of forgiveness and closure. Those kinds of endings, she considers, make great magazine articles, but they aren't real life. Real life keeps going, with slow pacing, unresolved conflicts, and confusion. But also happiness sometimes, too, if you allow it for yourself.

"You're so lovely," Alex says, kissing the top of Carolyn's head, then her cheek, then again closer to her ear. "You're a really lovely person. And your relationship with your mom will never diminish that."

Carolyn turns her head to Alex's. Before Alex can react, Carolyn kisses her. Before she can get in her own way, Alex kisses back. She doesn't think of Kate or her mother. She forgets she's irritated at Owen and Johanna. She doesn't remind herself she's having dinner with Juliette tomorrow or how fucking hot it suddenly is in this car. She only thinks about Carolyn's lips, which are also warm, her hair, which smells like honeysuckle. She thinks about how nice it feels, kissing Carolyn, how nice Carolyn is. How nice it is to feel something nice. She doesn't think about how at some point it will have to be more than this or less than this.

She awakens later, in the coolness of Carolyn's sheets, to the sound of Billie clucking in the yard. It sounds like a cartoon chicken: "buck-buck-ba-gawh!" over and over. She turns over, still in her bra and underwear, and runs her hand over Carolyn's empty side of the bed. They didn't sleep together, although they fooled around a little, cuddled. Mostly they talked, Alex about Kate, Carolyn about her ex, Carrie, a nurse, in Philadelphia.

"I'm sorry." Carolyn appears in the doorway, a mug of fresh-brewed coffee in each hand. "I tried to feed her before you woke up, but she was still noisy. I don't know why she does it—she doesn't even lay eggs anymore."

"What do you mean?" Alex makes room for Carolyn in the bed. She takes one of the cups from Carolyn and absently blows on the liquid. "She has an egg-laying song?"

"All chickens do." Carolyn smiles, sipping at the coffee. "It sounds like that."

"Buck-buck-ba-gawh?" Alex makes the noise Billie just made. "That's the egg-laying song?"

"They're very prideful." Carolyn laughs. "They love to brag they're laying an egg."

"I feel like I'm writing the wrong article here at home." Alex laughs too.

"Maybe you can come back and write another one," Carolyn answers. She brushes a strand of hair away from Alex's face. Alex takes a long sip of her coffee. She doesn't owe Carolyn an explanation about anything, at least not right now. Does she?

"I'm surprised you've never written about it," Alex says finally. "I mean, you know Billie best."

"I'm not a writer." Carolyn's hand lingers on Alex's shoulder. "It's an editor's life for me."

She looks at Carolyn, her mussed-up hair, her clear, green eyes, her smile. She thinks of Carrie, the nurse in New Jersey who cheated on Carolyn. She doesn't understand how that was possible—Carolyn would make a really great girlfriend. For someone. Alex isn't really looking to start over so soon after Kate. Not that she wants to get back with Kate, necessarily. Now that she thinks about it, she was more enthralled by the fact such a sophisticated and somewhat-powerful woman found her interesting and attractive, considered her worthy of the beltway class. She had finally arrived. She'd fed off the reflection of herself in Kate's eyes and had considered herself worthy in her own. Kate was the ultimate Sugarman's Pharmacy ribbon.

What exactly Carolyn sees in her, she's not sure. Carolyn, who is reliable and kind, whose self-worth isn't tied up in her career. Carolyn deserves someone much better than Alex.

We miss you. Johanna has texted her. *Where are you hiding? Let's talk this out like adults.*

"I should get home," Alex says, reaching for her shirt. "My family finally realized I was missing."

"Before I take you back." Carolyn presses her hand on Alex' thigh, keeping her in place. "What are we doing?"

"I don't know what we're doing." Alex pulls her shirt on. On that, she's honest.

"Well," Carolyn smiles. "Do you want to keep doing it?"

Alex rubs the bedhead out of her hair. She's home on bereavement; Carolyn can't expect her to be thinking for the long term right now.

But she can change her mind before it gets too far. It's not as if anything is going to happen between her and Juliette, anyway. Juliette, who she's come home to see. Juliette, her fateful journey, with whom she must have her final reckoning, or something.

"Well," Alex says after a moment. "Why don't we just take it easy and see what happens, okay?"

Carolyn pulls Alex into her arms back onto the bed, kissing her. For a second, Alex feels light, like she's eaten a delicious meal that's not too filling, or slept in on a Saturday, which is rare. She feels quiet, like a huge ball of cotton has absorbed all the thoughts in her brain. She feels blood pumping from her heart, continually washing over her body, a sustained pulse, so subtle you wouldn't even feel it unless you were trying to. Its rhythmic, slow beat tugs at the muscles in her neck and shoulders, making them feel like taffy. Almost like quicksand, if she gives in too much. Something you can drown in, she panics as she sits up quickly. Something, as all the muscles in her body clench back into their normal state of vigilance, she's not quite ready for yet.

Chapter Eighteen

"You could have texted." Alex says at the dining table as Johanna comes out holding a tray of pork loin. "I mean, I came outside and you were gone."

"We were looking for you everywhere, driving up and down the street." Owen drinks a bottle of beer. Instead of his usual T-shirt, he's wearing a green I-Zod polo shirt. "We thought you tried to walk home, so we went that way. Why didn't you just text us?"

"It doesn't matter now." She picks up her wine glass. Carolyn dropped her off out front before she headed back to work, and Alex was okay with that, not ready to embroil her in her own family drama. "Where'd you get that shirt?"

"You like it?" He brushes off the shoulders. "Johanna picked it out for me from Goodwill."

"Well, geez, I'm glad everyone got their shopping in while I was wandering around town with mom's clothes." Alex takes a sip of the wine.

"Johanna has great taste," Owen whispers across the table to Alex as Johanna bangs around in the kitchen. "I think it's because she was a man once."

Johanna comes out with a tray of asparagus and arranges it next to the pork. She's wearing a cute white peasant top that Alex recognizes from Goodwill.

"Do you say grace in this house?" Johanna looks between them. When they shake their heads, she reaches for each of their hands. "Well, maybe we should."

"I'll try." Owen looks across the table. When she shrugs, he continues, "It's not the best circumstances in which we were brought together. And it's been kind of tough, but I'm glad we're together, and I'm sure Mom would be too."

"Cheers." Johanna lifts her glass. "I'm going to add something. I'm really happy to have had the opportunity to get to know you two a little better. And I'm hoping the both of you feel like there's an opportunity to know each other better too. So we're going to talk this out, since I've had years of therapy while I was transitioning and am really good at this, about what happened today at Goodwill. Who wants to start?"

"I'll start." Alex takes another sip of her wine. "I've been a pretty ambivalent about coming home, which probably isn't a secret."

"We never not wanted you here," Owen interrupts.

"Owen—" Johanna holds her hand out. "You'll have your opportunity to speak."

"Because of Lewis," she continues. "No one believes me about Lewis—even though you saw us, Owen. It had to be you. Lewis had Mom's keys—it couldn't have been her who was home that day."

"I told you it wasn't me." He enunciates the words clearly, a twinge of anger peppering the end of each word.

"Does it even matter now? We all know Lewis is a terrible person, and he almost ruined Mom's life."

"Mom's life?" Alex gasps. "How about mine?"

"Yours too," Owen corrects. "But I didn't have anything to do with that."

"Yes, you did!"

"I think what Alex is trying to say," Johanna interrupts. "Is although it wasn't your fault, she needs you to support her nonetheless."

"I do support her—I text her all the time."

"That's not support—that's just cat pictures," Alex points out.

"Well, it's kind of awkward to even reach out." Owen looks into his beer bottle. "When your sister thinks you're a loser."

"Alex, do you think Owen is a loser?" Johanna looks at her.

"I don't think Owen's a loser," Alex says carefully. "I just think he's wasting his life here."

"I kept Mom out of trouble," Owen explains to Johanna.

"She didn't need you to keep her out of trouble." Alex shakes her head. "She was an adult."

"So I think I'm hearing two different approaches to parenting, to relationships." Johanna slices herself another piece of loin.

"Who's right?" Owen presses.

"I don't think either of you are right—or wrong," she answers. "I think you did what you did to survive. You did that—now what? Can you two have a relationship now?"

Alex stabs an asparagus stalk. Friction has been the static that's kept them together over the years and their mother the anchor that's has kept them docked at this sad little island. She worries if she's not angry at Owen she might just forget him altogether.

"I'm fine with that." Owen leans back in his seat. "I've never not been fine with it."

"Alex?" Johanna raises her eyebrows at Alex. Alex chews, stalling. If she does make nice with Owen, she can finish her business here and get home and not have to worry about any of this ever again. She deliberately keeps Carolyn out of this equation, preferring to break down each problem into smaller equations she can solve individually. And Juliette? She has penciled in Juliette to worry about tomorrow, when they have dinner together.

She nods at Owen, still chewing, as Owen holds his hand out over the table, and they shake. It's strange to think that everything that has mattered to her—her safety at home, her reputation, trust—suddenly doesn't matter. That the slate has been wiped clean, and she's supposed to be happy about it.

"So what else did you guys get at Goodwill?" Alex pushes her plate away. Suddenly she's not hungry. She still feels something unsettled, that amorphous memory of that person peering at her and Lewis in her bedroom—if not Owen, not her mother? Then who? Juliette? She had a key to the house too, that Alex had made her. But that doesn't make any sense. Does it?

They all look up at the knock at the door.

"I'll get it." Alex jumps up, worried Carolyn has decided to come back. She's not part of this equation. Not yet anyway. Maybe never.

"It's for me." Owen jumps up in unison, sending Tortoise scrambling off his lap and tearing through the living room. Owen brushes Alex as he passes, and she pulls on the back of his shirt.

"What if it's for me?" She nudges herself ahead of him a little, closing in on the door.

"Who would come see you?" He sticks out his arm, like a running back, and nearly clotheslines her. "You don't have any friends here."

"Neither do you." She lunges her foot forward, thinking she'll trip him, but that's madness. She stops in the hallway and watches Owen open the door.

"Hey!" He says to whoever's outside with the most enthusiasm she's ever heard him muster in their entire lives. "We've been waiting for you."

Owen steps aside, and a diminutive woman, whom Alex generously pegs in her late forties, but a hard forties—there's a lot of mileage on those tires—walks through the doorway, carrying a grocery store-bought dessert of some kind. She is lean and tough, like beef jerky, and the color of it, too, the result of what Alex is sure is too many years in a tanning bed. Her tight permed caramel curls helmet her head amorphously, like a half-blown dandelion. She's still wearing her Staples uniform.

"I'm Shelley." The woman grins at Alex. She hands Alex the box of cheesecake. "I'm sorry I'm late. Owen didn't give me much direction on dessert."

"This is lovely," Alex answers. She puts her thumb over the price tag, so she doesn't inadvertently stare at it. "I'm Alex, by the way."

"Of course you are." Shelley smells faintly of smoke, gum, and perfume. "I've seen all your pictures."

"Come on." Owen weaves his arm around Shelley's waist. "I want you to meet Johanna."

Alex follows them with the cheesecake. She watches Shelley visibly stiffen as Johanna stands up from the table. Did Owen even prepare Shelley about Johanna? Probably not. Although it's not as if Johanna prepared Owen about herself either. *Well*, Alex thinks, *at least I know they're really related*.

"Hello, honey." Johanna holds out her hand.

"My goodness," Shelley's voice starts normal but trails off high at the end. She glances quickly around before looking back at Johanna. "This...this room is certainly very brown."

"We call it the Hershey room," Owen says, nodding toward Alex. "Blame Alex—she and our mother painted the walls."

"Owen has told us so much about you and your impending nuptials," Alex says, ignoring him.

"Oh, that was certainly a surprise—right during our big desktop computer sale." Shelley looks at Owen. "He said he wanted to surprise me, and he certainly did. He's always surprising me."

"He's always surprising us too," Alex says, a little too glibly. She turns toward the kitchen. "I'll cut us some cheesecake. Shelley, do you want a glass of wine?"

"I'll help you." Alex feels Shelley behind her. She puts the cake on the counter and opens the cabinets and hands Shelley a glass.

"I'm so sorry about your mother." Shelley touches Alex's forearm. "I was with Owen at the hospital, and he was such a wreck. I was sorry you weren't there too."

"Oh." Alex is quiet for a minute as she tries to assemble four matching dessert plates from the cupboard. Had their mother known about Shelley? It seemed unlikely she could keep such a secret to herself. But the thought of Shelley being at the hospital takes her off guard. "He didn't mention that. Not that—it means anything. Owen's never been good with details."

"You can say that again." Shelley laughs. "Not that he doesn't mean well."

"What are you complaining about now, woman?" Owen comes in the kitchen with the dinner plates. As he drops them into the sink, he pats Shelley's butt.

"She's not property, Owen." Alex frowns as she cuts the cheesecake. She secretly wishes Owen will work out all his thoughtless, clueless, immature behavior on Shelley before he finds the actual love of his life. Shelley, she concedes, might be a good starter girlfriend for that purpose—she doesn't look like someone who takes a lot of shit from anybody.

"Oh, it's okay." Shelley wraps Owen's arms around her waist. "He's a very affectionate boy. I wish my own son was."

Son, Alex thinks as she carries two plates, hers and Joanna's, to the dining room. *Owen could almost be your son.*

"So, how many children do you have, Shelley?" Alex sticks her fork in the slither of cheesecake she's cut for herself.

"Just my son, Jimmy." Shelley glances at Owen as if seeking permission to divulge the information. "He'll be thirty next year. But I don't see him much—he lives in Virginia. He's had some struggles over the years. But I'm hoping he'll find his way. It's been a little rougher lately, now that I've been seeing Owen."

"He did threaten to come back and kick my ass." Owen shovels a forkful of cheesecake in his mouth. "More than once."

"How did you two, uh, start dating?" Alex presses.

"I needed someone to set up the DVD player I bought with my discount from the store," Shelley explains. "I doubt Owen said two words to me before then, even though I was his boss, but everyone said he was the one to ask, so I did. I made him dinner, since he wouldn't let me pay him, and, I don't know—we just got to talking, and it was real easy. Like I'd known him all my life."

"She made lasagna," Owen adds. "Different than Mom's, but still good."

"Your mother could make a lasagna," Johanna says suddenly. "She would make Béchamel and add it as a layer. I miss your mother's cooking after all these years like you wouldn't believe."

"I didn't know our mother cooked for you," Alex says suddenly, sensing an opportunity. "Weren't you always in Seattle?"

"Oh, no." Johanna drops her napkin on the table, along with Alex's hint. "I knew your mother quite well before you were born."

"This is nice, baby." Shelley leans over and rubs the sleeve of Owen's I-Zod between her fingers. "So much nicer than all those cartoon T-shirts you wear."

"You like it?" Owen glances up at Johanna. "Thank Johanna. She picked it out. And you know what else Johanna had me do? Buy an electric razor."

Owen brings Shelley's palm to his cheek. "Feel how smooth that is."

"I was absolutely appalled no one had taught Owen how to shave properly as a teenager. Not that he had much help, living with two women," Johanna explains, blinking her eyes, as she takes a deep breath. The moment is bittersweet, Alex thinks. It burns lightly in her chest. "Anyway, I figured it was the least I could do for him. For Adeline."

"Oh, that's nice." Shelley strokes Owen's face while beaming at Johanna. "Now maybe you can get him to pick his socks up off the floor."

Alex stares through the sliding glass doors. She doesn't want to think about this scrappy woman, who might have given her mother her money's worth in a fight, and Owen in any situation in which socks come off. At least, if he's trading one caretaker for another, Shelley doesn't seem anything like their mother.

"Do you like the wine?" Owen swirls his glass. "Johanna owns a winery outside Seattle."

"You two should definitely visit me," Johanna agrees, although it's unclear to Alex whether Johanna means her and Owen or Owen and Shelley. At least she seems to have risen from the doldrums of a few minutes ago and finished her slice of cheesecake. "I can give you the tour, and tastings."

"Well, maybe when my classes are almost over." Shelley nods, folding her hands. "I've been taking physical therapy classes at Shore Tech. I have another semester. I want to be a manager at Staples forever, said nobody."

"That's great," Alex says, and Shelley blinks, drinking in Alex's approval, and for a second, Alex is touched that her opinion, maybe even her blessing, matters to Shelley. Maybe she should stop being so superficial. *Maybe*, she thinks, *I've been living in the capital of superficiality and artifice for too long*.

"Yeah, and you could get a physical therapist job anywhere, like in Seattle," Owen adds, reaching over to spear another slice of Johanna's pork loin.

"What do you mean, honey?" Shelley reaches over and grips Owen's free hand. Although she's smiling, Alex can see the confusion in her eyes.

"Johanna said she'd get me a job at her winery," Owen answers. "Doing cybersecurity."

"Your degree's not in that." Shelley's knuckles are turning white. "What about the comic store?"

"What comic store?" Alex interrupts.

"The comic store Owen's going to buy part ownership in," Johanna explains. "The one here in town?"

"That place where you go play your games?" Alex thinks of the little hole-in-the wall storefront in an economically depressed strip mall a few miles away from the college, where a faded cut-out of Spiderman can be seen, wedged between the Dragon Wok Chinese restaurant and Curves, from the street. Why does everyone seem to know this information about the comic store but her? What other backroom deals have transpired as she's immersed herself in a silly love triangle?

"It's probably not a good investment." Owen looks doubtful. He pulls at his lower lip with his thumb and forefinger. "I mean, I can save the money from the sale of the house and put it toward our future."

"But our future is here." Shelley is practically cutting off the circulation to Owen's hand. "You know I can't be that far away from Jimmy—he needs me."

"Jimmy's an adult." Owen pulls his hand away. "He can take care of himself."

Alex looks at Johanna, who raises her eyebrows and shrugs as if to deny responsibility for any of these developments.

"It's kind of comical to hear you say that, Owen," Alex says finally. "After the way you babied our mother over the years."

"That was *different*." Owen rolls his eyes at her as if she's a child. "Jimmy's an addict and a jerk who doesn't want any help."

"Well, nothing's happened yet." Johanna pours herself another glass. "Everyone's just thinking aloud—no one's made any decisions about anything."

"I need to go and check on the dogs." Shelley stands up, her face clouded. She looks toward the door. "It was nice meeting you all."

"You just got here." Owen follows suit.

"I need to run to the bathroom." Alex stands up too. "It was nice meeting you, Shelley."

She goes to the upstairs bathroom so she can spy on Owen and Shelley, who appear a minute later in front of the house. They're standing by a beat-up tan Toyota truck with an orange racing stripe. Shelley's arms her crossed, and Owen is animated, his hands waving wildly. He reaches for Shelley's shoulder, but she shrugs him off. She then gets in the truck and drives away. Owen stands, stunned, for a second, before climbing into his ninja turtle car and squealing away after her. As Alex leaves the bathroom, she hears a buzz on the nightstand in Johanna's room. When she peers into the room from the doorway, Johanna's cell phone is lit up on the bedside table.

Did you find the photos? Someone named Cassandra has texted Johanna.

Chapter Nineteen

"I didn't know you talked to Owen about Seattle," Alex says when she comes back downstairs. She takes one of the boxes of photos by the dining room table and carries it over to the living room. "You going to tell him the big news before he gets out there?"

"Well, I can't spring it on him now that he's in the middle of a lover's spat," Johanna answers as she joins Alex in the living room with the rest of the wine. "To answer your question, I did talk about Seattle to Owen, but I didn't know at the time he was dating this Shelley woman—I found out the same time you did, remember?"

"Well, you may have just broken them up—I saw them fighting outside." Alex opens the first pack of photos and slowly flips through them. She doesn't know what she's looking for, exactly—or rather, what Johanna and Cassandra are looking for.

Johanna fingers a photo of Owen sleeping on his stomach on the floor. He's still in his Halloween costume—at nine, he went as a member of the Space Shuttle Challenger crew—and his plastic pumpkin is overturned beside him, Tootsie rolls and Smarties and Mary Jane chews scattered on the carpet. "Can I keep this one?"

"Sure," Alex answers, although now that she sees it, she kind of wants it too. Their mother found an old motorcycle helmet, spray-painted it white, and helped Owen paint on the decals. She could always be counted on the for the arts and crafts elements of their lives. Alex pulls out her phone and takes a picture of the picture. She tries to remember what she was for Halloween that year.

"Who were you?" Johanna picks up the next photo. Alex's hair is teased up. She's wearing an off-shoulder leopard print shirt. "Pat Benatar?"

"Someone from Cats," Alex suddenly remembers. "I don't remember which one."

"Jemima, *I* remember." Johanna holds it up. "Your mother told me all about your musicals phase. You want a picture of this one too? 'Cause I'm taking it."

"I hope Owen and Shelley don't break up," Alex says as she holds her phone over the picture of herself and snaps it. "I mean, I can't believe I'm saying this, but even though Shelley's a little—rough around the edges, she seems to have a good head on her shoulders. And I've never seen Owen so happy."

"If that's what he wants, I'll be supportive," Johanna remarks. "But if Owen wants a fresh start, I would be happy to have him in Seattle. There's room in my house."

"Do you have any roommates?" Alex presses, thinking of Cassandra. "Significant others?"

"I have been living with a woman for a year or so—Cassandra," Johanna admits. "We've been friends for years, and I guess we fell in love. So, yes, to answer your earlier question, I have been in love twice."

"I don't understand—you said you don't identify as lesbian?"

"I am a woman in love with Cassandra," Johanna answers. "It's hard for people to understand. I accept that. Your mother had a hard time understanding, too, and it upset her. But I don't think it's hard to understand love."

"Why did she have a hard time understanding?" Alex is confused. "I mean, I guess at first—but after all these years?"

"Well, because." Johanna clears her throat. "Because I wonder—maybe more than wonder—if she never stopped loving me."

"I could see that," Alex agrees. "She usually was the one who dumped people—for you to leave her must have been a big blow to her fragile ego."

"But she wasn't the reason I left—Adeline was my first love. And maybe my only, if she let me stay. But I had to transition—It was about being true to myself. Your mother was against it—she didn't think it would be appropriate for me to continue parenting, being married. Especially with her being an elementary school teacher. Her solution was for me to live in my birth body, stay married, and be miserable to make everyone else happy."

"I don't think Owen and I would have wanted you to stay if you were unhappy," Alex says. "I mean, Mom was unhappy, and she made our lives hell."

"I just wanted you to know I didn't want to leave. We could have worked it out, I think, maybe moved somewhere else where people would've been more understanding. I mean, love is just love."

"I understand—I think." Alex looks at Johanna. "Honestly, I don't know if I've been in love."

Maybe with Juliette, she thinks, but they were so young. And she doesn't know if her actions now have more to do with capturing that old feeling than about Juliette herself. But if she did capture that old feeling, maybe she would be happy for once.

"Love isn't the old razzle-dazzle, honey." Johanna pats her knee. "It's about what stays when the razzle-dazzle is gone. Or sometimes you don't even get the razzle-dazzle, but you have a connection that can't be explained. And being with that person makes you a better person, makes you want to be a better person."

Alex certainly wasn't a better person with Juliette back then. *But I can be a better person with Juliette now*, she thinks. Not that, her being married, it's even possible. Could Alex be a better person, anyway?

"Are there any particular photos you'd be interested in seeing?" Alex pulls out another packet. What was Cassandra's interest, she wonders, in the mysterious photos?

"Does Adeline have any of me?" Johanna picks up her wineglass casually.

"I don't know." Alex feels goosebumps on her neck. "Why?"

"There are some pre-transition photos that are a little racy. I know your mother, and I know she would have kept them. Frankly, I prefer neither you nor Owen see them."

"Like sex photos?" Alex is having a hard time closing her mouth.

"They're *artful* photos. Sensual." Johanna pours herself another glass of wine. "Still, there're not something I'd want my children to frame."

"We should probably find them before Owen does, then." Alex grabs more packets of photos. "At least before you tell him the truth."

"You know, the funny thing is, on the plane ride I was more worried about telling you than telling him." Johanna holds up another photo.

"Why do you say that?" Alex's shoulders stiffen.

"You had a lot of responsibility growing up, and your mother let you down a lot when you needed her. And sometimes, by her own admission, she was just plain mean to you." Johanna puts her hands on Alex's shoulders and looks into Alex's eyes. "And I don't think you've ever dealt with that—being abandoned, essentially, by both of us. You've been hurt the most."

"Well, no kidding." Alex looks away. "I've been waiting for my whole adult life for someone to recognize that."

"Do you recognize it?" Johanna asks.

"I don't even know what that's supposed to mean." Alex rolls her eyes. But Johanna looks through photos and doesn't answer her. Alex wonders if this is what years of therapy does to people, where they turn shit around on you and answer questions with questions. It feels like the same kind of gas-lighting that her mother threw at her all these years.

"You have a lot of Adeline in you," Johanna remarks quietly, not looking at her. "She could carry a grudge to the moon and back."

"I haven't carried a grudge." Alex reaches for her wine glass. "I've just tried to live my own life the opposite of the way she lived hers. All the success I've had, however small it is—is all despite her."

"I don't want to fight." Johanna holds up her the two photos she's kept of Owen and Alex. "I want to see all your Halloween costumes, so keep digging."

They don't find any photos of Jeffrey and Adeline Maas, in compromising positions, or even noncompromising ones. What they do find: Halloween pictures from the next year, when Alex is ten and Owen is nine. Owen is Doctor Doom and Alex is a Pink Lady from Grease. She remembers wanting to be Sandy but her mother insisting she be Rizzo. *Sandy was an uptight stick*, her mother explained not so gently. *On Halloween, you're supposed to be someone you're not.* There's pictures of tie-dye Easter eggs and her mother's elaborately wrapped Christmas gifts. There's a picture that Owen must've taken, slightly off center, of Alex and her mother on the sofa. Her mother is gripping her by the stomach, her chin burrowed into Alex's shoulder. Both of them are smiling.

Of course, there are no pictures of the fights, the groundings, the silent treatments, the screaming matches, the missed appointments and meals, the hours of being alone in places while their mother ran errands. But it was more than that, Alex remembers now. Like any life, there was more than that.

Owen comes home after ten. He blinks, frowning at them as he drops his keys on the table and picks up Tortoise, who has already wrapped herself like a scarf around his feet.

"Everything all right?" Johanna asks.

"I don't know." Owen shrugs, petting Tortoise. "Shelley can be such a...woman sometimes."

"Well, you did propose to upend her life in front of total strangers." Alex closes the box of photos. She has maybe twenty photos saved to her iPhone; Johanna, surprisingly, has set aside about 10 packets' worth for herself that encompass her and Owen's entire lives.

"Of course, my own sister wouldn't side with me." Owen frowns.

"Well, now you know what it feels like," Alex spits back.

"Women." Owen gives Johanna a look and heads toward the stairs. "Who knows why the fuck you'd ever want to be one."

"That was awkward." Alex corks the bottle of wine on the coffee table. She doesn't want to get drunk again, not like last night. "Should we go to bed now?"

Johanna takes Alex's hands in hers as Owen's door closes upstairs. "Let's do something else I learned in therapy. I want you to pretend I'm your mother. Now tell me whatever you want me to hear."

"I hope you have a lot of free time," Alex jokes, but Johanna doesn't laugh. She's looking at Alex intently, her attention completely focused. She doesn't even blink when Tortoise appears out of nowhere and jumps up on the couch between them, plopping down into Alex's lap. Not once in her life has she commanded this much attention from her mother for anything, much less her thoughts. She takes a deep breath and starts talking.

Chapter Twenty

"I'm not putting a lock on your door." Her mother stood by the wall in their dining room holding a fan-book of paint swatches. She held up a moss-colored swath against the wall. "Do you like Serious Sage, or should we go really bold?"

"I don't care." Alex crossed her arms. It'd been a week since she'd woken to find Lewis in her bedroom. He'd stayed over the last few nights, nights in which Alex slept in Owen's room, on a beanbag in the corner. She'd told Owen she'd had a nightmare and was too scared to sleep in her own room, but mostly she was scared of Lewis coming to visit her after their mother fell asleep.

"Of course, you should care—you're going to have to eat here for a little while longer." Her mother picked a deep red color and pressed it against the wall. "What about red? Red is supposed to make you hungry."

"No." Alex shook her head. "It looks like blood. Like we live in some 1960s art house horror film."

"Oh." Her mother turned to her, her eyes large in approval. "I like that—1960s art house horror film. I don't see what you have to hide anyway. You think I'm going to find your pot or something? You don't think I *could get much better pot on my own than that seedy shit you smoke?"*

"No, it's not for that—and thank you for confirming that you stole some of my stash."

Alex stared at the wall. The dining room didn't need painting, but their mother had gotten it into her head that the boring eggshell color they'd been looking at for years was the only thing keeping it (and not the fact she had no friends) from becoming the lovely Parisian salon she always imagined it to be, full of artists and writers drinking and smoking and maybe playing her mother's favorite board game, Parcheesi. If she painted it, she seemed to believe, they would come.

"Well?" Her mother sat down on one of the dining room chairs and lit a Parliament cigarette. "Why do you want it, then? Masturbation? Satanic rituals?"

"Lewis." It was one word, but the amount of energy it took to expel it from her lips made her imagine it was the equivalent of childbirth. Her mother glanced at Alex before turning her attention to her cigarette, picking at the filter with her thumbnail. The covers of her mouth quivered slightly before she pursued her lips tightly into a frown.

"Well?" Her mother practically spat at her. "Lewis what?"

"Lewis was in my room," she blurted out, the rest of the words tumbling over one another, like she was trying to outrun the avalanche that would follow them.

"Liar." Her mother stood up and, without warning, slapped her. "Why would he try to force himself on you? You're not even his type."

"I'm not lying." Alex took a step back and brought her hands to her face. "There's a mole on it. On his shaft. You know where."

"Stop it." Her mother grabbed her above the elbows and shook her. "Who do you think paid for your class ring? Paid for Owen to tour MIT? For his new computer? Don't you think you could be a little more grateful? But no, everything has to be about you. Honor roll, honor society, French club, 1,400 on her SATs, high school play, Swarthmore, Alex-Alex-Alex. That's all you care about— not that we could be on the street without Lewis."

"That's not true." She felt tears in her eyes. She thrived in school, even loved it, because, unlike at home, there were clear expectations, rules, and awards. It was the only place in her life in which she had control. "And you can get another fucking job."

"Get another fucking job," her mom mimicked her. "It's not so goddamn easy, Alex. You want me to work at Kmart on weekends and embarrass you? Lewis pays really well, and he treats me really well."

Her mother let her go and picked up her cigarette, almost burned down to the filter, from the ashtray. "We need the money, Alex. Don't fuck this up for us. Don't fuck this up for Owen. Don't fuck this up for me."

Alex reflexively put out her arms. She thought maybe her mother would try to burn her with the cigarette. Instead, she took a final drag and snubbed it out in the ashtray.

"Just get out of my face." Her mother waved her arm dismissively. "I don't want to see your fucking face the rest of the day."

"I'm leaving." Alex grabbed her purse and ran toward the front door. "For good."

Alex waited outside for Juliette to pick her up, walking up and down the sidewalk in front of the house. If she stopped moving, she figured, she'd know how much she was shaking. Her intestines felt like they were devouring themselves, but she didn't want to risk going back inside and using the bathroom. When she saw Juliette's Datsun at the top of the street, she ran up to meet it.

"Oh, Alex." Juliette threw the shift stick in reverse. "Your fucking mother. I hate her."

Alex cracked the window. She felt short of breath. Her chest ached. "I think I'm having a heart attack."

"You're having a panic attack." Juliette pulled over into the parking lot of the bingo hall across from the development of Alex's house. Then, she turned to her, taking her hands in hers. "Take a deep breath. Now hold it. 1-2-3-4, and let it out. Breathe again."

Alex closed her eyes and listened to Juliette's own, light, even breaths. She still smelled like flour and buttercream from her mother's bakery.

"You'll be fine." Juliette took her hands and squeezed. "It won't be forever. Just keep breathing, and it'll stop."

"I'm never coming back here." Alex choked out the words between her still-shallow breaths. "When I get to college, I'm just going to pretend this place never existed."

"I'm going with you," she heard Juliette say.

"What do you mean?" Alex opened her eyes.

"Let's go right now," Juliette said. "I have two hundred dollars saved up. We can drive to Philadelphia."

"I can't start classes at Swarthmore until I finish high school," Alex explained as Juliette started the car. "And besides, we'd have to find jobs, a place to live together—I can't just stow you away in the dorm."

"I don't care—we have each other." Juliette smiled, pulling out of the bingo hall parking lot. "That's enough. We don't have to ever come back. I don't ever want to make another Smith Island cake as long as I live."

Alex sat in silence, calling her bluff, as Juliette drove a few streets, past the mall, past the church the Spriggs attended, and their high school, until they got to the intersection for Route 13. If they followed, it, Route 13 would take them to 95, then Philadelphia. In a few short hours, they'd be in the clear.

Without speaking, Juliette turned right on 13, toward Philadelphia.

"Let's finish college first." Alex grabbed Juliette's forearm. "Okay? Then I'll go wherever you want to go."

"I want to leave now." Juliette kept driving. "Before you go away and never come back."

"You can come visit me at school," Alex said. "I'll write and call."

"Once you get to school, you'll be around all kinds of interesting people, smart people, and you'll forget about me." Juliette drove faster.

"Juliette, stop—" Alex reached over and grabbed at the wheel. "I don't want to throw my life away before it even starts."

Juliette said nothing, her face placid, as she took the first exit off 13 and turned around.

"I didn't mean it like that," Alex said quietly. "I just meant—"

"I understand," Juliette answered. Her lips were pressed tight as she pulled back on 13 South toward town. "You don't have to explain."

Alex thought about that last month. Although Juliette still talked about the apartment in Paris they were going to get, Alex had begun to think—to talk— about different things. Her scholarship, places she wanted to visit in Philadelphia, possible majors. The types of friends she would have, so different than the morons at school. Her actual future.

"Scott Mueller asked me to the prom," Juliette finally said as she pulled up in front of Alex's house.

"Oh my God," Alex laughed. Thankfully, Juliette wasn't mad at her anymore. They had never really fought; they had so little time left together, a few months, and had always planned to make the most of it. "What did you say to him?"

"I'm thinking I might say yes." Juliette stared through the windshield.

At the moment, Alex felt completely alone. And as the blackness of it started to swallow her, she swallowed it instead. She choked it down and built walls around it and dug a moat and then wove barbed wire around that.

"Fine." Alex opened the door and got out. She felt tears fighting their way into her eyes, but she blinked them back. Not turning, she waited for Juliette to pull away. Still, she heard Juliette's Datsun idling behind her.

Alex took one step, then another, toward the house, away from Juliette. When she finally got to the porch, she heard the wheels of the Datsun squeal away.

Alex hadn't meant to hurt her, but Juliette never thought things through. Her impulsiveness and Alex's practicality might work well in some cases, like deciding to get frozen yogurt instead of ice cream, to cut back on fat when Juliette's sweet tooth flared up, but maybe it would be hard to spend a life together with such competing personality traits. Especially when, if Juliette had had her way, they could be sleeping in some ratty hotel in a dangerous part of Philadelphia that night, her meager savings depleted.

Inside the house, her mother had moved the dining room table and chairs out onto the deck.

"I knew you'd come back," her mother declared, standing in the empty space, hands on her hips, as if she'd built the pyramids. "And before you say anything: truffle brown."

"Truffle brown what?" Alex dropped her purse on the floor near the door. It landed with a thud as heavy as her heart.

"The color for the dining room." Her mother sighed in exasperation. "Don't you remember anything we talked about this afternoon?"

"I remember the important stuff," Alex answered as her mother walked over to her.

"Come on." Her mother grabbed her arm. "We have to go to the hardware store, now that I'm inspired."

As she tried to pull away, her mother tightened her grip, her eyes pleading. It was the first time Alex considered her own power in their relationship, that her mother needed her more than she needed her. That she didn't have to take her abuse. That, after high school, she could (and would) just walk away.

Still, it didn't make her less angry at her. That her own mother, who'd raised them alone, albeit imperfectly, was weak. A woman who would get out of her car at a traffic light and chew out at the person behind them because they'd been following too closely. A woman who told a kid in Owen's Boy Scout troop she would personally cut his testicles off if he ever teased Owen again.

That woman couldn't protect her.

And now, without Juliette, either, Alex was really alone. She would have to prepare herself. At Lowe's, she followed her mother through the aisles as she dumped packages of drop cloths, paintbrushes, paint trays, and had a gallon of truffle brown mixed up.

"It'll kind of looked like a paneled room, like a Victorian study," her mother explained, shaking her keys absently at the paint mixing station. "Very Henry James. Or Edith Wharton, who I know you like better."

She tapped her foot and scratched the back of her neck, tipping the brim of her Walker hat into her eyes by accident and knocking it back with the palm of her hand. Alex wondered what pills her mother had taken, and whether this was the only apology that would be forthcoming.

"I have to use the bathroom." Alex walked away. "I'll find you."

Instead, she wandered through the aisles until she found the one housing doorknobs, deadbolts, and padlocks. She studied the instructions on a deadbolt kit and tried to remember whether her mother had a hole-saw attachment for her drill. Deciding to err on the side of safety, she picked one up. It looked like a metal cup the size of a doorknob, only with no bottom and serrated teeth around the edges.

If her mother could use power tools and not kill herself, so could she. At the checkout line, she dumped her items in the cart as her mother frowned.

"Do you think I'm made of money?" She stared at Alex's items but made no effort to take them out of the cart as Alex dug her wallet out of her purse.

"I'm paying for it," Alex answered, pulling out a twenty. "It's my lock."

"Who's going to install that for you? You've never used a drill in your life," her mother continued as the checkout clerk scanned the items.

"I'll figure it out it myself," she answered and looked her mother in the eye. "Isn't that what you always told me?"

"Touché." Her mother held up her hands in mock offense. She looked at the checkout clerk and jerked her thumb at Alex. "She thinks she's Bob Vila over here."

They stayed up half the night painting the dining room, covering the stains and scratches on the old white eggshell paint with several coats of the dark, murky truffle brown. Alex never spoke to Juliette again. Owen helped her install the lock on her door, although he never asked why she had gotten it, what it was for. And Alex and her mother never talked about Lewis again, either, not until Lewis was raided by the feds a few years after

Alex graduated college and was scraping by in DC, saving money for grad school, and by then it was a whole other can of worms altogether—legal fees and strategy, her mother's sudden unemployment, her sudden shortage of pharmaceuticals and the rollercoaster of rage and self-pity that followed.

However, after that night, Lewis had stopped coming to the house, although whether of his own volition or her mother's request, Alex never found out. It was the only small victory of the evening.

"It looks like we're inside a chocolate bar." Her mother sat cross-legged on the paint tarp, a smudge of paint on her nose. It was three in the morning; the walls glistened like a wet blister. She fished a joint out of her shirt pocket and lit it, taking a long drag, before leaning over and holding it out to Alex, who sat across from her. "Here, this is the really good stuff. Like, forget-today-ever-happened-and-the-day-before-stuff."

Alex sighed and took a drag—it was harsh, so skunky she could practically smell it in her pores—and held it in her lungs. It would be dark after that, day and night, dark and oppressive, in the dining room, probably like the Victorian salon her mother had wanted but depressing as hell and no one ever visited, anyway.

She finished the joint with her mother, inhaling, holding the smoke, feeling her lungs become numb, her limbs, until she felt something break in her. Her will to care.

Chapter Twenty-One

Juliette has bought fresh flowers, blood red dahlias and lavender asters, surrounded by baby's breath. Two white tapered candles burn on a white cloth table.

"This looks great." Alex runs her fingers lightly above the cloth. "You look great."

Juliette is wearing an off-the-shoulder smock covered with red, blue, and purple wildflowers, matching the ones on the table. Her gold hoop earrings nearly brush her shoulders.

"You too." Juliette smiles. "You haven't aged a day, I swear."

"Thanks" Alex touches her neck and glances toward the kitchen at the salad bowl. "How can I help?"

"Why don't you pour us some wine?" Juliette nods toward the bottle of pinot gris. "I just need to check on the rockfish."

"How's your family?" Alex asks as she pours the wine into the glasses Juliette left on the kitchen island. "It was, uh, nice to see your mother the other day."

"They're fine—my mother is getting ready to retire." Juliette eases the rockfish out of the broiler oven. "I've been thinking of taking the bake shop under the restaurant's wing. I know my mom would like that. Occasionally I include slices of her Smith Island cake on our dessert menu, but I didn't want to be so tied at the apron strings, so to speak. I feel like my mother has always sort of hovered over me, and owning the restaurant gives me independence and authority, you know? Something she can't question."

Alex pulls her digital recorder out of her purse. "You mind if I take notes?"

"Not at all." Juliette's deep in concentration as she brushes toasted pecan butter over the rockfish. "I see my family once a week, I guess. Of course, it's impossible to keep my mother from coming into the restaurant unannounced, as you saw the other day."

"And your sister?"

"She moved," Juliette says. "She couldn't wait to get away from the Sprigg compound. She's finishing her postdoctorate at Tulane, can you believe it?"

"She was always so shy," Alex replies, surprised. "Even shyer than Owen."

"She really blossomed at college," Juliette moves to the other side of the island, picking up one of the wine glasses. "I always regret I stayed home. Not that I could get a scholarship to a great school like you did. Remember when we were going to move to Paris or San Francisco? I always regret not being able to do that with you."

"You blossomed just fine." Alex blinks. Where Juliette's going with this, she isn't sure. Even if she wants to, she's decided she can't, in her journalistic or personal capacity, follow. She holds up her glass as well. "To being grownups."

"To reconnections," Juliette counters, studying her over her glass. "And second chances."

Alex chokes up a little wine. She dabs her lip with her pinky and refreshes their glasses as Juliette brings the dishes to the table. They sit in silence across from each other for an agonizing minute.

"We always had potatoes and asparagus in my mom's garden at home," Juliette remarks as Alex spears a stalk of asparagus from her plate. "And garlic. We don't usually harvest garlic until late July, so these are right out of the garden."

"This is delicious," Alex nods, relieved to talk about something. "I never cook at home and getting Owen to eat something that doesn't come from a can and have a cartoon character on it always has been a challenge."

"Owen mentioned he was still living with your mother." Juliette swirls the wine in her glass.

"He completely failed to launch." Alex bites into a green. "But maybe this'll be good for him, having to do stuff for himself. Johanna's been a big help."

"I think learning to do something gives one such pride, and agency." Juliette nods. "I was so scared to buy the restaurant—I mean, half of them fail. But I felt like, at least I did something. For years, my Mom wanted me to take over the bake shop, like I wouldn't be able to succeed on my own. She never thought I could do anything."

"Your mother could have been kinder to you," Alex agrees.

"You never came home after high school," Juliette says. "I always wished I could have done that."

"You could have." Alex picks up her wine glass. "I worked three jobs after school—I catered, I was a receptionist at a think tank, and I wrote theater reviews for the alt-weekly. I lived in a basement on the edge of Columbia Heights, which was a dump back then. And there was mold everywhere in my place. But I wasn't going back. I would rather have died of mold exposure than go back."

"That's why I've always wanted to be you." Juliette drags a square of rockfish around her plate. She looks wistful. "You're fearless."

"You're not wedded to fear. You can stop being afraid whenever you want." Although, she thinks, *part of my own fearlessness involves having complete amnesia of my life before college.* "And second, what are you even talking about? You started as a sous chef after culinary school and worked really hard and bought your own restaurant, which is incredibly successful. If that's not fearless, I don't know what is."

"Come." Juliette stands behind Alex after dinner, one hand on Alex's shoulder, the other holding the bottle of pinot gris. "The couch in the study is monstrous—we can spread out, kick our shoes off."

After a beat, Alex picks up her wine glass and follows Juliette into the study. She watches as Juliette turns on the bookshelf lights and the overhead off, giving the room a dim but warm glow. She picks up a remote, and, suddenly, Ella Fitzgerald's voice fills the room.

"I love Ella Fitzgerald," Alex says, sitting at one end of the sofa. She's always been more partial, though, to Billie Holiday—her graveled voice, her drug addiction, her earlier years of prostitution and later years of incarceration.

"I know." Juliette kicks off her sandals and draws her knees up at the other end.

"What do you mean, you know?" Alex grins.

"You do your research, I do mine." Juliette gazes at her over her glass. Alex mentally calculates how much information Juliette could have gleaned about her from Facebook. Enough to know Alex had gushed about hearing Ella Fitzgerald's 'My Romance' at the grocery store last month, and that she had some great rockfish at a restaurant in Georgetown. But it's the thought, she figures, that counts.

"So do you like living in the district, where you are now?" Juliette asks.

"Yeah," Alex says. "It's expensive and commuting can suck, but culturally and intellectually, it's great."

"And you meet lots of beautiful, professional women there, I imagine," Juliette continues. "Like your ex."

"There's more people in a city, but I don't think it's easy to meet people anywhere. At least people with whom you really connect at all levels."

"With Kate, you didn't?" Juliette studies her over her wine glass, very still, as if she's nervous.

"I thought we did at one time," Alex says after a minute. "But I'm not so sure anymore."

"Did you date a lot in college?" Juliette presses. "Or is that off limits, too? I mean, you're not seeing anyone now, right?"

Alex looks at a chip in her nail polish. She wishes she'd asked Johanna to do her nails the night before. She sighs.

She doesn't have to lie about Carolyn—she can just not answer. Her first commitment is to her assignment.

"Did *you* ever date any other women?" Alex asks instead. "Aside from me?"

"No." Juliette shakes her head.

Alex smooths the leather of the couch between them. Maybe she's a little happy that she's been the only one. But maybe she's also a little mad that, if that was something Juliette had wanted to explore, she didn't let herself experience it.

"I think living in a city is easier for a lot of reasons," Alex says, choosing diplomacy. She smiles. "You have more anonymity; it's easier to take chances on a lot of things—relationships, your career, trying a new hobby."

"I wish I could move to the city," Juliette becomes animated. "I mean, I love the restaurant, but a producer at Food Network who's interested in my doing a show for them, she's worried there just isn't enough dramatic interest in this town. It'd have to be smaller or bigger, or maybe focus more on my family instead—the whole tightknit Christian family thing. My mother loves the whole tightknit Christian idea, as you can imagine."

"You could open a second place in DC," Alex suggests. "It's definitely a high-end, foodie town."

Juliette nods. "That's what I was thinking. But Jack really likes that he's only one of two foot orthopedic surgeons here. In DC, he'd just be a small fish, you know?"

"Well, cities aren't for everyone." Alex shrugs. "That's okay."

"I shouldn't be telling you this." Juliette pours herself another glass. She looks up, horrified. "This is off the record, right?"

"Of course." Alex leans over and holds up her recorder. "It's been off. But why did you marry Jack, if you knew he wanted to practice here?"

"I was getting older. I didn't have any capital." Juliette pauses. "But then one night the hospital held a benefit at Sprigg, and Jack was there, and we fell in love just like that."

"A fairy tale ending," Alex says quietly.

"You think I married him for his money?" Juliette's eyes narrow. For a minute, she looks furious.

"No." Alex reaches over and touches Juliette's ankle in apology. "I meant it was fortuitous. Lucky."

"Sometimes you just have to go all in when you get an opportunity." Juliette's expression softens. She twirls a lock of hair near her ear. "And accept there are no perfect solutions."

"Then you should look for a place to open in DC, if Jack's not home very much, anyway."

"I don't know anyone in DC." Juliette shakes her head. Then, she smiles. "Except you."

"Well, I'm not really in the restaurant business." Alex moves away.

"But you know a lot of people," Juliette answers. "You have twenty-thousand Twitter followers."

Alex sips her wine. Because she's connected, in a way, she's always wary of what people want her to do for them. She can't get through a week at home without people asking her to write up their quirky boutique, or their underappreciated debut novel, or their underrated band. She doesn't theoretically see why Juliette would be any different, but the realization that Juliette may be playing her, too, sinks in her like a stone.

"I don't think I'm in a position to help you," Alex repeats tonelessly.

"I didn't mean to offend you." Juliette frowns. "I always seem to make you mad."

"I'm not mad," Alex says. "I'm just being honest. I always have been."

"Why did you take this assignment, since you're being honest?" Juliette puts her arm on the back of the couch, cradling her head in her hand.

"I didn't take the assignment." Alex leans back to face Juliette. "I volunteered."

"Really?" Juliette's face breaks open in surprise. She grins. "So you wanted to see me?"

"I just found out my mom died, and, I don't know." Alex rubs her face with her hands. "Maybe I thought I was going to have my own personal *A Christmas Carol*."

"I never thought about being the ghost of Christmas past." Juliette nods, laughing. "Of course, I'm not a writer like you are. So what have you learned so far?"

"Hmm." Alex traces the lip of her wine glass. "I don't know. One of the reasons Kate left was because she said I hadn't moved on from my past. And here I thought I was doing my best to put it behind me."

"Did you love Kate?" Juliette frowns.

"Yes." Alex blinks. Did she? She's not sure of anything anymore. "What I thought was love."

Juliette leans over. Alex moves her hand away, wondering, for a moment, if Juliette is going to kiss her, but instead she grabs her glass from the coffee table and gulps the last of her wine.

"A few years ago—after I got married, I told my mom about you and me," Juliette says, staring into the now-empty glass. "You know what she said? She said she had suspected and hadn't been happy about it, but she knew there was a lot going on in your life, so she just prayed to God to see everyone into the light of truth. And then you know what she said? *You see, you got married. Everything turned out just fine.*"

"It's what you wanted, wasn't it?" Alex puts her glass back on the table.

"Yes," Juliette says the word, quietly, without conviction. "My mom loves to brag about me to her friends, about my restaurant, how I might get a television show, my handsome doctor husband. That the daughter she put in the kiln had come out exactly how she hoped."

"Some parents think they're making a mug, but when they take it out of the kiln, it's an ashtray," Alex says. Or maybe, for her mother, it was the other way around.

"Sometimes I wish I'd come out an ashtray." Juliette swings her glass back and forth by the stem.

"Is that on the record?" Alex asks, laughing.

"It's not funny, Alex." Juliette stands up. She looks as if she'll throw the glass across the room.

"I'm sorry." Alex stands up and puts her hand over top Juliette's. She means to keep her from throwing the glass. But when Juliette leans in and kisses her, they both release their grip on it at the same time, and it shatters on the floor between them.

"Crap." Alex pulls away and bends to gather the pieces. As she collects the two biggest shards in her palm, Juliette bends down and takes them from her.

"Don't worry." Juliette guides her back up to a standing position, leaning in and kissing her again. "I'll clean it up later."

She pushes Alex back onto the couch with her body and settles in above her. Before Alex can argue, Juliette presses her lips onto hers, parting them. Alex rests her hands on Juliette's back. She remembers the feel and heft of her, surprisingly, the way you remember the feeling of an instrument you'd hadn't played in years. With a little practice, you could pick it up again. But would it be enough, playing the songs you'd learned years ago, or would you hope to make new music?

Alex wakes with her head pinned to the couch cushion. She'd dreamed Owen had been texting her, wondering where the hell she was. It's daylight. She feels Juliette's arm curled around her stomach, her bare breasts pressed against her own bare back, her breath, wet and heavy and metallic-smelling from the wine, on her neck.

"I need to check my phone." Alex turns over, almost knocking Juliette onto the floor.

"Good morning to you too," Juliette says sleepily, opening her eyes briefly before closing them.

"Owen might need the car for work," Alex lies, climbing over Juliette and rolling her gently into her vacated spot. She presses her feet on the floor and immediately feels a sharp pain in her right foot.

"Shit." She picks a slither of glass out of the ball of her foot, then squeezes with her hand to stop the bleeding. It trickles down the instep of her foot as she wonders if she will need stitches.

"Oh, no." Juliette sits up, swinging her legs to the right to avoid the glass. "I'll get some rubbing alcohol and bandages."

Alex watches Juliette move, naked, across the room, unconcerned with pulling on her clothes. Despite the throbbing pain in her foot, a warmth spills into her groin, sending a shuddering wave through her body. She has never been more attracted to Juliette than right now, and a small, happy laugh escapes her lips. Maybe she really is in love.

But she studies the artful, black and white photos of Juliette and Jack from their wedding resting on the bookshelves, along with the copies of *Grey's Anatomy* and books about Civil War history she knows aren't Juliette's, she feels like what she is instead: an adulterer.

> *Be home within a half hour,* she texts Owen. *I'm so sorry.*

She scrolls through the rest of the messages. Her stomach sinks as she reads one from Carolyn:

> *Good morning! Did you have sweet dream? How did your dinner go? Can I interest you in lunch?*

"Did it stop bleeding?" Juliette reappears. She's taken a moment to slip on a terrycloth bathrobe. As she sits down next to Alex, Alex's own arms cross involuntarily over her breasts.

"It's not too bad," she says, watching Juliette mop the blood away with one baby wipe, then another. She presses a square gauze over the cut and holds it there. Blood seeps through the middle. "I guess I shouldn't jog for a few days."

"I should have cleaned up the glass." Juliette removes the wet gauze and presses another on the cut. "I'm sorry."

"It's okay," Alex answers. "I could have done it myself."

Juliette looks at Alex. She kisses her cheek, nuzzling her face near her ear.

"I loved being with you again," she murmurs into Alex's ear. Alex hears her phone vibrate. She glances over at Owen's message pop up before it disappears:

No big. Glad you're OK.

"I need to get Owen's car back." Alex bends over and begins to tape the gauze to the bottom of her foot with the medical tape Juliette also had brought. "He's super mad."

"Of course." Juliette nods. Alex stands up tepidly. She probably should wait a minute, she knows, let the blood congeal, but she immediately steps into her underwear.

"Thanks for dinner," Alex says, her dress halfway over her head. "If I have any follow-up questions, I'll let you know."

"I'm going to see you again, right?" Juliette touches her forearm.

"Of course." Alex pulls her dress over her hips. "I'm assuming this is all off the record."

"That's a good way of putting it." Juliette nods. She stands, her hand still on Alex's forearm. "Can you stop by the restaurant tonight? After eleven?"

"I can't." Alex thinks of Carolyn. "I mean, I may not have a car. Owen may still be mad at me."

"Owen thinks you're the greatest person in the world." Juliette smiles. "When I ran into him about a year ago, he couldn't say enough good things about you. How you got the brains in the family. How successful you were."

"Well, now I've been here a few days," Alex jokes, "he probably feels a bit differently."

Alex limps to the front door, leaning on Juliette.

"Are you sure you should try to drive right now?" Juliette asks. "I can make us some coffee, cut up some fruit."

"No, no." Alex leans over and kisses Juliette, as if that will settle the matter. She puts her hand on the doorknob and opens it. "I'll text you later, okay?"

Juliette nods, not meeting Alex's gaze. Alex weaves her hand into Juliette's hair.

"I had a great time last night," Alex says. "I mean that."

She does mean it. She's obviously hoped about such a scenario since she's returned home, felt safe in knowing it had been, until last night, a complete fantasy. But the events aren't things to themselves; they happen in the context of other things, and Alex isn't sure how she feels about those yet, her culpability in them. She gets in Owen's car and presses her left foot on the clutch, then winces as she presses her right foot on the brake. She looks in her rearview mirror at a dog running toward Owen's car, barking. She holds her breath and punches it into first, moving down the street before he can catch the bumper.

Chapter Twenty-Two

Juliette Sprigg is a woman of many surprises, Alex types on her laptop. *When visiting her home in the tony neighborhood of West River, I am denied a tour of the Craftsman-style home she shares with her husband Jack, an orthopedic surgeon at Shore General. "If it's no big deal, I spend most of the time in the kitchen," she apologizes. "It's where I do most of my thinking." Extremely personable and highly unpretentious, she does not strike one as a woman with the hottest restaurant on the Eastern shore, who's been in talks with cable network executives about her own reality show, who wants to open a second restaurant closer to a different river, the Potomac.*

"You banged her?" Owen asks from the couch. He's wearing one of the button-up blue checked shirts Johanna bought him from the thrift store and watching some Japanese manga cartoon.

"I bought you a shirt just like that, new, for your birthday last year." From the dining room, Alex looks up from her laptop. "You probably didn't even wear it once."

"You wouldn't even know if I did try on the shirt," he answers. "You didn't come down to celebrate."

"I had to finish the fall arts preview," she reminds him, glancing over. Always the magazine—every holiday, every birthday, any milestone—she'd always been working on something for the magazine.

"So you really banged Juliette Sprigg, huh?" He picks Tortoise up off the floor, where she's been rubbing his legs, and sets her on his chest. "What was that like?"

"Seriously? I would never tell you."

"Who made the first move?" he asks.

"She did." Alex pauses. "But we both had had some wine and got a little carried away."

"So one and done, for old time's sake?" Owen shifts on the couch, letting out a fart. "Or are you a thing? I thought she was like, married."

"I'm really still processing everything, Owen." She drums her fingers on the table. "And for God's sake, you're thirty-five years old, and you're farting on the couch?"

"I'm not married yet," he answers. "I can do what I want."

"Are you still getting married?" Alex raises an eyebrow.

"I don't know—I guess." Owen frowns. "Shelley kind of has a temper. It usually takes us a few days to make up."

"Yeah, but, again, you announced to her you two were moving across the country without even asking her. It's a little different than, say, I don't know, farting on the couch."

"I love her," Owen says. "I would move across the country for her if she wanted to."

"Even so, I don't know what to tell you, Owen," Alex sighs as she begins to type again. "I'm the wrong person to ask about these things."

Juliette's lips are as soft and fragrant as they were in high school, when I fell in love with her.

She looks at that line for a few seconds and lets her finger hover above the delete button. As she does, her phone digs with a message from Juliette:

I found a hair of yours on my shoulder when I was showering. No I know it wasn't a dream. ☺

Alex blinks and reads the message again. Whatever she ultimately feels about last night, she knows one thing for sure: it can't happen again.

"Can you wake Johanna up?" Owen asks. "We need to run an errand."

"Why can't you wake her?" she takes a sip of her coffee, prodding her forehead with her finger.

"Because you're a woman, and so is she now," he answers.

"I doubt she's parading around up there indecent," she sighs, but stands up anyway. Upstairs, her mother's door is half open. Alex feels the moisture and heat in the hallway creeping out of the bathroom from Johanna's recent shower. Inside the bedroom she can hear the sounds of Joni Mitchell's *Court and Spark*, Johanna singing *He said he'd be here over three hours ago/I've been waiting for his car on the hill.*

"Johanna?" Alex knocks lightly on the door. "You decent?"

She waits a few seconds, and when Johanna doesn't answer, peeks in the crack. Johanna is facing the bedroom windows, her back to Alex. She's wearing nothing but a pair of lacy white Victoria's secret underwear. On her back is tattooed a huge lotus flower, and in the middle is a yin and yang symbol. Alex knows the image as well as she knows the moles on her forearm; her mother had a smaller, identical tattoo above her right hip bone. Alex discovered it when she woke her mother up in the middle of the morning for to take her to her dentist appointment, the one for which Alex had stayed home from school. Her mom had been sleeping with one leg out of the sheets, in her just underwear and a ribbed tank top.

Why didn't you tell me you had that? Alex pointed after her mother struggled to a half-sitting position in bed.

I didn't want you to get one, her mother said, reaching for her cigarettes.

What does it mean? Alex's fingers hovered over the skin of the tattoo, as if it might bite her.

It means I was young. Her mother lit a cigarette. *And stupid. Now forget you ever saw it.*

Alex steps away from the door and stands motionless, the only sound the pounding of her heart in her ears. She wonders if Johanna feels the same remorse about her tattoo, if that's why it's always covered. It depresses her to think that if her parents actually *had* stayed together, if Alex and Owen had two mothers, that they might have divorced just the same. Who could live with Adeline Maas that long, unless they were forced to?

And because everyone is changing all the time, she thinks more charitably. Even herself, although she's reluctant to admit it. If she's lived the first thirty-six years of her life wrong, what guarantee does she have she'd live the next thirty-six right?

When the song ends, she takes a few loud, noisy steps and stands outside the door again.

"Johanna?" She calls loudly this time. "Are you decent?"

"Just a sec." She hears Johanna moving around, and a few seconds later she comes to the door, only now she is clothed, in a crisp white button-down shirt open to her chest and tied at the midriff. A purple tank top underneath covers her breasts and also the tattoo. "Good morning to you, Miss I Did Not Come Home Last Night."

"It got late," Alex explains. "I heard you two were up pretty late too."

"Oh, not as late as you, I imagine." Johanna brushes a strand of Alex's hair out of her face. "Now, tell me everything."

"Did you tell Owen yet?" Alex whispers.

"He was out all night," Johanna whispers back. "With Shelley."

"Oh for goodness sake—I'm going down there right now and telling him." Alex turns to leave as Johanna grabs her arm.

"No, you will not—it's my story, and it is my responsibility to tell it." It's the first time Alex has seen Johanna angry. It's the same pinched expression Alex's seen on her own face in the mirror. It surprises Alex that they look the same, but it surprises Alex more that she looks that angry to begin with.

"You're right." Alex looks down. "I'm sorry."

"No, sweetie, I'm sorry." Johanna sweeps Alex up in her arms so tightly she inadvertently gasps. "I didn't mean to bark at you. I'm a wildebeest without my coffee."

"At least I can blame it on my genetics." Alex laughs when Johanna lets her go. "My temper."

"And also your predilection for secrecy." Johanna stands at the top of the stairs. "Now, tell me all about your ex-ex-girlfriend."

"Are you ready?" Owen yells from the landing. When they reach the bottom of the stairs, he's standing at the door, holding his keys.

"Let me grab my phone," Alex says, even though she has no idea where they're going. "Is today the day we pick up the urns?"

"No—that's tomorrow. You stay here—we're just running an errand," Owen holds up his hand. "Finish your article—I know you need to get home to DC."

"Oh, okay." She nods, disappointed for a second. But she remembers the sex photos. She doesn't want to find them, necessarily, but given Owen's ambition in getting rid of everything of their mother's, she probably should find them soon. Her mom wouldn't have hidden them where she hid her pot, because as a teenager Alex would be looking for it. The Bible, then? Was it sacrilegious to hide those photos in a Bible? Did her mom even have a Bible?

After she hears them drive away, she slips back upstairs to her mother's room. Before she does anything, though, she sees Johanna's shimmering gold hard-shell suitcase on her mother's bed. Like a hypnotic coin, it beckons to her. She's not sure what she's looking for, or what she even expects to find. She kneels in front of Johanna's suitcase and unzips it. She opens the flat pocket under the top and feels around, pulling out what turns out to be a plastic freezer bag. Inside are old postmarked letters and photos. Photos of her mother, smoking in the passenger seat of a car, looking at the photographer, one eyebrow raised suggestively. And another at party, dancing, wearing a yellow miniskirt and a white button-down with big lapels. There're all of her mother, the pictures. None of her or Owen. *It's a little*, she thinks as she puts the photos aside, *obsessive*. Did Johanna love her mother still, just as Johanna thought Adeline still loved her?

She opens a letter addressed to J. Maas in Seattle from her mother, Adeline. Inside is a birthday card:

> *Dearest J,*
>
> *I hope you're having a great birthday and finally feel like a real bitch! Seriously, your boobs look so much better than mine! This the nicest thing I'm going to say about the whole thing, because a part of me is always going to be mad at you for doing this. It was one thing for you to leave, but what you did to Jeffrey I'll never forget. Did you ever think about how I would feel? No, you NEVER did—why start now, right?*
>
> *Okay, I'm not going to talk about it anymore. Things are okay here, although we are always a little tight, but I got a second job, and I think I've found a way to get you the money. The kids are fine—of course, Alex got one freakin' B—in*

Civics—and you'd think she was on suicide watch. Owen hides in his room most of the time—I guess he finally discovered masturbation.

Kisses, A

Alex slides the card back into the envelope and goes through the rest of the cards. Her mother was never much of a writer, but it's clear, as she reads them, her mother and Johanna shared great intimacy. If she had known years ago, she would have lobbied for her parents to get back together. Maybe, even, it would have saved them from Lewis.

What money had her mother sent Johanna? And why did she, when she could barely afford to keep them afloat until she started the insurance fraud with Lewis? What else has Johanna not been forthcoming about?

She puts the packet back into the freezer bag and returns it to the suitcase, a little disappointed. She doesn't want to be confronted with even more mysteries. She straightens up at the knock at the door downstairs and flattens herself against the wall by the window, peering out below. She expects to see Shelley but is surprised to see Carolyn instead, holding a tray with coffees and a paper bag.

"Am I bothering you?" Carolyn grins at the door when Alex opens it. She holds up the bag. "There's a place by the office that makes really great muffins, and I thought you might need some writing fuel."

"Oh, uh, it's fine." Alex leads Carolyn into the dining room. "I can take a quick break."

"So how was dinner last night?" Carolyn dislodges a cup out of the carrier and holds it out to Alex. "Did you get everything you needed from Juliette Sprigg?"

"Yep." Alex takes a sip of the coffee, taking care not to choke on it. "I got everything I needed. I'm just finishing the article now."

"Did you want me to take a look at it?" Carolyn reaches for Alex's laptop.

"No." Alex puts her hand quickly atop Carolyn. "I don't like people to look at stuff that's in-progress."

Carolyn looks at her. "I shouldn't have bothered you, should I?"

"You're fine," Alex lies, taking her by the arm and leading her into the living room.

"It's just the closer you are to finishing your article, the closer you are to leaving." Carolyn settles on the couch, holding her coffee with both hands. "So maybe I have ulterior motives in being here."

"Didn't your mother tell you it's not a good idea to throw your lot in with people on the verge of existential crises?" Alex jokes as she settles in the other end.

"I'm sure you're questioning a lot of things since your mother passed," Carolyn, more solemn, rests one hand on the top of the couch. "I know I did."

"What did it feel like?"

"Oh, I don't know," Carolyn picks at a thread that Tortoise has clawed off the top of the couch. "I guess I stopped caring about things. At first in a bad way—like whether I wore makeup to work or a wrinkled suit. I slept a lot or not at all. I felt like the membrane between this life and whatever happens after was torn, and I was in danger of falling in at any second. But then I stopped caring in a good way—what people thought of me, whether I was successful enough. I stopped being afraid of a lot of things. I figured the death of my mother was the worst thing that happened to me, and if I got through it, nothing else would be as bad. And I think now I'm even more capable of allowing myself to love someone wholly, because I've learned to love myself."

Alex flinches as Tortoise suddenly jumps into her lap and settles. She pets her absently, wondering exactly what it is she feels. If she's capable of feeling anything. Except, as Owen puts it, indignation.

"Are you still here?" Carolyn's voice wavers with concern as she leans closer. Alex knows one thing: being with Carolyn makes her feel better, makes her want to be a better person in return.

"Yes." Alex nods, looking up. She puts her hand on the side of Carolyn's neck. "That was so beautiful, what you said. You're one of the wisest people I've ever met."

"That's not true." Carolyn waves her hand dismissively, although Alex can see she's pleased.

"It is," Alex reiterates. Carolyn, she realizes, is a keeper. "You've laid a good roadmap to try to follow."

"Just remember every journey is different. Even what love means to different people, I imagine, is different."

"What does it mean to you?"

"It's hard to put into words. I guess it's someone with whom I feel comfortable, who has my back, who isn't afraid to challenge my beliefs but at the same times respects them, who stimulates me, who I completely trust to enter any situation in my life with me."

"Wait—are you talking about your mother or a partner?" Alex kids.

"Both, kind of, I guess. I think, after Carrie—after learning to forgive Carrie, I should say—you have to accept everyone will disappoint you sometime, trust or not, love or not, blood or not. No one is perfect. Life is imperfect. You have to learn to love despite disappointment and imperfection. My mother was very awful to me when I came out to her, but I also remember all the wonderful things she did for me growing up. I can't have only the good or turn my back at only the bad."

"My mother didn't believe me when I needed her to," Alex says, picking at the piping on the couch. Maybe she does, as Johanna put it, hold grudges to the moon and back. "Am I just supposed to let that go?"

"Well." Carolyn studies her, almost with pity. "Your mother is dead."

"Exactly." Alex rolls her eyes. "What am I supposed to do now?"

"Isn't that for you to decide?"

Alex looks away. For years, possibly even her whole life, she's known two things: ambition and grievance, and at times just one thing, ambitious grievance. It's part of her identity: being an underdog, being scorned, succeeding despite those who've wronged her. How can she live without something to push against? To push away?

And then it hits her as sharply as Tortoise's claw in her stomach: Johanna is right—She *is* just like her mother.

At least she's proud of you, Alex had snarled at Kate after she'd complained her mother didn't like the blouse she'd worn one week on *Face the Nation*. Or when she didn't like her father's new girlfriend. *At least you have a father*, Alex had snarled again. *One you still see several times a year and paid for your education.* She'd often downplayed Kate's grievances because they seemed normal, and therefore, in her mind, petty to complain about. After all, Alex would have gladly traded places with her. And yet, looking back, it was not a good look for their relationship, not a good look for her.

"I didn't mean to sound callous." Carolyn puts her coffee down and slides closer to Alex. "I guess I'm just tailoring my message to your perceived need."

"I'm not offended." Alex sits up, as Tortoise digs in deeper. "I'm not a fragile flower."

"Well, you certainly have quick reflexes." Carolyn is next to her now. She strokes her face. "Like when you need to dive under a table."

"That's why I'm never coming back here," Alex jokes. "You'll never let me live that down."

"Come back." Carolyn kisses her cheek near her ear, and Alex feels goosebumps on the back of her neck. "Come back."

Alex takes a deep breath as she holds on to Carolyn. If she wants to continue seeing Carolyn, she needs to come clean about Juliette. But when she parts her lips to speak, Carolyn stands up.

"I've really got to get back to work," she explains, as Alex struggles to extricate Tortoise from her lap. "I shouldn't even be here now. Can I see you tonight?"

"I have something I need to take care of first." Alex pushes Tortoise onto the floor and walks Carolyn to the door. "But maybe?"

"Text me, okay?" Carolyn hugs Alex.

"Thanks for the treats," Alex holds on to her. "You're so thoughtful and conniving at the same time."

"I thought you would appreciate complicated gestures," Carolyn says back.

"They fit well into my character arc," Alex agrees. Carolyn fits into her character arc.

> *I've been thinking about last night.* She texts Juliette after Carolyn leaves, then pauses. *We should talk about it.*

> *That sounds ominous,* Juliette texts back a few minutes later.

> *I just think we should talk about it.* She types.

> *Me too.* Juliette responds, and Alex is relieved. It was all a mistake. A stupid, drunken mistake. *So can you stop by tonight? Or can I come get you?*

Alex closes her eyes. She feels the current of electricity dancing above the tops of her hands as she holds her phone. She thinks about Juliette's own hands, gliding over her back and hips, the brush of her curls against her collarbone. She feels her emotions gaining on her, like that dog running toward Owen's car. She harbors no illusions her and Juliette's future will align in any meaningful way; she can either retrace· her steps to the point of last night's detour, or she could go a little farther, enjoy the view, and hope that she could meet up with the main road—Carolyn—later.

> *Yes, come get me.* She types and then turns off her phone.

She sets her digital tape recorder on the table by her laptop and begins to replay her notes from last night.

Chapter Twenty-Three

She's almost finished the article when through the living room window she sees the U-Haul pull up in front of the house. She doesn't remember Owen and Johanna hauling anything away this morning, and she cringes for a moment at the thought of what Owen may be hauling in.

She opens the front door and watches Owen and Johanna go around the back of the truck.

"Close your eyes!" Owen pokes out from the back of the truck and points toward the house. "And go back inside!"

Or worse, she realizes they have hauled something back for her, which makes absolutely no sense and makes Alex wonder whose terrible idea it was. She expects it of Owen, but after reading her mother's letters, bad decision-making is no longer new information about Johanna either. It's almost like they're all related.

She backs into the living and sits down on the couch, listening to Johanna and Owen struggle at the front door with a large object.

"Are your eyes still closed?" she hears Owen ask as the object shudders with a thud to the ground about five feet away from her.

"Yes," she answers.

"Well, you can open them now," Johanna says.

Sitting in the middle of the living room is the wardrobe responsible for her mother's purported back injury. Only now it has all four legs and has been repainted a distressed white.

"What's this?" Alex blurts out dumbly.

"It's the wardrobe," Owen answers, rubbing his hands on his shorts.

"Yeah, I get it, but why?"

"Mom was going to get it fixed up for your birthday," Owen explains.

"My birthday was four months ago." Alex's mother had sent her a birthday card with a picture of a Chihuahua wearing a sombrero on it. Inside, she had written *I hope you are living a life worthy of those twelve hours of labor pains I had. The present is still in progress.*

At first, Alex thought her mother was trying to be profound or introspective—the present time is still in progress. Which, admittedly, was completely unlike her. But now the words made sense—her birthday present simply hadn't been ready yet.

"She said you told her you were looking at some armoires at West Lake or something," Owen explains.

"West Elm," Alex corrects. "It's a furniture store." It's true she'd been looking at armoires, but it had been for Kate's condo, a place where she could store her things, a step toward their eventual moving in together. Something she didn't need now.

Not that her mother had known that. Still, she thinks of her mother seeing this wardrobe in the thrift store and deciding to buy it on a whim for her, fix it up. Although the fact her mother hauled it upstairs to her own bedroom made her wonder if it was actually a gift for her and not an afterthought, a lie her mother had told Owen to justify having bought it in the first place. Owen had forbidden her from buying anymore furniture after a nest of baby spiders hatched in an old stuffed wingback chair she'd rescued from the dump.

Instead, the gift seems like a microcosm of their relationship: her mother making some great, completely unnecessary sacrifice Alex hadn't even wanted and then proceeding to being a martyr about it until Alex was forced to find a place for it. Like the time her mother had found a vintage leopard print fur-trimmed cropped jacket in a thrift store in Easton and painstaking altered it so Alex could wear it during her first winter in Washington, even though Alex, a vegan at the time, had told her repeatedly she didn't wear or consume animal products. Alex still had the jacket, even though she hated wearing it, and told everyone it was fake when she was complimented on it.

"It looks lovely," Alex says after a minute. "But I don't see how I'll even get it home."

"I'll drive it up," Owen says. "We can pay for the U-Haul for a few more days."

"Great." Alex swallows. She stands and runs her hand over the painted wood, letting her finger trace a large carved pineapple, one of two that rest flush with the door handles across the width of the doors. Its ornateness would be out of place in her modern, Spartan apartment— and does she even have room for it? She supposes she could move the armchair and ottoman near her bedroom window, maybe even get rid of them. But she likes the armchair and ottoman set—although she doesn't read in it much anymore, it was one of the first things she bought for her apartment, her first adult purchase from a real store, not Goodwill or Ikea.

"Your mother had great taste." Johanna touches Alex's chin. "You're a lucky girl. The restorer told us you could get a couple thousand dollars for it."

"Mom said she paid two-fifty," Owen adds, moving Tortoise away from the clawed legs with his foot. "I thought she paid too much for it then. Shows what I know."

"What a nice gift—parting gift, as it were." Johanna nods. "What a nice story."

"I'm sorry—I need to finish my article," Alex interrupts. She feels ganged-up on, forced to take something she's never wanted. Except it's not even her mother doing the forcing this time. When she'd told Johanna a few nights ago about what had happened with Lewis, Johanna held her in her arms for a long time, saying nothing. She had felt vindicated—she thought Johanna had understood the family dynamics, understood her how her mother operated. But maybe Alex was the only one who did.

She works in her bedroom well into the evening, finishing up a third draft of the article about Juliette before e-mailing it to Rowan. She hears Owen and Johanna talking downstairs now and then, watching a movie, laughing about whatever.

"Kitten, we're making spaghetti!" Johanna calls up around dinner.

"I'll have some later!" she calls down.

She can't wait to pick up her mother's ashes and go home. If she even allows the damn wardrobe in her apartment, perhaps she will store only her mother's urn in it and nothing else. Not much else could fit in there with her mother's ego, anyway.

But maybe she's overreacting. Owen and Johanna's intentions were good. It's just a piece of furniture. It's a nice gesture. She'll just have to find room for it, be a good sport, a team player. A nice girl. She pushes the nagging anger deep into her intestines and takes a valium for good measure.

At 11:30, Alex tiptoes down the stairs. Owen's in his bedroom now, playing video games, and Johanna is in her mother's bedroom, talking on her phone to someone at the winery about business. She opens the door and slips onto the porch, easing herself onto the front step. She took another half valium about an hour ago, to guard against any tearful breakdowns in Juliette's presence. She can't even remember the last time she's felt so many emotions at once, barring her breakup with Kate, and those ended rather quickly, in the space of the few weeks it took to load up on assignments and push her grief away. The regimen of her life usually saves her from the amusement park of emotions that lurk in the dark corners of her mind. Here at home, though, she feels like she's been wearing an unlimited rides bracelet.

Juliette's BMW glides down the street and stops. She's still wearing her chef's uniform. She grins through the window as Alex hurries over and gets in.

"Hey, sweetheart," Juliette says, executing a quick U-turn in the middle of her street. "What a night! We had a birthday group that was out of control—we broke our record in receipts at the bar."

"Sounds fun," Alex says as Juliette continues. She tries to imagine nights like this together—Juliette coming home late, except by now, Alex normally would be in bed. Would they even see each other, considering Juliette's restaurant hours? Probably not, she decides, knowing she should be relieved she won't have to consider how their lives would fit into each other's.

At the house, Juliette drops her keys in a bowl in the hallway, her tote on the floor.

"I have to take a shower," she apologizes. "To get the restaurant all off. You're welcome to join me."

"I finished writing the article today," Alex mentions, following Juliette upstairs.

"I can't wait to read it." Juliette glances other her shoulder. "I worry I said something stupid."

"I think you'll like it a lot," she answers. "I already e-mailed it to my editor, so you don't have to be nice to me anymore if you don't want to."

"You're kidding, right?" Juliette says at the top of the stairs. She blinks, putting her hands on Alex's shoulders. "I hope that's not what you think all this is."

"I was joking," Alex laughs, light, forced. But is she joking? Part of her is, but part of her isn't.

"Are you trying to push me away again?" Juliette's expression softens.

"What?" Alex shakes her head.

"You're still kidding, right?" Juliette rolls her eyes. "You shut *me* out back then."

"You weren't ready to come out."

"Are you serious? I offered to run away with you." Juliette fishes some towels out of the hallway closet. "I loved you."

How did you know for sure? Alex wants to ask. Instead, she hugs Juliette from behind, puts her head on her shoulder.

"I'm not trying to push you away," she murmurs into Juliette's neck. "It's just been an emotional week, and I don't want to think about any of it right now."

In the shower, she closes her eyes, letting Juliette soap her back. She clears her mind and follows Juliette into the bedroom, trying not to think about Carolyn at home, waiting for her text, or Jack sleeping in this same bed tomorrow night, being none the wiser she'd been here, sleeping with his wife.

She clings to Juliette as she kisses her. Something raw, almost primal, in her craves Juliette's physical closeness, as if Juliette's skin serves as a salve to soothe all of Alex's sadness, worry, confusion, and anger. If sex were a type of mindfulness meditation, Alex decided she would be a nymphomaniac.

She had been like that, too, at first, a nymphomaniac, with Kate. But sexual attraction is a sprint, she knows, and a relationship a marathon. Something one had to train for, to pace themselves carefully. To know when to push and when to coast. They had been seventeen when Juliette told her she loved her that day at the beach. They had known so little of the world, of each other, even themselves. She certainly doesn't know thirty-five-year-old Juliette; most days, she doesn't even know thirty-five-year-old Alex. She wonders whether they are merely trying to solve a puzzle they'd long abandoned, which, in the intervening years, had gained a thousand more pieces, with no picture on the box to guide them.

"Will you let me visit you in DC?" Juliette asks afterward, her head on Alex's chest. "Maybe we can scout out locations for a second restaurant."

"I don't think that would be a good idea," Alex answers after a minute, stroking Juliette's hair. "Unless you're planning to divorce Jack."

"So this is it, then?" Juliette exhales forcefully on her skin. "Just tonight?"

Alex knows the equation will never work. Still, she decides to dangle the carrot out there, just so she can tell herself she tried.

"I would be happy to explore this further," she says carefully. "I wouldn't even force you to come out. That's something you should do when you're comfortable, although I wouldn't give you a pass forever. But I draw the line at having an affair."

"So again you're dictating everything." Juliette lifts her head and sinks into the pillow beside Alex.

"I'm not dictating everything. I'm not threatening to tell Jack what happened or expose you in some way or blackmail you. I'm just telling you if you're serious about getting back together, I'd be happy to, when you're single."

"What if I said yes?" Juliette answers. Alex's stomach knots. Did she forget who she was playing cards with? Of course, Juliette would call her bluff. Alex turns on her side and looks at Juliette, her deep, dark eyes, the long, full line of her lower lip. Maybe, just maybe, if she resets her life back to seventeen, Alex thinks, she can do it the right this time.

"I'd say I believe you," Alex says finally. "I trust you."

Juliette is silent.

"It wouldn't happen overnight," she explains. "The restaurant loans are under mine and Jack's name, and I couldn't depend on any income from the television show because of the show is designed around a specific image, the Eastern Shore, my religious upbringing, my marriage to a doctor, and the charitable causes we have around town."

"I can wait," Alex strokes Juliette's face. "I've got time. When you file for divorce, give me a call."

"You could be seeing someone else by then," she pouts. "How will I know you'll wait around?"

"I could be seeing someone now," Alex admits. She feels Juliette stiffen. "But if you say this is what you want, I trust you."

"What do *you* want?" Juliette asks.

"I want to feel something again." Alex kisses her forehead. "I want to love you the way I did back then."

"I want those things with you." Juliette turns and curls herself over Alex. "We're going to figure this out. Things happen for a reason."

"You mean, my mother died to bring us back together?" Alex laughs aloud. Her mother did certainly try to take credit for everything.

"I didn't say that. But we're here right now, and we haven't seen each other in over fifteen years." Juliette puts her hand over Alex's mouth. "Now, please don't ruin the moment."

"Just don't flake out on me, okay?" Alex says under Juliette's hand.

"I won't." Juliette lifts her hand from Alex's mouth and kisses her. As she positions herself atop Alex again, pushing her tongue into Alex's mouth, Alex believes her.

Chapter Twenty-Four

The next afternoon, Juliette stands in the doorway of the kitchen at Sprigg as a supplier rolls in a new shipment of wines. Alex watches as she pulls a bottle out of the crate, examines its label, and begins to talk animatedly to the supplier, her eyes narrowing and widening as she arches her head back and laughs. She looks every bit the part, Alex thinks, of the celebrity chef on a cooking show, commanding and intimate and also a complete mystery onto which viewers of all demographics could project their own hopes, fantasies, and disappointments.

"She'll photograph well," says Steve, who wears a canvas pocket vest and looks every bit the part of a photographer. Alex has chosen him from the three photographers Carolyn had recommended, not because of his pocket vest, but because he had photographed for the *Metropolitan* before. Next to him at the bar rest black vinyl bags of camera equipment. As Alex lifts her vodka and tonic at the bar at two in the afternoon, she wonders if she looks every part the writer. Insecure, prone to drinking, unkempt curly hair, a nervous predilection for checking her phone.

"You think she'll be the next Rachel Ray?" Alex wipes the bar where her drink has begun to sweat. She hadn't planned to drink, but she's nervous. Now the article's finished, she'll have to leave. Back to her life traversing the city, highlighting DC's most talented, most successful, most photogenic. It hardly seems possible she might come back with her own trophy in Juliette. Just hours ago, they had left the house, Juliette dropping Alex home before she ran errands. She had to return some phone calls, Juliette had explained rather cryptically, but maybe Alex could stop by the restaurant later so they'd have a few moments together before her shift, before Jack got home?

I love you. Juliette had mouthed through the windshield as Alex stood on the porch.

I love you too, Alex had mouthed back. She watched Juliette's BMW drive away and tried to stay positive. But the farther away Juliette got, the more worried Alex had become.

"She's better than Rachel Ray." Steve slurps the rest of his iced tea through a straw. "She's got the folksiness of Ray but the optics of Nigella."

Alex finishes her drink as Juliette makes her way over, extending her hand to Steve.

"It's such an honor, Steve." She smiles, her hands resting loosely on her hips, below her white cooking smock. "Are you hungry? Can I whip you up a snack?"

"I'm all right, thanks." Steve stands up. "I was thinking I could use the bay windows, overlooking the river. I'll need a few minutes to set up."

"Great—that'll give me just enough time to freshen up." Juliette steps toward Alex and laces her arm through hers. "Come help me?"

Alex follows Juliette through the kitchen, where the sous chefs are chopping onions and slicing peppers and tomatoes. Juliette's office, which stores paperwork and employee files, is the size of a walk-in closet. Juliette locks the door and turns as Alex leans against the desk.

"You look great," Alex says as Juliette wedges herself between Alex's legs. She notices Juliette has changed out the locket she usually wears and has opted instead for a tiny, but noticeable, gold cross. She's also not, Alex notices, wearing Alex's bracelet. "Very, uh, wholesome."

"You're so beautiful." Juliette grins, leaning in and kissing her. She strokes Alex's chin with her thumb as her eyes flit around the room. "So, I got a call from Food Network."

"And?" Alex says between kisses.

"They want me." Juliette puts her hands on either side of Alex's face. "I'm getting a show! And there's already talk from Simon & Schuster about a cookbook."

"Oh my God, Juliette—that's wonderful." Alex wraps her arms around her. "Sounds like you no longer have any problem with capital."

"The Food Network likes the whole story—" Juliette pauses, still holding on to Alex. "The restaurant, my family—my mom, especially. And Jack, of course. That's how they envision the show."

"Did you agree to it?" Alex pulls away. Of course. Of course, she had known. It shouldn't have been a surprise Juliette would disappoint her. And yet her shoulders feel like she's carrying all of Steve's camera equipment.

"I said I'd run it by the people in my life." Juliette frowns, blinking.

"God dammit, Juliette." Alex looks at the floor. She wonders whether Juliette had already known about the show before last night and had only wanted to hear Alex say yes to her. Her mouth tastes sour, but not from the vodka.

You're a fucking idiot. She sighs and looks up. "Well, you should do it."

"What do *you* want?" Juliette guides Alex's face up to meet hers.

"I want you to be happy—I really want that for you," Alex says. She always thought she'd been the one to get away from their pasts, their towns, and their mothers, that she'd won. But it wasn't a competition. If she loves Juliette, had loved Juliette, she should want her to escape too. Even if it meant they were farther away from each other than ever before.

"I want you to be a part of this." Juliette looks around the room, at the file cabinet of orders, employee files, OSHA regulations laminated and pinned to the wall. All the unglamorous parts of the business. All the things Alex would have been happy to be a part of. "I just don't know what to do."

"You know, I am a part of this." Alex takes Juliette's hands. "I wrote a story for the magazine. I'm cheering for you on the sidelines."

"That's not what I meant," Juliette answers. "I want us to be together."

"Are you going to tell Jack about us?" Alex squeezes Juliette's hands harder, as if she's extracting a confession.

"I can't tell him." Juliette shakes her head. "The whole show—"

"Celebrity chefs get divorced. Some of them are even gay."

"This is not that kind of town. That's not my family." Juliette glances back toward the door. "I can't disappoint them."

"I know you won't," Alex says quietly. Her own career has comprised building a fiction of successful people, with their inner demons, their disappointments, their complicated families left off the page. What had Carolyn said about loving disappointment and imperfection? Had she meant it in situations like these? What would be the Christian way of putting it—love the sinner, not the sin?

Alex straightens up and hugs Juliette.

"That's your choice," she says, pulling away. She has no one to blame but herself for diving into this wreck. "It doesn't mean I'll hate you. It just means I'm disappointed and hurt, and I won't ever be able to see you again."

"Alex, no." Juliette clamps her hand atop Alex's. "We'll figure this out—we agreed last night. Stop running away again, please—You haven't changed at all."

"Yes, I have." Alex looks at her. "Good luck with everything, Juliette. I'll make sure you get some copies of the magazine."

She lets herself out of the office and walks through the kitchen. It feels cramped, full of dangerous objects—ways to cut yourself, burn yourself, slip on the floor. Yet Juliette works here every evening and doesn't even think about it. Alex puts her hand on a large silver refrigerator to steady herself. Her blood's pulsing in her neck and her fingers. Her legs are like crepe paper.

"Is she ready?" Steve looks up from his light meter when she finally makes it back to the dining room.

"Since the moment she was born," Alex jokes. She walks out of the restaurant, toward Owen's car, and gets in. She's not going back in there. She feels stupid and humiliated, big dumb tears rolling down her face. She had run away from Juliette the first time over fifteen years ago exactly so this wouldn't happen. How stupid was she that this time she completely invited heartbreak in?

She opens her mother's purse, figuring there's probably a joint in it somewhere. Even if it's decomposed down to a crumbly rolling paper and flakes, she doesn't care. It'll be enough to take the edge off and get her home in one piece. She wipes her eyes and nose with the back of one hand as she digs around in the Chanel bag. There's a thin pocket on one side, and she unzips it, digging around with her finger. Instead of something stiff and papery, however, she touches something metallic.

Keys. She holds them up in disappointment. A set of spare keys, it looks like, to the house and the old Subaru. And one smaller one, to a post office box or lockbox or something. Of course her mother would have spares. Even if she was largely disorganized, she had the good sense, as a single mother without much of a support system, to recognize it and plan for situations in which she may misplace them.

Or maybe even when someone like her boyfriend steals her keys from her.

Alex's palms sweat. She thinks back to that afternoon in her bedroom, the shadow in the doorway. It had been her mother's size, not Owen's. Maybe she'd come home as usual, using the spare key to the Subaru and house, surprised that Lewis's Volvo was parked out in front. Surprised at what she had seen inside and had gotten out of there, fast. Maybe she'd taken a valium and driven around, wondering what had just happened and what she should do about it. She was already knee deep in their insurance fraud scheme and dating Lewis and not with a lot of good options to extricate herself from either.

Still, it was no excuse for leaving her own daughter in that situation. If she, in fact, had.

Alex will never, ever know for sure. And she can't let this be the thing that defines her mother for her the rest of her life.

Or her. She shoves the keys back into the purse and closes her eyes, trying to think of the nicest thing her mother has ever done for her.

You're not going to school today. Her mother stood in the doorway. She was dressed in ballet tights and an oversized white Oxford shirt. *You have a fever.*

Are you drunk already? Alex glanced over at her alarm clock. It was 6:50 in the morning.

No, I'm not drunk. She sat at the edge of Alex's bed. *I called school and told them you were sick. We're having a girl's day.*

Mom, I have a calculus test. Alex sat up. *Now they're going to think I'm trying to get out of it.*

A year from now, you'll realize how little of this all matters. Her mother looked around at her posters. *And you'll be in college, away from your poor dear mother, who will miss you terribly, and just wants to have some mother-daughter time before you go.*

Can't we do it another day? Alex got up and pulled off her nightgown.

You were positively going to stay in bed the rest of your life yesterday. Her mother was looking at her breasts with what looked like admiration. *Did you get over prom that fast?*

Alex hadn't gotten out of bed the day before. All she could think about was Juliette and Scott at the prom that past Saturday night. How Juliette had looked at her when she came up to her on the dance floor. With embarrassment and shame but also sadness and hurt.

She couldn't not attend the last month of school or avoid Juliette. But she could humor her mother for a day.

What did you tell them I had? Alex asked as she drank some orange juice in the kitchen. Her mother would write outlandish explanations on their absentee notes, like "Owen had yellow fever. By the grace of God, he survived" or "Alex got her period. You wouldn't have wanted her there, anyway, believe me," prompting the principal to ask for a meeting, because he'd thought Owen and Alex had been writing the notes themselves.

I told them you were suffering from the delusions of youth. Her mother started the coffee pot.

I was hoping you said I had rabies or something. Alex smiled.

I'm saving that for Owen, her mother answered.

Outside in the yard, her mother's workstation (an old industrial hard plastic picnic table she used to sell some of her homemade candles at the swap meet) was teeming with plates.

New project? Alex picked one up. They were inexpensive, probably from the thrift store, some with delicate patterns, others Fiestaware, some china, some porcelain or earthenware.

Here. Her mother handed her a hammer and a pair of goggles. *Let's break some shit.*

Why? Alex watched her mother strap on pair of goggles, her hair spiking out over the strap.

Because you need to learn how to break shit. Her mother picked up a plate and threw it down on the carport. The sound of impact, like a gunshot, raced up Alex's back. Shards of plate shot out in all directions. *You will never be able to leave people, leave places, move on with your life, if you can't break shit.*

I don't want to break shit. Alex sat at the table. *People could use these plates. There's nothing wrong with them.*

You don't force form on situations. Her mother picked up another plate. *You change form to fit situation. Would you wear that freaking yellow mustard jumper I bought at the thrift store? No, but you wore the scarf I made out of it.*

But this is different. Alex watched her mother put a plate on the end of the table and raise a rubber-headed mallet. *This is just pointless and wasteful.*

It's just form. Her mother pounded the plate with the mallet. The plate cracked in all directions. *Everything changes. You can't live your life on form.*

I don't see what this has to do with Juliette. Alex stood and scooped up a shard of plate before her mother pounded it again.

It doesn't. Her mother stepped away from the plate. She picked up a new plate, one with painted yellow roses around the border and held it out toward Alex. *It's about you.*

Alex sighed. She took the plate from her mother and, after counting to three, threw it as hard as she could against the back steps. It exploded into seemingly a thousand pieces.

Do another one. Her mother pointed to the stack.

I don't want to, Alex whined.

You need to keep breaking them until, at worst, you're indifferent to it or best, you get a feeling of power from it. Her mother jutted her chin toward the plates. *Do it.*

Mom... Alex shook her head.

Would it help you if I said I needed the shards for a new art project? She sighed.

Her mother sat on the steps of the deck, smoking a cigarette, as Alex picked up another plate. She stared at the pattern, and then, silently apologizing to the plate, threw it on the ground. She took a third and smashed it on the table with a hammer. After a while, she got used to the plates exploding under her hands. She looked for different ways to crack them, make patterns. She threw them at the ground at different angles or pitched them way up in the air and watched them drop. She felt a little excited, a little edgy. She felt as if she should have skipped more school, taken up smoking. Kissed Juliette in the auditorium during prom in front of everybody and apologized for being a coward, promised to look for an apartment together in Philly, leave that summer after graduation. Walked into Lewis's office on Main Street and confronted him in front of his patients instead of watching Juliette write ASSHOLE CREEP CHILD MOLESTER on his window in lipstick in the cover of night.

I lied. Her mother stood up after she'd broken the last plate. *I didn't need those for any project.*

They both watched as a police officer appeared from the side of the house and walked unsurely up to them.

Can we help you? Her mother flicked her cigarette butt on the ground.

We received a complaint, he explained, surveying in the detritus of their project littering the carport. *About noise.*

Of course, you did. Alex's mother peered up and down the street at the neighbors' houses. *Fascists!*

Chapter Twenty-Five

Alex isn't sure where she's going. There are only so many places to go in this town: the mall, the satellite college that's part of the state university system, the community college, the hospital. And the newspaper office. *That one's going full bell jar*, her mother would say of her in Owen's car, crying at the traffic light, "Arthur's Theme" blaring on the light rock radio station to drown out her thoughts. She pulls into the parking lot of *The Shore Times* and grabs her phone. If she's going to go full bell jar, she may as well burn it all to the ground. She doesn't deserve any consolation prizes, certainly not Carolyn.

I'm outside. Do you have a minute? She texts Carolyn and waits.

A minute later, Carolyn appears at the entrance, scanning the parking lot. Alex beeps and cracks open her window as Carolyn comes over.

"Oh, sweetie." Carolyn peers into the crack of the window. "Are you okay? Aren't you hot in there?"

"I'm fine—you don't have to get in. This'll just take a minute." Alex takes her sunglasses off and wipes the tears and sweat off her face. The heat is making her tired; perhaps it'll stop her from crying all together, keep the cauldron that's her stomach from boiling over, lull her to sleep in the newspaper parking lot. And, if she stays out here sleeping too long, she may qualify as an above-the-fold news item in the paper: WOMAN SLEEPS FOR TWO DAYS IN PARKING LOT OF NEWSPAPER TO AVOID GOING FULL BELL JAR.

She watches Carolyn make her way around the car and get in the passenger seat.

"Wow." Carolyn takes in the interior. She jiggles the stick shift that's shaped like a ninja sword. "It's even more...interesting...up close."

"You really want to get the full effect of its awesomeness, you need to drive through town and let people see you in it," Alex laughs through her tears.

"Well, let's go." Carolyn takes her hand and squeezes it.

Alex sighs and pulls her hand away, her hand on the ignition. But she doesn't start the car.

"I need to tell you something," Alex turns toward Carolyn. "I think you're a lovely person. It's just—I've made some stupid decisions since I've been here. Not that you were one of them, but I have no business getting emotionally involved with anyone right now."

"So what are we doing?" Carolyn frowns.

"I'm doing you a favor," Alex says. "You're a wonderful person who deserves so much better than me. I'm a terrible person."

"You're not—"

"Don't argue with me." Alex sighs. "I am a terrible person. At least I am right now. If we met in the future and you lived in DC..."

"I could move to the city," Carolyn presses. "It would give me a reason to finally get out of here."

"No, that's a terrible thing to do," Alex says dismissively. She takes Carolyn's hand and pats it, as if to soften the blow. "Because I know I wouldn't move back here for you. For anyone, actually. If you do move, it should be for yourself."

"So." Carolyn sits very still, staring through the dashboard window at the newspaper office. "I guess this is goodbye, then."

"I'm sorry." Alex wipes tears from her eyes. "I don't want to hurt you because I really like you, but I've been so selfish. I've done nothing but try to distract myself from my own damage since I've been here."

"This is my fault too," Carolyn says, teary eyed. "You came home because your mother died. I should have respected your boundaries."

"Stop." Alex grabs her arm. "You didn't do anything wrong. You've been really good to me. More than I deserve. I'm sorry I wasn't that person to you in return."

"That's not true—"

"No." Alex glares at her. "Stop. Get out. Don't argue with me. Just go."

Carolyn sits quietly, lips parted, her hands on her stomach as if Alex has stabbed her. Alex looks away, focusing on an empty bottle of Yoo-Hoo rolling around in the parking lot.

"I'm going to go back to work now." Carolyn opens the door. "Good luck with your article."

Alex nods, closing her eyes. She's doing the right thing, she knows. Although it doesn't negate all the stupid things, including to Carolyn, she's done up to this point. She watches Carolyn head back into the flat, ugly building.

"You deserve so much more than all of this," Alex says quietly after her. Although she knows, in the end, that's all up to Carolyn. She also knows she doesn't deserve to be the one to give it to her. Still, she wants so much happiness for Carolyn. *Maybe*, she thinks as she starts the car, *that's what love feels like*.

*

At home, Owen and Johann have picked up the urns. They sit side by side on the coffee table, two gleaming pods. All that's left of Adeline Maas. Alex feels a lump in her throat as she touches the top of one. *Can this really be the summation of a life?*

"You look terrible," Owen says from the couch. Beside him lies a couple of their old high school yearbooks. "What happened to you?"

"Nothing." She shakes her head as she picks up one of the urns. It's heavier than she expected. She imagines riding home with it on the bus, hidden in a duffel or tote bag, and then on the metro back home. She puts it back down on the coffee table. It's then she notices the fireproof lockbox.

"Do you know where your mother may have been the key to this box?" Joanna asks as she comes into the living room, holding a pitcher of sangria.

"Maybe," Alex answers, thinking of the small key in her purse. She knows for certain, though, this is where the coveted pictures are kept.

"You okay?" Johanna presses. "You want to talk about it?"

"I'd rather just break some shit, if that's okay with you." Alex drops her purse on the table and studies the wardrobe, which is sitting in the corner of the living room like some dignified old relative.

One that's been talking crap behind her back for years. She stands before it, running her hand along the smooth panels. It is gorgeous, even if isn't her and never would be. Her mother might have known the difference between eighteenth-century and nineteenth-century French armoires, and Kate may have known, too, with a little practice, but Alex didn't care. Her dressers came from Ikea, and, in a one-time extravagance, a new sofa from Crate & Barrel after Kate left. She wants her mother, or rather the memory of her, in her life on her own terms, she realizes, and not this rehabilitated, varnished version.

And, as if to prove her point, as her palm rounds the back of the wardrobe, where the back panel meets the side, a splinter lodges into the pad beneath her middle finger.

"Dammit!" She whips her hand away, shaking it, looking irritated at Owen. "Can you help me take this outside? To the carport?"

"Why?" He looks up from the couch, where he's flipping through one of the yearbooks, like she has asked him to clean the bathroom.

"I have my reasons," Alex says over her shoulder as she heads into the kitchen. Her mother's toolbox is still under the sink, to Alex's relief, jammed underneath the U pipe. She pulls it out with her good hand and then rummages through the junk drawer for a pair of tweezers.

"Owen, help your sister," Johanna says from the living room. "High school will still be waiting for us when you're done."

"It's gonna get ruined out there," he complains as Alex comes back into the living room with the toolbox and tweezers. "Why can't you leave it where it is?"

"If you want me to freaking destroy it in here, I can do that," Alex says calmly as she opens the toolbox and pulls out a Philips head screwdriver. "Help me get the doors off."

"It's your birthday present from our mother," Owen says, jumping up off the couch and standing in front of the wardrobe. "What the fuck is wrong with you?"

"Everything," she answers, grabbing a hammer as well. "Now please help me take it outside or get out of the way."

Owen looks pleadingly at Johanna, who is studying Alex. After a moment, Johanna takes a sip of her sangria and flips her hair back over her shoulders.

"Let her do it," Johanna says. "She needs to do this."

"But you paid—" Owen starts as Johanna holds up her hand.

"Doesn't matter," Johanna continues. She smiles faintly. "Happy birthday, my dear."

Alex pauses. Maybe she's crazy. It's a perfectly good piece of furniture. But as she thinks this, her chest tightens. Her stomach twists, and her fists involuntarily clench. She nudges Owen out of the way with her body and begins unscrewing the doors from the wardrobe.

"I think you're bat-shit crazy." Owen crosses his arms as he watches her. "I always thought you were self-righteous and judgmental, but now I know you're just freaking bat-shit crazy, just like Mom."

Alex looks at him. It's what she's always feared, that somehow she would turn into her mother and not even realize it. But after this week, maybe there's no way she can even deny it. She removes one door, and then begins to work on the second. Owen slumps back into the couch and stares at the wall.

"You want to pretend nothing's wrong, go right ahead," Alex mutters as she rocks the second door loose.

"It's not about pretending anything's wrong." He rolls his eyes from her at the couch. "It's about letting it go."

"What do you think I'm doing?" She drops the door on the carpet.

Owen stares at the door, and then Alex. *Please*, Alex thinks to him, *do this one thing for me.* After a moment, he gets up and grabs the legs of the wardrobe as Alex lowers the top so it's horizontal between them. They navigate the living room and dining room before getting it out the French doors onto the deck and down to the carport.

"You can leave it here—thanks." Alex fans herself with the neck of her shirt as Johanna comes out with the hammer. She holds it out to Alex.

"It's an awfully nice wardrobe," Johanna says. She frowns, as if she's having second thoughts. "But it's your wardrobe."

On the carport, Alex circles the wardrobe as Johanna stands back on the deck. Even in its skeleton form, that is, sans doors and drawers, it's sturdy, probably able to withstand a blow.

This is for Juliette, she thinks as she pushes it over. It makes a satisfying boom as it hits the concrete.

"Oh." Johanna watches from the deck, her hand over her mouth. "Well, it's just a little scratch. Nothing you can't fix if you change your mind."

Alex picks up the hammer and lines it up with the supporting vertical beam in the middle of the skeleton before lifting it over her head.

This is for Lewis, she thinks as the beam splinters on the side and buckles.

"Okay, still salvageable," Johanna hurries down from the deck and stands over the wardrobe, surveying the damage. "It's fine. It'll be fine."

"I hate this stupid wardrobe!" Alex screams at her. "I've hated it since I first saw it. I don't want it in my life."

Alex moves Johanna aside with her arm and lifts up the hammer again. *It's great that you got a National Magazine Award*, her mother scoffed once over the phone. *But you write about quirky people for rich people. It's not like you do anything that matters.*

She hits the beam again until it collapses into the wardrobe. It's not that she wants to destroy her mother. It's just that she wants to destroy how her mother had made her feel. Like Alex, at worst, would never be good enough, and at best, was just an extension of her mother, a flattering bracelet that was nothing on its own.

She steps inside the wardrobe and bends over, banging out one of the sides. Owen, and even Johanna, may never understand the dynamic, but it doesn't mean she has to pretend, for their sakes, that it didn't exist.

The back panel of the wardrobe breaks loose. Alex's shoulders burn as she rests the hammer on the ground. Then she picks it up and bludgeons off the squat, scalloped legs.

"Okay, it's not salvageable," Johanna says as Alex drops the hammer onto the carport and bends over, catching her breath.

When she gets back to DC, she's going to do things differently. She isn't quite sure of the details, but she knows she wants to write about things honestly, not spend the rest of her life peddling puff pieces to subscribers of the *Capitol Metropolitan*. She wants to write about her own flaws, about her mother's, and put them somewhere outside of her where she can see them and let them go. Maybe she'll write a memoir. Or maybe just an essay—she should probably start small.

"It's totally not salvageable," Alex agrees, picking up a piece of wood that was once the top. "Its form was no longer useful to me."

"Oh Jesus Christ, did your mother spoon feed you that form crap, too?" Johanna looks at the sky and laughs. She rolls her eyes. "Do you how long she's pushed that? She even said it to me."

Johanna suddenly looks over Alex's shoulder with a frown. Alex glances to her right as Johanna gives the middle finger to one of the elderly neighbors three doors down and yells "Hey, this isn't your soap opera, Mildred!"

The sliding door to the deck opens and Owen peers out.

"Jesus, Alex." He looks shell-shocked. "Feel better?"

"Yeah, I kind of do," she answers, trying to catch her breath. Even though she's gasping for air, her whole body is light, relaxed. Completely different.

"Someone's here to see you," he says. "Why don't you come inside and stop being crazy for a minute?"

Juliette, most likely. But there's nothing Juliette can do, short of divorcing Jack, that will interest Alex, nothing worth her time.

But it's not. It's Carolyn who's now standing next to Owen at the patio door. As Alex stands in the carport, her eyes red, her cheeks flushed, her blood pressure so high she should be under stroke protocols, she understands Carolyn has come to fight for her. Although she doesn't understand why—her hill isn't one to die on. It's not even a hill—it's quicksand.

"Uh, hey." Alex takes a step toward the deck. "I was just...doing stuff. Have you met Johanna?"

"It's nice to meet you—I've heard a lot about you." Carolyn gives a little wave as Johanna waves back. Her face clouds as she surveys the wreckage. "Maybe this isn't a good time."

"No, it's okay." Alex nods, laughing, taking a step toward the porch. "I'm fine now—really. I'm great."

"Do you have a minute to talk, in private?" Carolyn glances at Owen and Johanna, who are looking at Carolyn as if she's an endangered species, a snow leopard or giant panda.

Alex suppresses a smile. After all that's happened today, Carolyn still likes her. *Maybe*, she thinks, *three hours isn't so far apart.* Maybe they could work something out—slowly—when Alex gets her shit together. But maybe she should try to look presentable first.

"Can you give me a second to wash up?" Alex climbs up the steps, brushing her hair, which is sticking to her cheeks and neck, away from her face.

"I'll entertain her," Owen offers as they go back inside. He sits on the couch and pats the cushion beside him, grabbing one of the yearbooks. "You want to see what Alex looked like in high school?"

Alex slips into the downstairs powder room and listens as she lathers her hands, her face, her armpits.

"That's Alex." She hears Owen say to Carolyn as she rubs the mascara and sweat off her face.

"She was pretty cute back then," she hears Carolyn say. "What happened?"

"Do you know Juliette Sprigg?" She then hears Owen ask. She ratchets up the faucet, trying to rinse her face as quickly as possible, but she gets soap in her eyes. She grabs for the hand towel and is practically wiping off her eyelashes now as she imagines Carolyn's reaction to his information.

"I didn't realize Alex already knew Juliette," she hears Carolyn say finally.

"Juliette and Alex secretly dated in high school," Owen explains as Alex bursts from the powder room, armpits still soapy with Jergens coconut liquid soap, and runs into the living room. He looks up at her. "Kind of still secretly now. Right, Alex?"

To this, Carolyn says nothing. In fact, she says nothing at all as she stands up walks to the front door.

"That's totally not true," Alex lies as Carolyn grabs her purse from the hall table.

"What, that you didn't secretly date her in high school?" Carolyn shrugs Alex's hand off her shoulder. "Or that you aren't secretly dating her now?"

"I didn't want you to know I knew Juliette at first, much less dated her, because I thought you'd think it would look unprofessional for me to interview her," she explains. "The other stuff kind of just happened—I wasn't expecting it."

"You could have mentioned it—that you already knew her, that you're involved with her—before I kissed you." Carolyn opens the door. "But you seemed happy enough to let me make a fool of myself."

"It wasn't that simple." Alex grabs her arm again. "I didn't come home to get involved with anyone. And I'm not involved with Juliette anymore, if that means anything. But I liked being with you and selfishly used that as an excuse not to think about my mother while I was here. If I was still being selfish, I would have continued lying to you. There was just no good option, except to let you go to find someone else."

"That's a good idea." Carolyn looks at Alex's hand clamped above her elbow. "Just let me go."

"You know." She releases her grip. "You're dodging a bullet."

"And to think I came over here to try to change your mind." Carolyn shakes her head, tears in her eyes. "I'm glad that got nipped in the bud quickly."

"You'll be fine." Alex swallows. "You're going to meet a wonderful person. And all this was just...the road leading up to it."

She watches Carolyn get into her Corolla. She knows all this is just the road for her, too, leading up to something. Although hers feels more like a dead end than a six-lane highway. Still, she realizes that if she doesn't do the work on herself she's never done, they'll all be dead ends, not matter how artfully she dresses them up, no matter how hard she convinces herself they're cul-de-sacs instead.

"So who was that again?" Johanna asks when she comes back into the living room.

"Somebody named Carolyn," Owen looks at Alex, confused. "I don't remember any Carolyn from high school."

"Oh." Johanna wipes her hands with a paper towel. "Well, she seemed nice."

Chapter Twenty-Six

"Alex." Johanna is knocking on Alex's bedroom door. "You alive? You decent? You want to talk?"

"Come in." Alex is sitting on her bed, holding her mom's keys. Her hands are shaking. She knows it wouldn't have ended with Carolyn any other way. At some point, she would have found out about Juliette. At some point, she would have felt betrayed. But Alex wishes she hadn't been so focused on changing the trajectory of her past with Juliette than seeing the present, Carolyn, right in front of her.

"I don't deserve nice things," Alex says as Johanna sits down next to her.

"Oh, that old thing wasn't you." Johanna squeezes Alex's knee. "Definitely a mom choice."

"Wait—are you talking about Carolyn?" Alex asks in surprise.

"Carolyn?" Johanna brings her hand on her mouth. "Oh no—of course not. I was talking about the wardrobe."

"Oh—well, I guess I didn't deserve either." Alex laughs. But she's laughing more about the uncanny habit that she and Johanna have of sticking their feet into their mouths.

"I feel like I hardly knew Carolyn," Johanna continues. "I guess I hardly did. Why didn't you tell me about her? Why didn't you tell me about your love triangle that happened right under my nose?"

"I don't know." Alex shakes her head. "I wasn't supposed to be here for that. I thought you'd think I was selfish."

"You were here to grow." Johanna takes her hand and squeezes it. "I think you did that, a little. But, in the future, I want you to feel like can tell me things. Let me know how I can help you feel like you can."

"I don't know." She shrugs. "I guess I just never trusted anyone, after Mom. Or Kate. Or maybe it's just genetic, you know, like the way you haven't told Owen the story of Jeffrey and Johanna?"

"I am doing it right after we finish talking." Johanna squeezes Alex's hand harder. "But I want us to talk more—a lot more. Even though I'll be heading back to Seattle soon, we can always video chat."

"Wait, you're leaving?" Alex feels a lump in her throat. "I mean, I guess I have to leave too. But it feels like we just got here."

"We just did," Johanna agrees. "But we're not going to not see each other again. This time, you won't be able to get rid of me."

"Sometimes I don't even want to go home," Alex continues. "There's nothing for me there. And now that Mom's gone, and I've scared off all the women in my dating pool, I don't really have anyone in my life either."

"You have me, dear," Johanna says. "And if you really feel that way, why don't you come out to Seattle with me?

No one will know you out there. You can totally pretend to be someone else."

"Like, transition to a nice person?" Alex grins.

"First of all, you are a nice person. You just had a lot buried in there—you were constipated. Everyone's fussy when they're constipated, and it comes out in the worst way. And second, if you do 'transition,' you won't need surgery, or hormones, although your new therapist may change your antianxiety medication."

"We'll see about therapy," Alex answers.

"Well, what about Seattle?"

"We'll see about that too."

In the past few days, Alex has had enough change to last her a few years. Maybe she should just go home, be alone. Figure out who she really is. What she really wants. She makes a fist with her free hand and grimaces, not realizing she's still holding her mother's keys. When the sting goes away, she holds them up to Johanna.

"I found them in one of my mother's old purses," she explains. "We should see whether the photos are in the lockbox."

Johanna leans over and picks up something off the floor. The lockbox.

"I came prepared," she says, a little sheepishly. "I might've even let you hammer it open, despite what you did to your mother's wardrobe."

"I'm sorry if I hurt your feelings about that. I know you and Owen meant well, getting it restored."

"Don't worry." Johanna waves her hand. "You did what you needed to do. I'm all about catharsis, honey."

"Well, speaking of catharsis." Alex nods at the lockbox. "Let's see what's in there."

She stares straight ahead as Johanna opens it. From the corner of her eye she can see Johanna go through the papers, some jewelry, then a manilla envelope. She sees Johanna sit up straight.

"In the event of my death—destroy!" Johanna reads what Adeline has written, with a sharpie, on the front of the envelope. "I think we're getting hotter."

"I'm not looking," Alex says, unfocusing her eyes. She can still, see, however, Johanna open the packet and pull out a packet of photos. She can see her hold one photo a few feet from her face.

"I should really get my readers," Johanna says, bringing it closer and then holding it away again.

"Wow—are you guys looking at porn?"

Johanna and Alex whirl around together to see Owen standing in the doorway of Alex's room.

"My door doesn't close all the way," Alex explains to Johanna apologetically as Owen leans in for a better look.

"You don't want to see these." Johanna shoves them back in the envelope. "Unless you want to see your mother having sex."

"With you?" Owen raises his eyebrows as Johanna hurries past him with the lockbox. When she hears her mother's door shut, Alex laughs aloud.

"You know who she is, right?" Owen shakes his head and laughs too.

"I do," Alex answers. "I didn't know you did too."

"Johanna's our—was—our father. Duh," Owen says, as if he hasn't heard her. "When did you figure that out?"

"When—" Alex pauses. "Wait, when did you?"

"Mom told me years ago." He shrugs. "During the trial. A lot of the money from the insurance fraud she sent to Johanna, you know, to pay for the surgeries."

"What? How did I not know? I did her checkbook for years." At least now what her mother said in the birthday card to Johanna—*I think I've found a way to get you the money*—makes sense. It's actually quite a nice gesture from her mother, even if it was something for which she wound up sacrificing her career. The one she was worried about keeping when Johanna first brought up transitioning to Adeline so many years ago.

"It happened while you were at school," he says. "Toward the end, she was sending Johanna a lot of money."

"But why didn't you call Johanna on it when she gave you that poop story?"

"I don't know." He shrugs. "I guess it's her business what she wants to tell us. So I just played dumb and decided I was going to spend some time with her when she was here, even if she didn't know it."

"I guess Mom really did love her—Johanna," Alex says. *Enough*, she thinks, *to almost go to prison for fraud*. She crosses the room and hits Owen's arm. "Why didn't you tell me any of this at the time?"

"Well, for one, Mom swore me to secrecy about everything—"

"That sounds about right."

"And two, you always acted like you weren't interested. That you had your own life."

"That sounds about right too." She looks at him apologetically. "I still can't believe you were capable of such secrecy."

"I'm not a moron." He hits her arm back. "I have a PhD."

"Well, I'm glad you're using it." She laughs. He gives her a look. "I was just kidding."

"I wasn't frowning about that," he says. "I'm sorry about, uh, what happened with Carolyn. You have every right to be pissed."

"It's okay." She shrugs, wiping tears from her cheeks with the back of her hand. For a second, she'd actually *forgotten* about that particular humiliation. "It's not like you ever even met her."

"Yeah, but I didn't need to open my mouth about Juliette. I mean, I don't want to ruin whatever's going on between you. I wasn't thinking."

"There's nothing going on." Alex says. "Not anymore."

"Oh." His brows furrow. "Well, I'm sorry if you are."

"I don't know." She shakes her head. "I have no idea what I'm doing. I thought maybe if I could change what happened between me and Juliette, my life would turn toward the right trajectory this time."

"Well, that would require time travel."

"I know, but…"

"Besides, the longing you seek is not behind you, it is in front of you."

"Owen." Alex grins. "That's the most profound thing you've ever said to me. Thank you."

"Actually, it's from *Star Wars: The Force Awakens*,"

"Of course, it is." She rolls her eyes. "But the larger point is that my life to this point has sucked, and I'm going to make it better myself instead of blaming other people or trying to rewrite the past or just being a workaholic and ignoring it completely."

"Hey, at least you did something with your life." He frowns. "My only use to Mom was carrying groceries and filling prescriptions under my name. I shouldn't have done that—I feel terrible. I enabled her. But I just wanted her to get off my back. She could be such a bummer to live with and be around."

"You weren't Mom's keeper." Alex sits down on the bed. "She probably would have found a way to get those pills without you anyway. You shouldn't feel guilty now. Your life is just beginning, with Shelley. I'm sure she'd be happy for you."

"Do you think Johanna likes Shelley?" Owen looks at her.

"Are you still thinking about going to Seattle?"

"I don't know." He slumps down next to her. "There's nothing for me here. Except Shelley, I mean."

"From now on, I want you to tell me everything." She grabs his forearm tight. "About Shelley, about Johanna, about Mom, about getting fired, about your life plans. Okay? I want to know about everything. Because I'm your sister, and I'm the only one you have."

"Okay. Are you going to let go of my arm now?"

Alex loosens her grip but doesn't let go. "Are you going to talk to Johanna now? Don't be as much of a chicken as she's been."

"Yeah." He stands up. "You're not angry at her, are you? For not saying anything?"

"Well, if we're going to tell each other everything from now on—Johanna already told me. On the way back from the airport."

"Oh." He raises his eyebrows. "Who's keeping secrets now? You, dear sister, have totally surrendered the right to be angry at me ever again."

"I'm not even sure I'm capable of any more anger." She frowns. "I think I got it all out on the wardrobe."

"Better the wardrobe than me or Johanna or Lewis," Owen says.

"Shit, *is* Lewis still in town?" Alex jumps off the bed. Her vague sadness has morphed into a very specific panic. "You haven't seen him, have you? Don't lie."

"Nope. And if he was, you're leaving soon, right? What chance is there that you'll run into him?"

"With my luck, very high."

"I wish you weren't going." He pauses in the doorway. "I know I've said some mean things, but they're not true. I actually miss you sometimes."

"Well, you have a car—why don't you ever come up and visit me?"

"No way I'm bringing Donatello to DC," Owen laughs. "He'd be stolen in a minute."

"Are you happy, Owen?" Alex asks.

"What, do I look unhappy?" He brushes his T-shirt, as if she's pointed out a stain.

"No." She shakes her head. "It's just—I *do* want to be happy. And I have no idea how to go about doing that."

"A big freaking pizza would make me happy right now." He pats his stomach. "Hey, do you want to do something for Mom, now that we've gotten the urns back? Like a memorial dinner or something?"

"I need more information than *memorial dinner*." In her mind, a plan Owen is in charge of could go very weirdly south very quickly.

"If you don't want to, I won't make you. But I've never asked you for anything, and this is the only thing I'll ever ask you—that the whole family, all four of us, have one meal together before you leave."

"What do you mean, the four of us?" she calls after him as he heads toward their mother's room to see Johanna.

Chapter Twenty-Seven

"Don't put her on the table," Alex says as they're seated at the Dough Roller on Coastal Highway. "It's unsanitary. Put her on the seat."

"She can't see anything from there," Owen replies. He pats the top of the urn. "You know it would piss her off if we didn't."

"I'm more concerned about it being a health hazard." She reaches over to grab back the urn, which is now resting on the table, but Owen smirks and moves it slightly out of her reach.

"Children, honesty." Johanna stands up and walks toward the entrance of the restaurant.

"What, she's mad?" Owen looks after her in surprise. But instead of going outside, she lifts up a high chair and brings it back to the table.

"Put her in here." Johanna pulls the straps out and pats the seat.

"Because she'd really enjoy being in that." Alex rolls her eyes as Owen hands Johanna the urn. "Although, honestly, she could be a big baby."

The waitress near the kitchen who's been keeping an eye on them makes her way to the table.

"Good evening—what can I get for y'all?" She glances at the urn. "And who's dining with us this evening?"

"My dead husband," Alex says. "The Dough Roller was his favorite place."

"Oh, I'm glad to hear." The waitress nods and blinks. "I mean, I'm sorry to hear about your husband. So, uh, what kind of pizza does your husband like?"

"The Meat Explosion." Owen hands their menus back to the waitress. "I guess that's why he had a heart attack."

"You guys are awful." Johanna unrolls the paper from her straw after the waitress leaves. "It's easy to see why you're siblings."

"We're not usually this weird," Alex admits. If Owen had tried to pull this off in DC, she would have been mortified. But she's never going to see these people at the restaurant again. There's something freeing in that. It almost, maybe, makes it enjoyable.

"It's cool that our whole family is finally together." Owen takes a sip of his water.

"I just want to say, now that we're all in the *know*." Johanna nods at both of them and winks. "I was a little apprehensive about meeting you, that you would judge me for not being here until now. Goodness, and the way Adeline talked about you sometimes—you'd think you were the second coming of Damien from *The Omen* and Regan MacNeil from *The Exorcist*. Well, I mean, I guess I mean I heard the good and the bad—your mother never minced words. But it's been surprisingly lovely to spend time with the both of you."

"Well that's good, I guess." Alex takes a pizza plate and napkin as the waitress puts the hot pie on a stand in the middle of the table. "I mean, we certainly haven't been on our best behavior while you've been here."

"And, since we all seem to be prone to secrecy, I want us to pinky swear we'll never keep secrets from one another again," Johanna continues. "We don't actually have to do a pinky swear. Whatever adults do when they swear to do something."

"You'd think, as bad as we are about being tactful, this shouldn't be a problem for any of us," Alex laughs.

"Speak for yourself, daughter." Johanna bites into her pizza.

"So I thought we'd release some of Mom's ashes after we eat." Owen looks up.

"Mom hated the beach," Alex answers. And, she thinks, *she didn't care much for pizza either*.

"Well, actually, we'd drive here every once and a while on Sunday nights and get French fries with vinegar on the Boardwalk," Owen explains. "And we'd go on the Haunted House ride because she thought it was cheesy. It's kind of like my favorite memory of her."

Alex doesn't have those kinds of memories with her mother, or really any the past few years. It seems unfair Owen got all the good memories. Except he didn't—their mother drove drunk, fell down steps, almost set fire to the kitchen after leaving a roast in the oven, all after Owen had moved back home. If anything, he deserved to have good memories.

"That's sweet, Owen," Alex says after a minute. "I'd love to go to the Haunted House later."

"What have you done with my sister?" Owen reaches across the table and feigns taking her pulse. "What is this earnestness that has replaced your deeply encroached cynicism?"

"It's just nice to spend time with Mom." Alex looks at the urn. "When she can't say anything."

"Fascist." Owen winks and holds out his glass. "Cheers."

*

It's crowded on the boardwalk, the height of summer family beachgoers riding the salt and pepper shakers and bumper cars at Trimper's Rides, eating fries with salt and vinegar, buying T-shirts and hermit crabs at the beach stores.

"I'm going to walk along the beach," Johanna says, undoing the straps of her sandals. "I'll meet back up with you."

"What's the matter, you scared?" Owen jokes. But Alex thinks maybe it's the stares and sidelong looks Johanna gets from some of the crowd. *It must be difficult*, she thinks, *to always be the center of attention one can't control, to be uncomfortable, all ironically so that one can feel comfortable within oneself.* Alex has spent years when she's not working not noticing people—glued to her phone, or the *Washington Post* or *New Yorker*. Now, she looks out among the crowd of families as she waits in line for the Haunted House with Owen and feels like she fits in less than Johanna, or even her mother, who at least had children. She wants to belong to something. Or someone. She pulls out her phone to text Carolyn about this revelation but realizes she can't do that anymore.

"Do you have a napkin?" Owen asks as they near the front of the line.

She nods, digging in her mother's purse. On the side, near her wallet, she sees a champagne-colored card. Kate's break-up note. Alex hasn't thought of it in days, and suddenly, she's not even sure why she's keeping it. As she hands Owen a tissue, she takes the notecard out. Without looking at it, she gets out of line and dumps it in the garbage can by the ticket booth. At least, she realizes, as she rejoins Owen, one good thing has come of her trip home.

She climbs into one of the cars, which is shaped like a coffin and clearly made for children and presses her knees tightly together so her legs don't touch Owen's. Owen stretches his arm across the back of the seat against her shoulders as her left elbow digs into his ribs.

"They added some new stuff a few years ago," Owen explains as the coffin jerks forward on the track. Chewed wads of bubble gum plaster the door that opens into the ride. A warbly soundtrack of menacing organ music plays emphysemically through the salt-eroded speakers. "But it's pretty lame—a guy in an electric chair, some Saw-like stuff."

After Alex's eyes adjust to the darkness, she can see that the car slides into a chamber that looks like a mineshaft, only the beams are slightly skewed. They're painted neon orange so that they stand out in the black lights, and the rails on which the car moves tilt slightly to the right, in Alex's direction, as a screeching sound now blares over the speakers. It gives the illusion they're skidding out of control and about to plunge into the open mineshaft at the end. Alex braces herself against the edge of the coffin car as they jut and roll downward closer to the end of the track.

"This was Mom's favorite room," Owen explains over the screeching. "The Creepy Chamber."

A few feet before they reach the wall, Owen pulls a baggie out of his shirt pocket. Alex just now realizes it's the button-up she bought him for his birthday last year. He untwists the baggie and shakes it onto the track behind them, although the car is so cramped his arm hits her shoulder as he reaches back, and she feels something like powder hit the back of her neck. She touches the skin above the back of her shirt and feels her mother's ashes there. Instead of brushing them off, she rests her hand back on the side door of the coffin. A second later, the car dips again, picks up speed, and bursts through the door into the next scene.

*

Johanna is waiting for them outside the ride. As their little coffin screeches to a stop, she takes a picture of them with her phone.

"I'm going to get this framed," she says. "I'm going to make a montage with all your Halloween pictures. And I'm going to make you copies."

"I'm going to play Golden Axe." Owen says as they reach Marty's Playland. "Anybody want to watch me?"

Before they can answer, Owen wanders into the arcade.

"My work is clearly not done here." Johanna stares after him.

"It's a job for Shelley now." Alex pats Johanna's arm. "And it is a job I would not wish on anyone."

Chapter Twenty-Eight

Alex wakes up to the sound of fucking. It's less grunting and moaning and more bed creaking and wall thudding, but unmistakably fucking. At first, she thinks she's at home in DC, where the early morning fucking usually wakes her from sleep, but her bedroom window is in the wrong place, and the comforter too frilly. It's then she realizes she's still at her mother's house, her mother is still dead, and either Owen or Johanna is fucking.

Owen, judging by their shared wall. Alex finds Johanna in the kitchen, brewing coffee. She's wearing one of Adeline's robes. Even though Johanna is thin, it's still too small, riding up mid-thigh, Johanna's broad shoulders pulling the collar open across her chest.

"I told Owen I needed a ride to the bus station this morning." Alex roots through the cabinet for a clean mug, clanging them together in irritation. "But he sounds busy."

"I can take you, kitten."

"You can't drive a stick." Alex turns around.

"I can drive the U-Haul," she explains. "And then Owen can pick me up after I drop it off at the rental center."

Alex mulls her options as she pours herself some coffee. It seems slightly better than the ninja turtle car, but not much.

"I guess it'll have to do," she answers after a moment. It's the sentiment that seems to summarize her life best right now. Still, she had let herself daydream this earlier morning that it'd be Carolyn who would take her to the bus station and kiss her goodbye, tell her to call her so she'd know Alex had gotten home okay.

They listen to a quick staccato of bumps above them before the house goes silent.

"Well, at least there's a happy ending up there." Alex blows across the lip of her mug and glances at the ceiling. "I think."

"It's been a tough week for you." Johanna kneads Alex's right shoulder. "You lost a mother."

Alex closes her eyes. Just like her mother's death, the realization that this woman before her, whether they continue having a relationship or not, has passed along her genes, is also her parent, is still jarring and will take some time to get used to. But this woman's been here all week, cooking pork cutlets, making Halloween montage photos, tentatively encouraging Alex's furniture decimation, driving her to the bus station.

Unlike Alex, she's tried.

"You know, I, uh, have been thinking of doing some more writing outside of work." Alex leans against the counter. "If you really needed someone to ghostwrite your memoir."

"Oh, you're so sweet!" Johanna holds up the creamer bottle with both hands, like a trophy. "I'd insist on paying you though."

"No, absolutely not." Alex shakes her head. "It'll give me a chance to learn about your life and about...your journey."

"Oh, you can just watch my YouTube channel for that," Johanna answers, pivoting to the fridge. "I post a new video every week about the ups and downs of transitioning."

"Oh." Alex pauses. "How did I not know about that?"

"Sweetie, your mother just died." Johanna explains, patting her shoulder. "I was here for you, not to upsell."

Alex hears footsteps on the stairs and rinses her coffee mug in the sink. When she turns around, Shelley is standing in the doorway. She's wearing one of Owen's Star Trek T-shirts, only on her it looks like a nightgown.

"I'm sorry—I don't mean to interrupt." Shelley looks down. "I just wanted to get a glass of water for my pills."

"You're not interrupting anything." Johanna closes the refrigerator and smiles brightly. "I'd better hop in the shower, though, if I'm going to get Alex to the bus station."

"I heard you had a good time at the beach last night," Shelley says, opening the cabinet, finding a glass on the first try.

"Are you guys still getting married?" Alex asks. "Sorry to be so forward—I don't have much time left here."

"Oh, well," Shelley laughs. She studies the glass if it were the one who asked the question. "I don't think we never weren't—I just don't like being surprised like that."

"Are you going to Seattle?" Alex grips her hands. A prickly jealousy crawls over her that her family might move away and leave her all alone.

"I don't know." Shelley looks up. "I want to finish my classes. But if Owen doesn't want to wait around, I'm not going to force him to stay."

"Well, I'm happy for you guys, I mean, if you stay together. I mean—God—that was stupid. I'm sorry."

The story of my trip home, she thinks. As she turns to leave, Shelley reaches over and pulls her into her arms, squeezing Alex so tight that she involuntarily gasps. She feels tears in her eyes, as if she's been the recipient of an emotional Heimlich, and everything she's tried not to think about this morning rushes out in whimpers. Of all the things she would never have predicted on this trip home (and there were many), this was probably the most unpredictable of all—being comforted by the manager of her hometown Staples in her mother's kitchen.

Right now, she's so okay with that.

*

"We'll be fine." Johanna stands by the door of the U-Haul.

"Are you sure?" Owen asks. He's standing on the porch in his boxers, holding Tortoise.

"We've got to go," Alex says by the passenger door.

"I'll meet you at the U-Haul place," Owen says to Johanna. "Just text me when you've dropped Alex off, and I'll come pick you up and we can pay up for the rental."

Once Alex is in the truck, Owen waves Tortoise's paw goodbye from the porch. A strange paradox settles over her—wanting to get away from this town as fast as possible and forget again that it exists but also wanting to linger.

But maybe that's life, she thinks. *There's always a razor hidden in one of the candy bars. But you don't ever stop eating them.*

"That's a terrible analogy," Johanna says as she rolls out of the development at five miles per hour and makes a wide turn toward the highway. "I'm not so sure I want you to ghostwrite *The Grapes of Maas* after all."

"What if I buy you breakfast at Panera?" Alex spots the familiar sandstone building with the green sign about a quarter mile up. She has a terrible craving for Panera. Specifically, their sausage, egg, and cheese breakfast sandwich, and there's time to indulge it before Johanna drops her off at the bus station to go home.

"Can you get me the cinnamon crumb coffee cake?" Johanna asks as she guides the empty U-Haul into the parking lot adjacent to the Panera, since the parking lot of Panera is almost full. It's Johanna's maiden voyage driving a light commercial truck, and she needs lots of room to maneuver. She's already run over two curbs and scraped a corner mailbox on the way over here.

"Really?" Alex frowns as she digs her phone and wallet out of her purse. "That's the most senior citizen thing on the menu."

"Alex, I'm eligible for Medicare next year." Johanna reapplies her lipstick, glacier pink, in the rearview mirror, even though she's only going to go inside to use the restroom. "I need to refine my taste for it before I have to play bingo at the senior center."

Alex watches Johanna ease out of the truck. She can't imagine Johanna, who's wearing a white spandex tank-top dress and her platform wedges, among the shrunken, doughy women with embroidered sweaters and orthopedic shoes the color of old taffy. She can, however, imagine Johanna inviting those women to her winery for a tasting, or giving them a makeover, teasing their hair up like the women they probably used to watch on *Dynasty* or *Dallas*. Johanna seems to know more about hair and makeup than any woman Alex has ever known.

Inside Panera, Alex places their order and leans against the wall. How can she be so exhausted? She's only spent the week at home—it's not like she climbed Mount Kilimanjaro. Still, she's like a tampon that's been in too long, water-logged and bloody and unable to absorb any more.

But then, there he is, the big clot that she already thought she'd hemorrhaged out: Lewis Mahoney. It's been sixteen years, but she'd know him anywhere: his angular frame, preppy khakis, and longish brown hair, now peppered with gray, that creeps over his ears and falls in choppy bangs over his deep-set eyes and aquiline nose. He couldn't have gotten his medical license back—could he? The two years of prison for felony prescription fraud hadn't been nearly enough—she's avoided therapists for years because of therapists like him, men for years because of men like him.

At the very least, she should be able to get out of here without *this* ghost of Christmas past, get her sausage, egg, and cheese breakfast and dark roast coffee in peace.

She watches him type on this laptop, pausing to sip his coffee. She's already burned her bridges from one end of this town to another, at least with women. Better to lay low, slink out of here, and get on the bus back to DC, where she can sabotage nobody but herself.

"Goodness, kitten, I practically had to toilet paper the entire ladies' room." Johanna is twenty feet across the store from her, near the restrooms and drink station, but she speaks with such projection that everyone looks up. "I was going to write my own initials on the maintenance log."

Everyone including Lewis, Alex realizes as she glances back toward his table. Their eyes lock for a second, two. Neither has changed much, except they are older, so it's hard to pretend they don't know each other. But both of them know it's better to pretend they don't.

"He's cute." Johanna is standing beside her now, looking at Lewis also and smelling of the Paul Mitchell awaphui wild ginger high-gloss primer she's combed into her hair. "He's not my type though."

"It's. Lewis," Alex whispers through clenched teeth, elbowing Johanna in the side through her spandex tank dress. "Just turn around."

"That's Lewis?" Johanna has no inside voice. Her voice is reliably capable of penetrating cement walls and probably high-velocity weather systems.

"Shh." Alex is now pushing Johanna back the way she came. "Just get our order—please?"

"No one messes with my daughter and gets any with it." Johanna reaches into her woven purse. Is she going for that steel nail file again? But she pulls out her phone instead and points it at Lewis, who briefly comes into focus on the screen before he gets up and walks toward them.

"You can't do that." Lewis covers the lens of Johanna's phone with his palm. "Who the hell are you?"

"I'm Alex's parent," Johanna explains. "Adeline's ex? Adeline, who almost went to prison because of you?"

"Adeline Maas." Lewis studies Johanna, as if wondering what else she knows. "I didn't force her to do anything. She was equally to blame."

His eyes are sunken, so dark underneath they're almost purple. His polo shirt is pilled and fading. Alex is almost a little sorry for him.

"And if you and your tranny friend don't put your phone away and stop harassing me." He's looking at Alex now. "I'm calling the police."

"Johanna, let's go." Alex is sweaty, her throat tight. In the movies, women kick guys like Lewis in the balls, or at least spill coffee all over their laptop keyboard.

In real life, though, women, Alex at least, just want to get the hell away and never, ever have to think about the existence of guys like Lewis again.

"I'm watching you." Johanna points her French-manicured fingernail at Lewis. "Stay away from Alex or I swear to God you'll look worse than you already do."

Alex grabs their order from the counter, not stopping to get sugar or cream for coffees. The entire store is watching them now, maybe someone even filming on their own camera phones for social media exploitation later. Thank God Alex is going back to DC, even though Lewis could figure out easily enough that she lives there, she writes for a freaking magazine, for goodness sake, if he doesn't already know. *There is no anonymity from your past*, she thinks, as Johanna leads her out of the store, her arm linked through Alex's.

"Can you drive?" Johanna hands Alex the keys. "I've got something in my contact lens."

Alex takes the keys without answering and gets in the driver's seat. Of course, her trip home for her mother's death would end like this. Now, she doesn't even have the appetite to scarf down the stupid sandwich that made them stop here in the first place.

"Are you coming? I can't miss my bus." Alex looks out the window at Johanna, who's staring, her hazel eyes narrow, her brow heavy and nearly slouching over her eyes like a bloodhound, at the Panera in the next lot.

"I left my high-gloss primer in the bathroom." Johanna smiles and puts on her butterfly sunglasses. "Pull around over to the entrance ramp, and I'll meet you there."

Even though the parking lot at Panera has emptied a little, Alex doesn't argue. She has less experience driving a truck than Johanna, who's only had twenty minutes. But they assured her Owen they could handle it. And after this, they'll go on with their lives. Will they see each other again? There's what people say and, of course, what people wind up doing instead.

Alex adjusts the seat and backs slowly out of the space.

Surprisingly, it's easier than Johanna made it look. Although there are blind spots everywhere, the steering wheel turns easy, and she hopes any retirees who decided on Panera this morning instead of Cracker Barrel can see the Huge. Fucking. Truck. inching out of the parking space at one per mile per hour. She rolls around the back of the restaurant, thinking none of this would have happened if Panera just entered the 21st century and installed a drive-thru, and coasts up to the exit that will take them back onto Route 13 and the bus station. But when she glances into the side mirror, she sees Johanna coming out of the restaurant, more specifically running out of the restaurant with a laptop, Lewis running after her. Johanna holds the laptop over her head as she runs before heaving it toward her left down a row of cars.

"Shit." Alex leans over the cab of the U-Haul and opens the passenger door for Johanna. They definitely should have gone to a place with a drive-thru.

"Go, go, go!" Johanna's woven purse hits the seat and Johanna claws herself in after it. Alex glances at the rearview mirror to see Lewis has given up pursuit, attending to his laptop instead. Still, Alex floors it from the entrance ramp until the next traffic light.

"What the hell?" Alex glances at Joanna as they idle, waiting for the light to turn green. "You want him to press charges?"

"You didn't see any of that, okay?" Johanna sprays a little more high-gloss primer onto her bangs and flattens them back over her forehead. "I'll handle it if the cops show."

"Thanks." Alex takes Johanna's hand. She glances into the rearview mirror again before easing on the gas.

"We're not going to do some Thelma and Louise thing now, are we?" Johanna holds up Alex's hand. "Because I have a different dress I want to die in."

"Are you kidding?" Alex smirks. "You know how pissed I'll be if we have to pay for another day on this rental?"

But she's not angry. Not anymore. This whole week will be funny, kind of, maybe a hundred years from now.

As they near the gas station where Greyhound has a small terminal, she squeezes Johanna's hand again. "If I did drive us over a cliff, though, I'd tell you I love you first."

"Oh, I love you too, Alex." Johanna squeezes back. "I always have. Don't worry, we'll be fine."

With her other hand Johanna unwraps Alex's breakfast sandwich instead of the coffee cake she'd requested and takes a bite.

"Oh, I'm sorry—can I have some of this?" she says, her mouth full. "I actually hate fucking coffee cake."

Chapter Twenty-Nine

The card that arrives in the mail four months later is pink and bears an interlocking J and S, presumably Juliette's new branding logo, on the back flap of the envelope.

> *Dearest Alex, Thank you so much for the amazing article in the Capitol Metropolitan.* Juliette has written in her big, girlish handwriting on the card inside. *It's always wonderful when someone knows you so well and can translate that onto the page. I was so happy to see and spend time with you over the summer, and I'm looking forward to spending time with you again, if you're ever back in town. Please, please don't be a stranger. Love, Juliette*

She had cried for Juliette when she'd gotten back to DC, but it had been mixed with tears for her mother, for Carolyn, for herself, and even for Kate (the few times she'd stumbled upon her on the Sunday morning political shows while channel surfing)—one big sloppy wail that began when she got home from work in the evenings and didn't stop until she was almost ready to get up the next day. It's hard to know how much she had cried for each individually, whether the whole episode was instead one amorphous black cloud that would, just as it had rolled in, roll away in one dark, gloomy clump.

Aside from a sharp intake of breath, a small heartburn, she looks at the card and doesn't feel much of anything. Instead, like most mornings, she's just tired and empty, her only plan to get through the day, the week, the month by faking it until she makes it to the other side. To what other side? Her therapist, a woman named Sarah, won't say, only that Alex will know it, feel it.

Unlike the Kate's card, Alex doesn't put Juliette's in her purse, doesn't plan to carry it around for the next four months. Instead, she slips it neatly back into its envelope and drops it in her neighbor's recycle bin on the way to work so she won't have second thoughts and dig it out later. At the metro station, she gets a copy of this week's *Washington City Paper* out of the newspaper stand and settles on the train, scanning the contents for the essay she'd sold to them.

> Instead of taking me shopping for clothes or making me chicken soup, my mother took me into our back yard, where a stack of plates she'd bought at the thrift store rested on the picnic table. She then ordered me to break them. When I refused, when I said it was stupid and wasteful, when I couldn't understand the connection between my heartbreak and this physical act of destruction, she lit a cigarette and said, "You will never be able to leave people, leave places,

```
move on with your life, if you can't
break shit."

My    mother   died   recently.   And,
finally, for once in my life, I am
ready to break some shit.
```

Alex skims through two-thirds of the article until her eyes catch one line:

And Carolyn, if you're reading this, if I could do things over with you, I'd do them so differently.

Alex doesn't harbor any hopes of reconnecting with Carolyn; her admission, for all readers of the *Washington City Paper*—and hopefully Carolyn—to see, is an apology. An apology because she hurt Carolyn. Of all the things that happened while she was at her mother's, it's hurting Carolyn that stings most of all.

When she gets to the offices of *The Capitol Metropolitan* she e-mails the link to Carolyn with the subject line "My article." She doesn't write anything else. She figures, as she hits send, she's already said everything she wants to say.

"You were pretty brutal on yourself," Owen says later that evening on the phone, after he's read the article too. "I mean, people make mistakes."

"I needed to be honest with myself in a forum in which I couldn't take it back," Alex answers, reaching into the cabinet for a can of cat food. "It's time for Tortoise's dinner. That's the real reason you called, isn't it?"

"No." She hears Owen laugh at the other end. "Although maybe I thought I'd kill two birds with one stone. Can you put her on the phone?"

As Tortoise circles Alex's ankles, Alex puts the phone down so Tortoise can see Owen on the screen. When Owen and Shelley left for Seattle a month ago, Owen dropped Tortoise off at Alex's house. *It'll only be for a few months*, he'd explained. *Until we get a place and get settled. Besides, she really likes you.* Although she hadn't admitted it to Owen at the time, she really needed the company—someone to hold on to in bed at night while she tried to beat back the ever-cresting waves of her thoughts, someone to come home to in the evenings, to talk to as she sat on the sofa on Saturday mornings drinking coffee. She might even get her own cat if she's forced to give up Tortoise. She has her at least until Christmas, for which Johanna has already bought Alex a ticket to Seattle. And, of course, she'll have to go back in April for Owen and Shelley's wedding, which Johanna is hosting and catering at the winery. She's happy, mostly, for all of them, Johanna, Owen, and Shelley, how well they've adjusted to the big changes in their lives—Owen working on updating the winery's online ordering system, Shelley finishing her classes at an accredited physical therapy school outside Seattle, and Johanna surpassing two million subscribers on her YouTube Channel "My Maasive Transformation."

But she's just as proud of her own small steps—life with Tortoise, her weekly appointments with her therapist, the yoga class she attends on Tuesday and Thursday evenings. The journal she's begun keeping, not only to jot down things she wants to talk about in therapy, but also just her memories, and how she feels about them. How she feels about having Johanna in her life, to whom she talks to once a week, Johanna, who is always shipping her bottles of wines from the winery or new makeup products she's tried and liked. Johanna, who is her real, actual parent. It still feels so weird to say to herself.

Alex doesn't delude herself that her life is interesting or important enough for a memoir, but she likes writing regularly in her journal now, especially letters to her mother. At first, they were (predictably) about old grievances, but more and more have they been about things Alex has done or seen that her mother may have enjoyed, like the Ingmar Bergman film festival at the Silver Theater, an exhibition on Chinese textiles at the Freer Gallery of Art. Things Carolyn may have enjoyed too.

Every day that week, Alex refreshes her e-mail every few minutes, waiting to hear back from Carolyn. But she doesn't. After the first week, she checks less frequently but also checks her spam. A month, and then another month, passes. Three months later, she adds another activity, a meditation group on Sunday nights. Not to meet anybody, but to try to figure out a way to move on from it all without pretending it never happened, her usual way of dealing with things.

> *You should just get a cat,* Owen texts when she tells him about the group. *Tortoise would really like a brother or sister, she told me.*

Chapter Thirty

Alex never goes on Facebook anymore, but she receives an email notification someone has tagged her in a photo, and she wants to untag herself from it the same way she's been untagging herself from her former life the past six months.

It's an old photo of her old friends having cocktails at a bar in DuPont Circle. Kate's in it, too, but Kate isn't the one who had posted it. Alex wonders if it is a sign. Maybe the friend who has posted the photo wants Alex to know, from Kate, that she should text her, show up at the old Friday night bar. Be visible.

Or maybe the friend is just careless. Thoughtless is more likely. The friend probably had liked how *she* had looked in the photo, not caring Kate and Alex were in it. Still, Alex wonders whether she should be more visible, whether she's ready.

Instead, she types in Carolyn Pusey's name. She'd only visited Carolyn's profile once or twice when she was home at her mother's, when they were still speaking. She's surprised to find now that Carolyn has updated her photo. Her hair curls at the bottom now and sweeps off her forehead. It looks good, Alex thinks, even as it hurts to consider that Carolyn suddenly cares about how she looks not to attract Alex, but someone else.

She glances at some of Carolyn's other photos. To her relief, she hasn't uploaded any new ones. Alex clicks on the photo of Billie peeking outside of her chicken coop and smiles. Her fingers freeze on her mousepad when she glances at Carolyn's city of residence. It's changed; it now says Washington, DC.

She closes the profile, then opens it again. Still Washington, DC. She closes her eyes, feeling her eyelids ache from the force required to keep tears from escaping them. Carolyn had come after all, started a new life for herself. And she hadn't even bothered to tell her.

She should move on too, Alex knows. This half year, she knows she has tried. She wonders whether Carolyn moving here is a sign. But maybe it isn't the sign Alex is looking for.

She pours herself a glass of wine and stares at the message button on Carolyn's profile. At least Carolyn hasn't unfriended her. Maybe, Alex thinks, as she clicks on the message button and begins to type, this is the thing that would make her.

> *Hey! Congrats on your new city! I'm so surprised that you made the leap. It feels weird to find out on FB. So many things feel weird, like the fact I'm typing this. That I'm still thinking about you. If you want to block me, I'll understand. And maybe it'll help me to move on, too, if you do just that. But, on the chance you're free and looking for something fun to do, I've been writing a profile on this improv group, and I'm checking out their monthly show on*

Friday night. It's kind of up your alley. Maybe I'll see you there?

She attaches the event link to the message and sends it. She closes Facebook and downs the rest of her wine, pours another glass, and gives Tortoise some treats. She waits for what seems like an hour but is only a few minutes, then opens Facebook again and checks her messages. Carolyn has read the message. She smiles, closes Facebook, then walks around her living room, drinking her second glass at a more leisurely pace. After ten more minutes have passed, she checks again. Carolyn hasn't responded. She closes Facebook again and takes a long shower. She clips her toenails and paints them, then gets ready for bed. Under the covers she reaches for her phone and checks her Facebook messages. Carolyn hasn't responded, but she hasn't unfriended her either.

Alex can't not go to improv night, so it doesn't matter if Carolyn stands her up. But she doesn't invite anyone from the paper at the last minute, either, not because she's hopeful, but because she doesn't feel particularly social. *It's an assignment*, she reminds herself. *Assignments only require her to be professional.*

Still, she puts on her favorite skirt and silky blouse, her heels. She puts on weekend makeup and her favorite perfume. She gets to the venue early but decides not to linger in the lobby. Instead, in the theater she chooses a cabaret table in the front, one with two chairs instead of four. She sips her vodka and tonic and fiddles with her iPad, ignoring her email and Facebook. Suddenly, the lights dim, and she's still alone.

The improv group is good. They do a skit with Albert Einstein, a pregnant woman, and a zombie on an airplane, and one at the department of motor vehicles. Alex keeps her iPad in her lap and types a few notes. At intermission, she goes into the lobby to get another drink.

It's then she sees Carolyn. She wears a sand-colored cashmere sweater and a plum-colored plaid skirt and tights. And then she sees the woman Carolyn is with, slightly older, with short salt and pepper hair, trendy glasses. It isn't like Carolyn to send a message this way, Alex thinks, but it sure as hell is working. Alex walks past them to the bar, looking absently at a message she'd gotten from Owen a few hours before, her entire body hot with embarrassment.

"Alex." She hears her name, in Carolyn's voice, and suddenly Carolyn is there, standing in front of her, her date to Alex's right.

"Hey!" Alex summons all the excitement she can, from the vodka she'd just drank and what she's learned from drama classes past. She shoves her phone into her purse. "It's great to see you."

"You too." Carolyn smiles. She grabs the straps of her purse with her hand. "Thanks for the recommendation. I can't wait to read your article on the group."

"Thanks." Alex's lips purses. *Like you read my other one?* She glances at the bar. "Congratulations on making it here. I can't believe you did it."

"I can't believe it either." Carolyn nods, glancing at the woman with the glasses. "It feels like a dream."

"I'm Alex." She holds out her hand to the woman. She'll be cool with this, and when she gets home she'll unfriend Carolyn. But she'll have a life again, she decides, cocktail Fridays and culture Saturdays, one that she'll post all over Facebook.

"Nancy." The woman's handshake is firm. Is she sending a warning?

"Are you getting a drink?" Alex asks Carolyn, ignoring it. "These intermissions go so fast."

"No," Carolyn says. "Just getting some fresh air."

"I hope you enjoy the show." Alex's smile is so big her lips start to crack. "If you ever need any more recommendations, I'd be happy to give them."

"I might take you up on that," Carolyn answers. She holds Alex's eyes for a minute, but Alex is already looking at a mole on the side of Carolyn's face, something neutral, so that she won't have to decipher Carolyn's expression. She leaves them and goes to the bar.

You're a fucking moron, she tells herself as she pulls a twenty out of her wallet. *Serves you right.*

She turns with her vodka and starts back to the theater. Carolyn and Nancy are standing where she's left them. Can she walk by them without having to talk? She stops for a moment, waiting for them to make their way back to the theater, but they remain, daring her, she thinks, to go past them, to get back to her seat in the front before the theater fills again.

Alex grips her drink and walks toward them. The lights begin to blink, and Alex breathes a sigh of relief, knowing they'll have to return now too. Nancy turns toward the theater, but Carolyn whispers something to her, and Nancy makes her way to the theater without her.

"Thanks again for letting me know about this," Carolyn says as Alex reaches her. "I'm sorry I didn't answer—I wasn't sure if I'd be able to go because I was supposed to be going out to dinner with Nancy."

"It was nice of her to change her plans," Alex says lightly. "See? I told you that you'd have better luck dating if you moved to the city."

Carolyn doesn't answer. Alex takes a sip of her drink.

"It was brave of you to move," Alex continues. She's a little dizzy. The usher closes one of the doors. She takes a step toward the theater. "I can't believe you left the paper."

"You were right," Carolyn says. "You shouldn't move because of someone. All this time, I was looking for something—someone—to save me from my life. But all it took was me applying for another job. I'm doing some editing for the government now. It's not as exciting as covering the state fair, I guess, but it pays better, and the hours aren't all over the place."

"We should get back inside," Alex says. Her throat is tight. She no longer wants to make small talk. "You know, if you want to meet for coffee sometime and catch me up, that would be great."

"Thank you," Carolyn says. "I might take you up on it."

Alex takes a step backward, and then another, away from Carolyn, finishing her drink as she does so.

"Actually, don't," Alex says, noting the surprise on Carolyn's face. "It would be too hard for me. I'm sorry. I shouldn't have contacted you."

"I finally read the article you sent me, a few days ago," Carolyn says. "I'm sorry I didn't read it before."

"That's okay." Alex shrugs. But she's relieved to know Carolyn hadn't read it months ago and chosen not to respond.

"It's just—I thought it was the profile of Juliette," Carolyn explains. "Which I had absolutely no interest in. I wasn't expecting what you wrote instead."

"For me to announce to the entire world I'm a fuckup?" Alex laughs. "I'm a writer. You have to have a little flair in your work."

"Speaking of brave." Carolyn smiles.

"And now you're here...it hurt so much to find out on Facebook." Alex shakes her head. "But you didn't have to tell me. You don't owe me anything. I know that. Still, God, I'm an idiot for reaching out. And now you're missing the show, and your girlfriend is going to be mad at me."

"Girlfriend?" Carolyn laughs. "Nancy's my co-worker. She's married to a man named Gregg."

"Oh." Alex feels a little better again. *But even a dull knife in the heart*, she thinks, *is a knife nonetheless.*

"More importantly, *you're* missing the show," Carolyn points out.

"I think I have enough for the piece." Alex looks at her glass. "And now I just want to go home."

She initially thinks about going to the bar across the street, but she has some wine left at home. Enough to put her to sleep, but not enough that she'll be monstrously hungover when Rowan stops by tomorrow to pick her up for the Capitals game. The magazine had gotten comp tickets—no one in the office was interested in hockey, it seemed, and Alex, following her new mantra of getting out of her comfort zone, offered to go with Rowan.

Carolyn pulls out her cell phone and types a message.

"I just texted Nancy I'd meet her in the lobby after the show," Carolyn explains, looking up. "Seems rude to try to get back to our table now."

"Just go." Alex grabs Carolyn's arm and lightly tugs her toward the theater. "Don't bail on your friends. Or people you care about. Didn't you take away anything from my article?"

"Actually, I did." Carolyn pulls back. She steers Alex toward an overstuffed bench in the lobby, and they sit. Alex shakes the ice in her glass until Carolyn takes it from her and gently places it on the floor between them.

"What did you do with Billie?" Alex asks suddenly. "Did a big chicken come to the city?"

"One chicken did," Carolyn answers. "Speaking of chickens, I've been looking at your Facebook, too, since you left. At first, I was afraid to see pictures of you having a good time here with your friends, maybe dating. But you've posted hardly at all, which made me feel a little better. I wondered about contacting you. I wanted to contact you for some stupid reason, tell you I was here."

"And now here we are, doing the lamest skit of the night." Alex squeezes Carolyn's hand. She lets it go before Carolyn can respond. "You should go back to Nancy. I don't want you making a bad impression on your new friend."

"Why don't you come sit with us?" Carolyn stands up and takes Alex's hand again. "There's room."

Alex looks at Carolyn, who smiles at her. She wants more than anything to fold up Carolyn in her arms and not let go. But she hasn't earned it. She doesn't know if she ever can. She'll have to have smaller expectations. She promises herself, at the very least, she'll find out what happened to Billie. Everything else, she thinks, will have to be as dark and murky in her mind as the theater they've just entered. Alex follows Carolyn as she slips past the tables, the other patrons. She stays as close to her as she can, trusting Carolyn to lead them, as she fumbles in the dark.

Acknowledgements

So many people are part of a novel.

Thanks to Chelsey Emmelhainz for shepherding this book through many revisions and for having such an amazing sense of what it needed.

Thanks also to Rahne Alexander for help for with sensitivity issues and insightful suggestions that helped transform the final draft, as well as my editor Liz Borino for making me a sharper writer. Oh, and many thanks to Michelle Stevens for proofreading and catching all the important things! I am indebted to Raevyn McCann for an amazing publishing experience, and also Natasha Snow for her great cover design.

I'm also thankful to Rosalia Scalia, Jennifer Lee, Lalita Noronha, Kathy Flann, Jen Grow, and Gabrielle D'Souza for their input on first chapters.

Thanks to all the writers on Twitter for commiserating and also sharing their triumphs and setbacks. When one of us moves forward, we all move forward!

Finally, thanks to my family, especially my brother Scott for being supportive and comforting (and always ready with a meme from "Planes, Trains, and Automobiles") and Phuong for being my everything.

About Jen Michalski

Jen Michalski is the author of three novels, *The Summer She Was Under Water*, *The Tide King* (both Black Lawrence Press), and *You'll Be Fine* (NineStar Press), a couplet of novellas entitled *Could You Be With Her Now* (Dzanc Books), and three collections of fiction. Her work has appeared in more than 100 publications, including *Poets & Writers*, *The Washington Post*, and the *Literary Hub*, and she's been nominated for the Pushcart Prize six times. She lives in Carlsbad, California, with her partner and dog.

Website
www.jenmichalski.com

Facebook
www.facebook.com/jen.michalski.35

Twitter
@MichalskiJen

Also from NineStar Press

Stray by Nancy J. Hedin

Lorraine Tyler should be in vet school, but she stayed behind in her home town of Bend, Minnesota to care for her nephew, spend time with her lover, Charity, and give her momma a chance to complete nursing school.

Lorraine is content until her momma brings home a steady stream of bachelors to *straighten* her out. Charity is out of town more and more, and Lorraine's brother-in-law is looking for a new mom for Little Man. To make matters worse there're new people in town. A politician is drumming up fear and hate, a social worker is flirting with

Lorraine, and Lorraine's new friend, Ricky, is beaten into a coma.

Lorraine suspects Ricky was beaten because of being gay. Lorraine is determined to find out who did it, protect Ricky from the hater who might try to finish the job, and she's worried she might be next on the hater's list.

Stray is a story of politics fueling hate, competing romantic interests, and regular people examining their hearts, souls, and hormones. Will the people of Bend harbor the fear-rattled haters of some, or will they provide sanctuary for all?

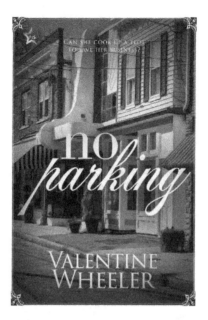

No Parking by Valentine Wheeler

When Marianne Windmere's bakery customers begin complaining that her parking lot is always full, she assumes it must be customers for the new restaurant next door. She's never met her neighbor, and with the parking lot situation, she has no interest in doing so. But when a snowstorm knocks out the power and traps both women in the building overnight, sparks fly—until the next morning, when the buried argument comes to a head.

Can they find a way to reclaim the magic of that night? And as decades-old secrets about the history of the town and Marianne's family come to light, can they work together to save both their businesses?

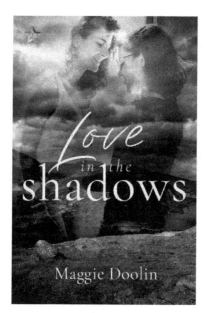

Love in the Shadows by Maggie Doolin

Meg Mitchell is about to enter her final year of secondary school in the small close-knit village of Tullybawn in rural Ireland. But even at eighteen, she has never had the joyful experience of first love with any of the boys she has met or gone out with.

However, that's about to change with the arrival of dynamic young English teacher, Harriet Smith. Under the charismatic Harriet, Meg blossoms and discovers that she has a real talent for English. She also finds herself inexplicably drawn to Harriet.

Over time, Meg's feelings deepen, but this is 1970s Ireland where homosexuality is still a crime, where sex of any description is never discussed, and where an all–powerful harsh and repressive Catholic Church holds sway over every aspect of family life.

In this climate, Meg will face many challenges, from her family, her community, and her own desires. She will have to choose a path forward despite difficulties that, at times, seem insurmountable.

Connect with NineStar Press

www.ninestarpress.com

www.facebook.com/ninestarpress

www.facebook.com/groups/NineStarNiche

www.twitter.com/ninestarpress

www.instagram.com/ninestarpress